TRICKSTER

BOOK THREE OF THE ANGELBOUND LINCOLN SERIES

CHRISTINA BAUER

CONTENTS

Dedication	vii
Author Preface	ix

TRICKSTER

1. Lincoln	3
2. Myla	5
3. Lincoln	10
4. Myla	16
5. Lincoln	22
6. Lincoln	26
7. Myla	30
8. Lincoln	33
9. Myla	36
10. Lincoln	40
11. Myla	45
12. Lincoln	53
13. Lincoln	57
14. Lincoln	62
15. Myla	65
16. Lincoln	70
17. Myla	74
18. Lincoln	78
19. Myla	85
20. Myla	92
21. Lincoln	96
22. Lincoln	98
23. Lincoln	102
24. Lincoln	103
25. Myla	105
26. Lincoln	108
27. Myla	111
28. Lincoln	115
29. Lincoln	120
30. Lincoln	128

31. Myla	130
32. Lincoln	135
33. Myla	137
34. Lincoln	142
35. Myla	145
36. Lincoln	149
37. Myla	152
38. Lincoln	154
39. Myla	158
40. Lincoln	160
41. Lincoln	162
42. Myla	165
43. Lincoln	167
44. Myla	170
45. Lincoln	174
46. Lincoln	176
47. Myla	180
48. Lincoln	183
49. Myla	184
50. Lincoln	186
51. Myla	189
52. Lincoln	192
53. Myla	194
54. Lincoln	197
55. Lincoln	200
56. Myla	203
57. Lincoln	206
58. Lincoln	208
59. Myla	211
60. Lincoln	215
61. Myla	218
62. Lincoln	221
63. Myla	224
64. Lincoln	228
65. Myla	230
66. Lincoln	232
67. Myla	236
68. Lincoln	239
69. Myla	242
70. Lincoln	244
71. Myla	247
72. Lincoln	250
73. Myla	255
74. Lincoln	259

75. Myla	262
76. Lincoln	266
77. Lincoln	268

EPILOGUE

1. Lincoln	273
2. Myla	277
3. Lincoln	281
BACULUM	283

ALSO BY CHRISTINA BAUER

ANGELBOUND	287
OFFSPRING	289
FAIRY TALES OF THE MAGICORUM	291
DIMENSION DRIFT	293
BEHOLDER	295
PIXIELAND DIARIES	297

APPENDIX

If You Enjoyed This Book…	301
Acknowledgments	303
Collected Works	305
About Christina Bauer	309
Complimentary Book	311

| *Afterword* | 313 |

COPYRIGHT

Monster House Books
Brighton, MA 02135
ISBN 9781946677518
First Edition

Copyright © 2020 by Monster House Books LLC
All rights reserved. This book or any portion thereof may not be reproduced or used in any manner whatsoever without the express written permission of the publisher except for the use of brief quotations in a book review.

DEDICATION

For All Those Who Kick Ass, Take Names
and Read Books

AUTHOR PREFACE

Dear Readers,

I am so psyched for TRICKSTER, I can't even tell you! Here are some key points to consider before you get started.

Point One. There's A Dual Point of View

Myla and Lincoln's voices are back in this novel!!! The core conflict just wouldn't work unless readers got to know both their inner thoughts. Plus, it's fun to write.

That said, the story is very much centered in Lincoln's world and his character arc, so get ready for a deeper view into the inner workings of our favorite Mister the Prince.

Point Two. This Takes Place After SCALA

Please note that this book also takes place after the events of SCALA (Angelbound Origins Book #2). There are no spoilers here if you read out of order. I also wrote it so you can enjoy it as a stand alone.

Point Three. What Is My Problem?

At this point you may wonder: why do I write things out of sequence? Wasn't SCALA published a while ago?

Here's my honest answer: *I have no idea.*

This is just how my gift works. I know it's different from everyone else, and sometimes Business-Me wants to take Author-Me out and kick my own ass, if that makes sense. But then I drink coffee and get back to writing. Self-distraction is a very useful skill.

Point Four. Beholder Bonus

If you read my Beholder series, you'll recognize some backstory on the characters of Mlinzi and Walinzi. Again, not necessary to have completed that series to enjoy this one; it's more of an easter egg for power readers.

Enough of my preamble, let's get to the Angelbound fun. I hope you enjoy TRICKSTER!

CB

TRICKSTER

1

LINCOLN

When it comes to fighting, everything's more fun with a battle lion.

Case in point: I now stand in the Royal Gymnasium, ready to teach my nobles the latest in combat. Around me, there looms a tall and rectangular space made from gleaming wood. Gilded balconies line the walls. Leather mats cover the floors. And the best part? A supernatural white lion named Rufus towers just a few yards away. Golden beads gleam in his braided mane; modified armor arches over his spine.

A vision of feline power.

Plus Rufus sports quite the attitude. That's a decided bonus.

"Give up, demon biter," Rufus bellows.

See what I mean? Fun.

By saying *demon biter*, Rufus refers to my being thrax. My people are part human, part angel, and totally committed to fighting demons on the Earth's surface. Meanwhile our homeland of Antrum lies miles underground where we enjoy a secure and medieval lifestyle. As High Prince, I give regular combat lessons to nobility. Today's session is called *Fighting the Four Legged*. For the occasion, I wear human-style body armor instead of my regular tunic, chain mail, and high boots.

Rufus bares his teeth. "I shall shred you with ease," he growls. To emphasize the point, Rufus drags his claws over the practice mat, tearing open fissures of white fluff.

Low gasps echo in from the gym's balconies, all of which overflow with my top nobles. The royal court stares at Rufus, their eyes wide and mouths open. I could explain that Rufus and I are friends, but my nobles won't believe it.

Two reasons why.

One. The court thinks Rufus is a demon. He's not. Rufus' family originally came from an alternate reality called the Primeval. It's a place where animals speak, but aren't necessarily good or evil.

Two. Rufus and I always talk trash before a fight. This way, the nobles pay closer attention. The idea came to me from a wrestling program I viewed while on demon patrol. *Ah, television.* Humans are rather creative with technology, considering how they can't wield magic.

I inspect the gym's many balconies, my gaze locking onto one with an eagle pennant. Thrax are divided into different clans—what we call houses. The eagle banner signifies my own house, Rixa. I scan the balcony's front row, skimming past the familiar forms of my mother, Octavia, and father, Connor. My chest warms with affection.

There she is.

My fiancée, Myla Lewis.

The rest of the world fades into a blur of brocade gowns, leather jerkins, and formal manners. Myla shines out as a figure of life and light. Energy vibrates in her clear blue eyes, long auburn hair, and amber skin. Today she wears the fitted robes that mark her as the Great Scala, the only being who can move souls to Heaven or Hell. The dress is as unique as the woman. All in all, I detect only one imperfection; Myla's not staring at me.

I'm man enough to admit the truth. I like my fiancée's attention.

And I know exactly how to get it.

Turning, I focus on Rufus once more. "Less talking," I say with a wink. "More fighting."

Rufus bares his teeth. "If you insist."

"That I do." I whistle a series of low notes—that's our signal.

Then I lunge for Rufus' throat.

2

MYLA

I've gotten myself into some awkward situations, but this one? It's the pits. Everything started when I spoke some fateful words to my fiancée:

Sure, I'll visit your palace in Antrum.
Yeah, I'd love to watch you teach battle stuff.
What a disaster.

As of this moment, I sit on a gilded balcony with the nobles of Rixa. Surrounding me are sweaty guys in tunics and women whose puffy gowns get caught on everything. I'm crammed by the front edge with Lincoln's mother, who looks petite and lethal in her dark velvet dress. Beside her sits Lincoln's father, who's the definition of a medieval king with his barrel chest, black tunic, and chin-length white hair.

All that remains is watching the fight. Everything is good, yes?

That's a big no.

Here's the issue. I'm a mix of angel, demon, and human. The good news is, that mix makes me a supernatural dynamo called the Great Scala. The tricky bit is how my demonic side comes with two deadly sins, lust and wrath. Of the pair, my control over lust is zilch. Plus when I get all lusty, my eyes blaze with red light, leaving my carnal urges pretty obvious. And what revs me up more than anything?

Ogling my fiancée as he jumps around in his body armor.

See the issue here?

I'm stuck in a balcony with no easy way to reach the exit... all while my man hangs one story below me in his *second skin of rahr*. Any second now, Lincoln will leap about and look hella hot.

Talk about your danger zones.

Even worse, all the major nobles from other thrax houses sit nearby, ready to watch the Red-Eyed Demon Fiancée Show. Not that I care a ton about them. It's the parental issue that really makes my skin crawl.

Some things your future in-laws simply don't need to know.

Down on the gym floor, Lincoln chats up Rufus, the battle lion for this class. It takes a feat of personal will, but I stare at the ceiling.

This is me. Not looking at Lincoln.

Octavia nudges my elbow. "Myla?"

"Hmm?"

"Lady Bentford asked you a question."

"Sure." Considering how that lady's right behind me, I welcome the chance to turn away from the Spectacle Du Man Candy. Lady Bentford is a classic House of Rixa type, namely the elderly maven. I'm talking lots of wrinkles and years of poor dental work. It's a kind face, but I don't let it fool me. Old Rixa ladies are mean as snakes if you misstep one toe on their beloved traditions. Girls like me were created to bug the crap out of them.

Lady Bentford bows. "Greetings, oh fiancée of the High Prince Lincoln Vidar Osric Aquilus."

"You can call me Myla." *As in, I have my own name.*

Lady Bentford's mouth contracts so much, it disappears into her face. "I gave the correct opening for initiating contact with the High Prince's fiancée. Now you must provide your formal greeting in return. It is the Rixa Way."

Whoa. I don't know any of that stuff.

So I make shit up. Clearly Lady Bentford wants some formal blah blah blah. How hard can it be?

"Okay." I close my eyes. "I greet thee, I greet thee, I greet thee. Huzzah. Woot woot." I don't wait for a comment before launching into my next question. "What can I do for you?"

Beside me, Octavia stiffens. The reason? Octavia's been taking the *nasty old lady factor* pretty hard these days. Lincoln's mother always knew that Aldred, the evil Earl of Acca, would loathe me. If anything, the earl's hatred was a relationship bonus. But now? Octavia's old geezer girlfriends have been shooting her the stink eye 24-7, simply because I suck at formal manners and the infamous Rixa Way.

Lincoln's Mom is going twitchy.

And I get that. Friends can affect you. There's no way I'm changing how I act, but I *do* get it.

Lady Bentford offers me a goblet. "Would you like some saffronia?"

There's a hidden trap in this question, but I don't know what it might be. *That said, who cares?* I take the cup and smile. "Thank you."

Lady Bentford continues to look not-pleased. "It's customary to sip from your goblet the moment it touches your hands. My family brews this particular vintage. I wish to ensure it is pleasing."

"Oh." I down a mouthful. My eyes almost bug out of my head. *Whoa. Tastes like warm pee.* My cheeks bulge out while my tongue tries escaping down my throat.

"You don't like it." All the color drains from Lady Bentford's face.

I force myself to swallow. *Gah, that was gross.*

"No," I totally lie. "That was super yummy."

Lady Bentford isn't buying it. Not that I blame her. What a crap performance on my part.

"Thanks for the drink," I say quickly. "I'll watch my fiancée now. Buh-bye." Turning around, I hope Lady Bentford gets the hint.

Beside me, Octavia sips her own goblet of *yellow snow juice*. "You must learn to enjoy saffronia."

"I'll add it to the list." I don't volunteer how said list happens to be super-long and urine bevs sit at the tippy bottom.

"Saffronia is the favorite drink of Rixa," explains Octavia. "The fortunes of Lady Bentford's family are built upon its popularity."

"Good for her."

Octavia sips her own drink without gagging. Total achievement. "May I give you some advice?"

"Can I stop you?"

A small smile curls Octavia's mouth. "I'm afraid not."

"Then shoot."

"The Rixa Way is an important set of manners and traditions. It may seem silly to you, but it's crucial for Antrum."

Sure it is. "I thought you guys were all about fighting demons."

"We are. And the Rixa Way supports everything. Manners. Traditions. Formalities. It all weaves together into the greater fabric of thrax society."

"Huh." *That's really all I have to say.*

"You're nineteen; Lincoln is twenty. In Antrum, that's rather old to get married. The Rixa Way is expected of anyone so up in years. "

"Hey, I'm the poster girl for manners right now."

In reply, Octavia merely raises her brows. It's a small move that means, *you are so full of it.*

"Come on," I declare. "Who just DRANK WARM PEE and didn't spit it out?"

Okay, I might have used my outdoor voice just then. The entire Rixa balcony goes unnervingly silent.

Oops.

From the gym floor below, a great roar sounds. That would be Lincoln's combat lessons. Moving as one, all the nobles focus on the fight instead of me.

Yay.

For my part, I stare down at my pee drink and not at my guy. As long as I keep inhaling through my mouth, it's not a problem.

Another roar sounds. The battle must be getting goooooood.

Not looking. Not looking.

My tail perks up from its resting spot by my ankle. This is a total bonus of being part demon, by the way. I have a long tail that's covered in dragonscales. *Major badassery.* Right now, that tail arcs over my shoulder. The arrowhead-shaped end points toward the fight.

I get the hint. My tail wants me to watch Lincoln.

Still not happening.

A series of *oohs* and *ahhs* sound from crowd. Connor taps my shoulder. "Did you see that?" he asks. "Such an amazing strike."

Not looking. Not looking. Not looking.

Screw it. I'm looking.

The moment my gaze locks on Lincoln, my inner lust demon

wakes up with a big *HELL to the O*. Blood heats in my veins. Lincoln talks while fighting—it's all stuff about battling lions or whatever—yet his words fade into the background. All I catch are a rhythmic set of movements.

Lunge... swipe... back muscles ripple.
Jump... bend... excessive butt flexing.
Punch... twist... ripped arms bulging.

Rufus bites Lincoln's shoulder. The crowd gasps. I'm not worried, though. Rufus' jawline isn't even taut. Zero brawn lies behind that bite.

A moment later, Lincoln breaks free from Rufus. Then it happens—the Mona Lisa of battle moves. My breath hitches as Lincoln somersaults over the lion's back. The flip even includes some choice straight-leg slicing action.

Oh, my.

It's what my best friend, Cissy, and I call a BAEJS.

Body Armor Enhanced Junk Show.

My guy is one hundred percent beautiful; that's all I'm saying. And it's good to have a bestie that I can share this stuff with. Cissy's boyfriend, Zeke, serves in Purgatory's new guard, so she gets the whole body armor scene.

Heat rises behind my eyes. I fight it, hard.

No demon irises, Myla.

That's when Lincoln pauses. Our gazes lock. Desire blazes in his mismatched eyes. Like all thrax, he has one brown iris and one blue. Totally hypnotic.

Is the battle over? Do I really care?

Enough is enough. I'm having a lusty moment with my fiancée, end of story. My irises flare red as Lincoln and I continue our stare-a-thon. The crowd may notice or not. I'm no longer paying attention.

Mmmmm-mmm.

3

LINCOLN

It took a little doing, but I got what I wanted. Myla looks straight at me, her irises flaring with crimson light. *The demon spark.* Our connection lasts a second and forever, all at once.

Slam!

A heavy wooden door thuds against the gymnasium wall. I frown. There are two ways on and off the gym floor. The first is the main entrance; the second leads to the locker room. Either way, no one should enter at this time, let alone make a ton of racket while doing so.

As disappointing as it is, I break my gaze with Myla. Turning, I find none other than Aldred standing framed by the gym's threshold. The earl is a hefty fellow in a yellow tunic decorated with Acca's emblem, a closed fist. A thin comb-over of red hair stretches over his skull. Aldred marches across the gym floor, his belly shaking with each step.

Which brings me to a turning point.

There are a number of options here. I could order Aldred to leave the gym. Or I might ask him why he's interrupting my lesson. Finally, I could simply punch him in the throat. Over the years, I've learned that none of these work where Aldred is concerned. Best to hang back until the earl reveals his true plans. Then I act accordingly.

Thus for now, I must wait.

My Master of Arms, Nat, follows behind Aldred. Essentially, a Master of Arms acts as personal trainer for me and my top guards. Nat looks the role as well, considering how he's middle-aged with graying hair and a compact body. And the way Nat's mouth pulls tight? My Master at Arms is fuming about something Aldred-related.

This will be interesting.

All the nobles turn quiet. No one wants to miss a thing.

Aldred kneels beside Rufus. With a dramatic swoop of his arm, the earl runs his hand over the lion's armor. "Ha! I thought so. This clasp is loose." Aldred turns to the crowd. "Battle lions are under the exclusive mandate of the House of Acca. This error brings unspeakable shame upon me!"

Time was, Acca used to rule Antrum. Then Rixa kicked them off the throne. To have a bloodless transition of power, Rixa allowed Acca to keep certain battle rights. Bottom line? My family can't force Acca into war or dictate anything related to combat. Battle lions fall under Acca's—and therefore Aldred's—absolute control. I suspected the earl might use today's event in order to grab attention for himself and his house. I took the risk because, well, Rufus is simply that cool.

Aldred scans the room. "Who set this armor?"

That's when I see the real problem.

Aldred holds a rope in his pudgy fist. The other end of that cord encircles the neck of a scrawny nine-year old boy. The child's too-large yellow tunic is decorated with the image of a threadbare lion. The clothing—shabby as it is—means the boy is a servant of Acca who cares for Rufus and his extended family. A long scar runs from the child's right eye to his chin. My gaze snaps to Nat, who still glares at Aldred. No question about it. My Master at Arms is enraged by Aldred's treatment of this child.

Nat's not alone, either. Watching that cord dangle about the child's neck? White-hot fury burns through my soul.

"I said, who set this armor?" yells Aldred. To accent his point, he yanks on the line around the boy's throat.

Fresh waves of outrage careen through me. I round on Aldred. "What's on that child's neck?"

Aldred sniffs. "It's a traditional minder system for battle lion caretakers which—as you know—falls under the exclusive rule of the House of Acca."

My skin chills over in disbelief. Sure, Aldred's treatment falls under battle rules. Yet there are larger laws at work here. Tying up children is an abomination.

Aldred yanks on the cord once more. "Answer me!"

This time, the boy falls onto his knees, his skinny limbs quaking with fear. "I was the one who set the armor, Lord Aldred." His voice breaks with a sob. "Everything seemed fine."

Aldred focuses on the crowd once more. "According to ancient law, battle lions are solely subject to my rule. I do not tolerate sloppy work when it comes to matters of formal combat." Aldred stares at Myla as he says the words *sloppy work* and *formal combat*. Not a surprise. Aldred is forever painting my fiancée as *thrax tradition breaker extraordinaire*.

In fact, this entire interruption could simply be Aldred wanting to show how he follows formalities while Myla does not.

Somehow, I doubt it will be that simple, though. Aldred is notorious for layering plans within plans.

Even so, Aldred's schemes are not my main concern right now. This child is. I take a pointed step closer to Aldred. "That's enough. Release the rope."

Aldred's thick mouth pulls into a sickly smile. "Of course." The earl drops the rope to the gym floor before winding up his arm, ready to slam his fist into the child's ear. "Botched traditions and combat errors must be punished!"

Shock rattles through my nervous system. A single thought appears in my mind, the realization written large. *Aldred plans to strike this defenseless child.*

Moving swiftly, I grip the earl's wrist before it connects with the boy's head. When I next speak, my voice is a low growl. "I said, *enough*. Try that again, and you'll land in the infirmary. Am I clear?"

"Always," whispers Aldred. His smug grin stays firmly in place, however. After years of sad experience, I know Aldred is still scheming. Whatever the earl is up to, it's about more than hurting small boys.

Releasing Aldred's wrist, I kneel before the child. Up close, it's clear how another scar runs over his scalp, dividing up his hair crossways. He's been injured before. Often. The realization makes my heart sink.

"What's your name?" I ask.

"Baptiste, your Highness."

"And your house?"

"I have no mother and father. Officially." Baptiste twists the folds of his dirty fellow tunic. "I am fortunate to be a servant in the House of Acca."

"Would you rather officially join a house?"

The child looks up, his mismatched eyes wide with shock. "Yes, your Highness."

Rising, I address the gym. "Let it be known that Baptiste is now part of Rixa."

Nat steps forward, his face split into a wide grin. As Master of Arms, Nat trains young thrax for Rixa guard duty. He's taken in a number of orphans so far. Long story short, there's no way Nat will leave this gym without Baptiste in his care.

Aldred moves to stand between Nat and Baptiste. "This whelp has no house. He's lucky to serve Acca." Reaching forward, Aldred goes to smack the base of Baptiste's skull.

Fast as lightning, I grip Aldred's wrist and twist. Hard. Snaps sound as bones break. "I warned you."

"And I defy you." With his free hand, Aldred sets his hand on the hilt of his golden long sword.

A voice echoes from the balcony. "Nuh-uh, buddy."

I grin. That's Myla speaking. In a single swift movement, my girl leaps over the balcony's edge to land right beside me. The moment her feet hit the floor, Myla's robes transform from a fitted sheath into white body armor. It's one of her supernatural talents as Great Scala. At the same time, Myla's tail juts forward to grip Aldred's free hand.

"Who are you to touch me?" cries Aldred.

Myla's tail twists. More snaps sound as Aldred's other wrist breaks. "Who am I?" asks Myla. "A true thrax warrior."

The implication is clear. Our people live by a code. Thrax don't hurt those who aren't attacking, especially if the other party is less powerful, let alone a child.

The lines of Aldred's face pull tight with pain and rage. "This boy still has no house."

"False," counters Myla. "Lincoln just said it. Baptiste is now in Rixa."

"But there is no approved ritual for transferring someone without official parents," snaps Aldred.

Here we go. For most thrax, you can ruin almost anything by simply dropping the words *no approved ritual*.

Myla rolls her eyes. "Whatever." She twiddles her fingers at Baptiste. "Bippity boppity boo. You're Rixa."

I raise my free hand. "I second the motion."

"Done," states Myla.

"And dusted," I add.

We share a grin. One thing about my Myla. She can make any occasion fun.

I look to Aldred. "May we release your wrists now, or must things get uglier?"

"Do it," grumbles the earl.

Moving in unison, both Myla and I set loose Aldred's injured hands. "There's a magical infirmary around here somewhere," says Myla. "They'll fix you, easy peasy."

Aldred scurries out the door to the lockers. *Which makes sense.* Magical first aid is located there, and they heal broken bones in seconds. For his part, Rufus follows Aldred out with slow and regal steps. No question about it. Today got a little dicey because I added Rufus into the mix.

Yet fighting with a battle lion? Totally worth it.

With the earl gone, I pull out my baculum. These are short silver rods that I can ignite into any kind of weapon created from angelfire. This time, I form them into a dagger made of white flame. Stepping over to Baptiste, I cut the rope from around his neck. Angry red marks encircle his throat. *Deplorable.*

I pat his shoulder. "You're free now, little man."

Genuine relief shines in the boy's dirty face. "Thank you, your Highness."

"Nat?" My Master at Arms marches up to my side. "Do you have room in combat prep for a new recruit?"

This is all for Baptiste's benefit, by the way. I already know the answer to this question.

Still, Nat silently counts on his fingers as if he is truly unsure. "As a matter of fact, I do have a place available. That is, if the young lad wishes to be trained."

At these words, Baptiste's face brightens. I kneel before the child once more. "Would you like to learn how to become a Rixa solider with Nat?"

The boy nods quickly.

"Excellent," I declare. "It is now so."

"Your Highness." Nat beams, takes the boy's hand, and turns for the exit.

"One last thing." I lower my voice so only my Master at Arms can hear me. "Do the regular."

Nat nods. "Absolutely."

This isn't the first time we've run across a rogue house that mistreats children. Nat has become a self-taught expert on righting certain wrongs.

As Nat and Baptiste step out the main door, I raise my hands to the audience. Silence follows as all the nobles focus on me. "Everyone, thank you for attending today's class. In the end, it covered more topics than battle lions, which is a good development. As you all know, children have rights here in Antrum. Every house must respect that fact or pay the consequences."

Myla taps my shoulder. "We have a guest."

Sure enough, Aldred now stomps out onto the gym floor. He looks fully healed and ready for trouble. The earl scans the balconies before raising his arms. "Do not leave yet! I have something to say!"

I fight the urge to groan. *Of course, he does.*

4

MYLA

Aldred parks his big old butt on the center of the gym floor, ready to open his massive yap and cause trouble. Everyone hates the guy, but they say zero. Why? Aldred has a talent for gathering blackmail. The earl has something on every major house, and a bunch of minor ones too. I don't even want to know what he's keeping on Lincoln's father, but Connor does whatever Aldred commands. All that's missing are the marionette strings.

Note to self: see if there's a way to slow down magical healing for creeps like Aldred.

The earl sets his fists on his hips. "I had a lesson to share today as well. Everyone here should have seen how a true thrax disciplines those under him."

Viva la irritation! Aldred couldn't have set me up better if he tried.

"Seriously?" I gesture across the balconies. "Did y'all *really* want to watch Aldred punch some poor orphan in the head? No?" A long pause follows, which I take as a big *yes*. "Good."

Aldred's beady eyes focus in on me. "You're not queen yet. There's no tradition that allows you to voice your uninformed opinions. Stand aside."

That comment won't land well. My fiancée gives new meaning to the word *protective*.

Sure enough, Lincoln steps forward. Every line in his body is tight with rage. "What did you say?"

I rest my palm on the center of Lincoln's chest. It's a movement I've used before and it says, *I got this.* Where before his eyes were bright with fury, Lincoln's gaze now gleams with held-in amusement. My guy is the best.

"I should step aside… where?" I ask Aldred sweetly.

"Wait by the water bucket."

That would be in the far corner.

"Humph." I don't move a muscle.

"Well?" Aldred lifts his chins.

"This is me, standing wherever I freaking want to."

The chamber falls so silent, my breathing seems to become super-loud. For their part, all the nobles stay totally glued to the Myla V Aldred Show.

"Freaking?" repeats Aldred. "Freaking?! What did you say to me?"

"Sorry, did I say freaking? I meant to say this." I clear my throat. "This is me, standing wherever I *fuuuuuuckinnnnnng* want to."

There, that showed him.

A long pause follows where Aldred's beady little eyes scan between me and the nobles. He's judging their reaction. The silence is pretty much a big fat stamp of *You Go Myla* from the court. Even Connor and Octavia stay quiet. Considering how Connor fears Aldred—and Octavia's all anxious about her lady nobles—I consider this another item for the *Myla win column.*

"Fine," huffs Aldred. "Stand wherever you wish. I only wished to spare you the embarrassment of being beside me while I shared my news. My next announcement shall upset you." Aldred shoots me a smarmy look that says, *here's the part where you beg for mercy.*

I shrug. "M'Kay."

"You wish to become Queen of the Thrax," declares Aldred. "That means you'll have a say in battle matters." He points right at my nose. "Do you deny it?"

"Nope. Guilty as charged. I absolutely plan to boss you around." Some chuckles sound from the balconies. I tally another *win for moi.*

"Good," Aldred states. *He so thinks he's got me by my lady balls.*

"Therefore, per the First Rixa Treaty of Acca, my house may test your battle worthiness. I can even invite others to add their own ideas, including your home realm of Purgatory. The testing shall be called… the Trials of Acca!" Aldred slaps on a simpering grin. "Sorry if that saddens you."

Wow. If this is Aldred's big plan, it sucks ass.

"Let me get this straight," I state. "These Trials of Acca are supposed to test my battle skills as future queen?"

"Yes," answers the earl.

"And maybe these trials have a little something extra thrown in? Like non-combat stuff?"

Aldred bobs his overly bushy eyebrows. "Possibly."

"So that's another *yes*."

"Come now," says Aldred slowly. "This news must concern you slightly."

"Let me put it to you this way. When I was growing up, Purgatory was run by ghouls. I wasn't much older than Baptiste when they chucked me into the Arena to fight a Class B demon to the death. No warning. No training. I skewered the beast through its rib cage and went on to win three more matches."

My tail perks up to tap my shoulder. "Excuse me, *my tail* skewered the first demon." I slap the arrowhead shaped end in a modified high five. *Go us.*

"Bring on your trials," I continue. "I won't cower. What's tougher than a class A demon? Not much. And I've killed so many of those on demon patrol, I've lost count."

"Thirty-six," deadpans Lincoln.

I do a double-take. "Really?"

"I've been keeping tally for you."

My heart melts. "Aw, thanks."

Knowing Lincoln, he's probably recorded all the battle details, too. *Perfect.* I haven't updated my demon notebooks in weeks. My father, the archangel Xavier, and I do that together. It's like father-daughter scrapbooking only with demons and death. Good times.

Aldred's cheeks turn pink. I love it when he gets all pissy. "If you fail the Trials of Acca, you may not be queen. That *must* worry you."

I allow a long pause to follow because drama *plus* earl *equals* fun. "Oooo? I'm so scared of the big bad Aldred?"

Come on, douchebag. Spill whatever it is you're really up to.

"You speak of yourself as a great warrior," says Aldred. "Yet the Trials of Acca shall display *my* combat prowess."

I make my *eek* face. "Your battle skills? Are you sure that's a good idea? Didn't you get a ton of warriors killed when you mistakenly went after…" I snap my fingers, trying to remember.

"A soul slasher," finishes Lincoln.

"Right. So *not good.*"

Aldred rolls his eyes. "That was one time."

"Then you shot a limus with a crossbow," I add. "Those demons are like evil gummy bears. The bolts zipped right through."

Aldred glances away. "I recall no such a thing."

"Oh, I find that incident hard to forget," injects Lincoln. "The limus consumed you whole. Myla saved your life."

Aldred's pink cheeks now flare into a bright shade of red. When the earl next speaks, little bits of spittle fly from his mouth. What a lovely sight.

"You two think yourselves so clever," snarls the earl. "But when it comes to the Trials of Acca, I shall be the smart one. *Me.*" He pounds his chest, as if anyone was unclear about the *me* in this scenario.

At this point, I could shut my yap and give Aldred a chance to cool off. That might even be the mature and queenly thing to do. In fact, there's probably a traditional speech for leaving this whole scene behind. *The infamous Rixa Way.*

Nah.

Besides, there's still a bigger Aldred-centric scheme here. I can smell it, the same way that I scent the mothballs and stinky feet from Aldred's direction. It's on the tip of the earl's sausage-like tongue to blab his true plan. One more sarcastic nudge in the right direction and he'll snap.

"Go on," Lincoln whispers. "Break him. You know you want to."

And with that, it's clear I have the best fiancée in the universe.

I step super-close to the earl. *Take that, personal space.*

"Lay it on me, Aldred." I gesture to the still-packed galleries. "In fact, show us all how smart you really are."

There, that should do it.

"Open the gateway," calls Aldred.

I frown. The way the earl said the word *gateway*, it's clear that's his true plan. *Yay me.* Trouble is, I have zero idea what Aldred's yakking about.

A gateway. What?

Here's the deal. Ghouls can create portals, which are door-like holes that connect one part of the after-realms to another. When it comes to undeadlies, that's really their only serious skill. Even then, ghoul portals are pretty limited. For instance, you can't open one directly into Antrum. But gateways? Beyond the sort that connect to white picket fences, I've got nothing.

An electrical charge fills the air. Orange-colored mist pools around Aldred's feet.

Magic.

I take a half-step backward. Whatever this gateway is, it's definitely not of the white picket variety. We're talking some serious spellwork here. Yet since when does Aldred wield magic? The man can barely shoot a crossbow. Plus, no one in Antrum uses orange power. There's purple for thrax wizards. Red for demons. Even white and blue for angelic stuff.

But orange? What the WHAT? Who's casting this spell anyway?

The colored haze swirls into a round and flat disc that stands ten feet tall. My breath catches. This is definitely veering closer into ghoul portal territory, meaning this gateway looks remarkably portalesque, only it's bigger, rounder and way orange. A woozy feeling settles into my stomach.

"Any moment now," says Aldred. "This spell shall reveal the Primeval!"

My mouth falls open in shock. I'm talking the kind of wide open that only happens when a dentist scrapes random gunk off my molars. I thought we were maybe dealing with a mega ghoul portal. Perhaps something that allows outsiders to sneak into Antrum, which is a big *no no*.

This is much worse. Aldred has found a way to connect our reality to a totally different world. And not a happy place called

Butterflyland or something. This is the freaking Primeval, AKA the place that already spat out nothing less than Rufus the battle lion.

Crap on a cracker.

Forget sexy battle-gaze time. Now Lincoln and I have a new goal in life: dealing with Aldred's Trials of Acca while preventing him from opening a gateway into trouble.

5

LINCOLN

I knew Aldred was scheming something. Still I held complete faith that Myla would crack him like a coconut. But finding out that the earl's plan is to open magical passage to the Primeval?

That's rather a surprise.

Before me, the round gateway changes. The colored edges solidify into what looks like a thin metallic loop. In the center of the disc, the mists lighten until they vanish completely.

A view to the Primeval appears.

It's as if a circular window opened in the center of the gymnasium. If I step to check the gateway from the side, I only see a thin line hanging in the air. It's when I stare straight-on that I view the Primeval.

And what a sight it is.

Heavy clouds churn overhead. Dark rock walls loom in the distance. The dead remains of a forest stretch off in every direction. Broken trunks jut up from the dark ground, reminding me of blackened teeth. In the center of this wasteland, there stands a hulking stump of a tree that reaches six feet high. Instead of bark, shifting threads of tar wind up and down the trunk.

Aldred gestures to the gateway. "Behold the Primeval!"

At these words, the oozing sludge on the trunk shifts. A long face forms, one with deep holes for eyes and a jagged gash as a mouth.

"Who awakens the wizard Contagion?" cries the tree. "Prepare to fight!"

Back in the gym, Aldred speaks yet again. "Close the gateway!"

Instantly, the view clouds over in an orange haze. The mist swirls, pinwheel-style, as it moves in ever smaller rounds. I blink hard, not believing what I'm seeing. No magic of the after-realms looks like this. *Orange pinwheels?* Within seconds, the gateway vanishes completely. I try to process what I've seen. It isn't easy.

The gateway to the Primeval is gone.

And a new world of trouble has opened wide.

Stunned silence fills the gymnasium. Aldred grins. "Did you see that magical tree? I shall defeat it at the Trials of Acca on Friday." His voice takes on a growl. "It be... a demon arbor named the Contagion."

"Did he say, *it be*?" whispers Myla. "What is this, Thrax Talk Like A Pirate day?"

I shake my head. "Aldred's on a roll."

Which is bad news. After all, I thought the soul slasher was a horror. At least that demon type is well documented. I knew its powers and how to fight back. But a talking tree? That's unheard of.

The earl holds up his pointer fingers. "In two days time, the Trials of Acca will begin. Then you'll see my true power... as well as the failings of others."

Applause breaks out from the balconies. The nobility lovingly gaze upon Aldred. Some even cheer. No question why, either. My people adore a good fight. The stranger the opponent, the better. And the promise of a Contagion battle? That waves red meat before the hungry wolves at court. Sadly, the fact that Aldred will also use this fight to humiliate my fiancée doesn't register. Even my parents clap like mad.

Unacceptable.

Protective instincts for Myla charge every muscle in my body. At this point, I'd love to wring Aldred's floppy neck. At the very minimum, I want to educate my court on how Aldred's plans to open the Primeval are beyond dangerous.

Yet I know the thrax.

If I speak now, my nobles will believe I only wish to spoil their fun. Not to mention the fact that most of the court is terrified of Aldred dropping blackmail on them. Even if they did disagree with the Contagion battle—which they most certainly do *not*—then it would still be extraordinarily rare for anyone to openly defy Aldred. Sadly, that includes my parents.

The truth is both clear and unavoidable. As long as everyone backs Aldred, I can't keep this gateway closed. In order to stop the earl's plans for the Primeval, I must find hard facts about the threat and push them hard. And to accomplish that end, I need more information. Sadly, that can't happen right now. Taking in slow breaths, I force my body to calm.

Patience, Lincoln.

While waving to the cheering crowd, Aldred stomps off gym floor and through the main exit. Just outside, I spy Connor and Octavia. What a shame. My parents must have raced away from their balcony seats to wait in the outer hallway, ready and eager for Aldred to pass by.

Sure enough, the moment Aldred enters the passageway, my parents engage the earl. Father even pets Aldred's shoulder. A weight settles into my soul. I know my parents think that by placating the earl, they protect both me and Myla.

They're wrong.

I turn to the balconies one last time. "Thank you for attending today. This concludes our combat lesson."

The cheers die down. Instead, low grumbles sound as the crowd leaves. All I did was stop their applause for the earl's battle, and the court acts as if I spat in their collective mead goblets.

No question about it. This will be tricky.

Turning, I scan Myla's beloved face. She wears her contemplative expression, which means there's a little vertical line between her brows.

"We need to talk," I say.

"Do we ever."

Hand in hand, Myla and I march for the locker rooms. With every step, my thoughts whir through everything that just happened. All in all, Aldred just tore open a trio of problems.

First, there are the Trials of Acca.

Second, let's not forget the gateway to the Primeval.

And third? There's dealing with whatever that gateway unleashes. Knowing Aldred, it won't be anything good.

Still, beyond everything, my hunter's sense tells me another, even larger danger lurks in the shadows. I picture Lady Bentford offering Myla that foul drink... my parents applauding the earl's Contagion battle... and Aldred smirking as he announces the Trials of Acca.

An image appears in my mind. I picture smoke curling above a night forest. It's something I often see on demon patrol. *Smoke.* A small sign that might herald a large and destructive fire. That vision encapsulates the risk I now face. It's far off, undefined, and can drive disaster.

No matter what, I must uncover the true risk and soon.

LINCOLN

Myla and I slip into the locker room. The place has low ceilings, wooden floors, and walls lined with cubby-style spaces for belongings. The scent of old sweat hangs in the air. Happily, the chamber lies mostly empty. Only a few workers hover around Rufus, but they're off in a far corner.

Myla and I huddle by the opposite wall. "Aldred is opening the Primeval," I begin. "It's beyond belief."

"Your court was salivating at the idea. You'd think the circus was coming to town."

I rub my neck and think things through. "We need concrete proof of a threat. It's the only way to stop this or—in a worst-case scenario—to be fully prepared for protecting Antrum. Sadly, two days isn't much time to grab that kind of intel."

"It's more like one day for me, considering how I have that huge Scala Bleugh in Purgatory tomorrow."

In *Myla speak*, Scala Bleughs are public appearances where she must act otherworldly. Unfortunately, her people tend to lose their minds if anything about those events goes awry. Last week, Myla was one hour late to a grocery store opening. As a result, quasis took over the local news station to demand that whoever kidnapped their goddess come forward and name a ransom. Turns out, Myla got stuck in traffic.

This points out a number of limitations for Myla's home realm, including the fact that Purgatory really needs cell service.

"I'd cancel the Scala Bleugh," adds Myla. "But you know my people."

"That I do. Besides, this is a classic Aldred move. He doesn't want us to have time to counter-plan. I'm sure he checked your schedule and knew you'd be stuck in Purgatory. And with this revelation about how Aldred is treating orphans like Baptiste? He also knows I'll want to rescue any other affected children right away."

Myla sets her fists on her hips. "It's all a distraction from Friday and the Contagion. There's got to be information about the Primeval somewhere."

My thoughts whirl through my last trip through ancient scrolls. "There's nothing in the royal archives. I checked when preparing for today's lesson with Rufus."

"What about the Dark Lands? The ghouls stole a ton of books. Maybe something is in there."

"It's a fine idea. Sadly, Walker is the only one who can enter the ghoul libraries on short notice." By the way, Walker is our mutual friend and the only ghoul that both Myla and I trust completely. "Unfortunately, Mother sent him on vacation yesterday."

"Oh, yeah. That ghoul cruise through the Bermuda Triangle." Myla glances over to the battle lion. "What about Rufus?"

I bob my head, considering. "We can ask, but his family came to our reality many generations ago. Lions don't exactly keep records the way we do."

"Ugh." Myla rolls her eyes. "Aldred is such a pain. Sometimes I just want to ship him off to Hell."

At the mention of the word *Hell*, a dozen small lighting bolts materialize around Myla's palms. *Her igni*. These supernatural bits of energy help send souls off the Pearly Gates or an eternal inferno. Igni also speak to Myla in her head, giving visions and pointers. That's rare, though. Mostly they're just noisy little buggers.

Myla winces. "Quiet down, guys. I'm not sending Aldred to fry this very second. I get that you hate him. Now vamoose."

The igni arc and dive around Myla's fingers. For a moment, they flare more brightly. After that, they disappear. It may have been a short visit, but that doesn't mean it wasn't painful.

I cup Myla's face in my palms. "Are you all right? I know they can get loud."

"Deafening." She kisses my palm. "But I'm good."

I lower my hands. "Did they give you anything more?" Sometimes Myla's igni give her hints about how to best solve problems.

"Not this time." Myla snaps her fingers. "Although the whole igni-n-Aldred situation brings up a good point. This is one sweet example of *yours truly* following traditions. I won't send Aldred to Hell without having a thrax court trial first. Maybe I should get T-shirts made." Myla frames up her thumbs, as if picturing the finished product. "They could say... *Myla Lewis. Still not sending Aldred to Hell.*" She lowers her hands. "The back side would say, *Yet.*"

I chuckle. "I'd wear one."

Myla purses her lips. "That still doesn't answer our big question."

"Right. What awaits us in the Primeval?"

A strange voice sounds from the floor. "Hello."

Looking down, I discover the speaker. If I thought the gateway to the Primeval was a shock, this one is far worse. I do a double-take.

Nope, it's still there.

A small monkey sits by my boot. It has large blue eyes, orange fur, and a wide grin.

"I'm Ukapeli from the Primeval," he says. "You can call me Peli."

I frown. As far as I know, the only Primevals in Antrum are Rufus and his extended family of lions. Peli isn't setting off any thrax intruder alarms, so it's possible he's from a different reality. Thrax systems would have no way to detect Primevals. Still, I've never witnessed anything like him before.

Myla looks to me. "Are you seeing what I'm seeing?"

"That I am."

Peli's smile widens. "You're the Great Scala."

"Uh huh."

"So young and full of life." He hops on all fours while making ooo-ooo noises.

Myla hitches her thumb in my direction. "He's young too, you know."

"True." Peli chatters his teeth in an odd kind of chuckle. "You've no idea what you're into, do you?"

If you'd asked me some seconds ago, I'd have answered that Myla and I have a good concept of what's happening. Or as much as we always do when Aldred is concerned.

But now? *I'm not so certain.*

7

MYLA

A talking monkey sits by Lincoln's feet.
With orange fur, no less.

I'd say that's weird, but this is my life here. For my day job, I use little sentient lightning bolts to move souls around. Strange is normal for yours truly. It's the thrax who should be shocked by Mister Monkeypants.

I scan the locker room. In a far corner, some workers still fuss around Rufus, chatting in low voices as they clean his armor and whatnot. A few glance our way.

None react to the very orange monkey. It's like they don't even see him. *Whoa.*

Thrax keep a tight lid on security. When you're a demon hunter, enemies want to sneak in and kill you in your sleep. It's why Lincoln's people live deep underground. It's also why anything out of the ordinary makes all of Antrum lose their collective minds.

Take last week, for instance. A thrax warrior returned from demon patrol with an unexpected friend—namely a field mouse who'd camped out in the warriors' backpack. The moment the Pulpitum transfer platform reached Antrum, the whole place went on lockdown. Red lights flashing. Voice alerts yelling up a storm. Total drama.

If a field mouse causes that much worry, then an orange monkey should definitely launch superfreak fests all over the place.

Yet no one's reacting.

Maybe they just can't see Peli from a distance.

I cup my hand by my mouth. "Hey, Rufus."

The lion lifts his mighty head. "Yes, Great Scala?"

"Come here for a sec?"

Rufus rises onto all fours and lopes over. All the while, Peli picks bits of *who knows what* from his fur. Rufus pauses beside us. "How may I be of service?"

I gesture toward Peli. "Do you see anything here?"

Rufus scans the floor. "No."

"Really?" asks Lincoln. "You don't see a small orange monkey? He claims to be from the Primeval, just like you."

Rufus rechecks the spot. "Nothing is there. Are you playing games with this old lion?"

"I'm a trickster," says Peli. "Every inch of me comes packed with magic. I only show myself when and how I wish."

Lincoln refocuses on Rufus. "What do you know about tricksters? Are they common in the Primeval?"

Rufus snuffles, which is his version of a laugh. "My people left the Primeval many generations ago. We don't write history on scraps of paper like you. I've nothing to tell. Excuse me." Rufus saunters back to his corner.

I stare at Peli. *This little monkey is playing us somehow. And I should know. I love doing the exact same thing.*

"So, you're magical, eh?" I ask. "Did you open that gateway for Aldred?"

"Of course." Peli does a kind of curtsey that morphs into a him spinning around in a circle. Odd little dude.

"Why help Aldred?" asks Lincoln.

"Not telling," says Peli.

"Let me get this straight," I declare. "You're just now appearing to me and Lincoln, you announce you're behind the whole Primeval gateway, and you won't say why?"

Peli mock claps. "Yay for the girl with the pretty tail. She understands a trickster!"

At these words, my tail perks up to arc over my shoulder, whereupon it starts waving at Peli. *Total ham.* I smack it lightly on the arrowhead-shaped end. "Not cool, bud. This is really serious. Friday could be a disaster."

"Maybe they will," says Peli. "And maybe they won't." He lets out a long and dramatic sigh. "Don't take this is the wrong way, but I do hope Friday is a horror show."

"Any details?" asks Lincoln. He's now using his regal voice, which usually gets results.

"To answer that, I must first check something in Purgatory," replies Peli. "Or rather, some*one*."

I make my yuck-face, because this conversation is the pits. "That's not really specific."

"How's this?" Peli hops closer. "The fate of Friday depends on a ghoul. He or she will have the mark of an orange skull here." Peli taps his right shoulder. "If I find this ghoul, then your day of trials shall be a beautiful catastrophe… one that I have worked for ages to bring to pass."

I sniff. "You're kind of irritating, has any one ever told you that?"

"And you don't ask the right questions," counters Peli. "You should be wondering what Aldred's done in Purgatory for your trials." Peli giggles. "Someone's been a busy earl."

I debate threatening Peli bodily harm. Nothing serious, mind you. I'd just wave my tail around and see if that gets me anything more specific than *ghoul with an orange tattoo*. Like an actual name, for example. But before I get the chance, orange mists surround Peli's small body.

A moment later the monkey vanishes, leaving nothing behind but questions.

8

LINCOLN

The colored mist disappears and with it, Peli. A long pause follows before Myla breaks the silence.

"What. A little. Dick."

I can't help but chuckle. "Well said."

Myla's eyes blaze red while she paces a line by the wall. Across the room, Rufus and company stop to watch.

"Is your fiancée all right?" calls Rufus.

"She's about to tirade," I explain. "It's a demon thing. Not a problem."

And it's almost always enjoyable, if I'm being honest.

Rufus nods, shrugs, and goes back to getting his fur brushed.

"I can not believe this," rails Myla. "Did we—or did we not—just rid Purgatory of Lucifer's Orb?"

The answer is *yes*, but I don't reply. Tirade time is not interactive.

"It took for-bleeding-ever, but we finally chucked that stupid orb into storage. What a pain in the ass *that* was. And at the same time, Aldred gets his own daughter possessed by the King of Hell. Nightmare! And what was that, ten minutes ago?"

"I heard it was last month," calls a worker from across the locker room. *Interesting.* This place has better acoustics than I thought.

Myla throws up her arms. "Now that douchebag earl wants to open a gateway to another freaking reality to fight an evil tree that does fuck-knows-all. And we have a trickster monkey running around who's helping Aldred but clearly has his own agenda. And-*and* I have a Scala Bleugh tomorrow which is always a pain. And-*and-and* there's a ghoul in Purgatory who could be a key to this whole thing on Friday. I hate ghouls. Except Walker, who is on a cruise when we need him most." She lets out a long breath with a 'hoo' noise. "Okay, I'm good now."

I do my best golfers clap. "That was one of your best."

"Thank you. My inner demon needs to come out and play sometimes, you know?"

"I do."

Myla frowns. "Guess this means I must mosey back to Purgatory. Peli was right about one thing. I need to focus on Aldred's schemes for the Trials of Acca."

"Clearly, he's looped in the quasi people somehow."

"Well, we both know who tracks everything in Purgatory." That answer would be Cissy, who's now Senator for Diplomacy and has her own spy network. "Care to join me?"

"I wish I could, but I should visit the Royal Archives again. Perhaps there is something on the Primeval that I missed previously. After that, I must check in on Baptiste, Nat, and the other orphans." A vague memory kicks at the back of my mind. I stare off into space, trying to capture the thought. Suddenly, a word appears in my mind.

"Wictus," I say aloud.

Myla purse her lips. "What's that?"

"Not a what, it's a *who*. Wictus were thrax who lived in the Acca caverns long before Aldred's people settled there. They kept records." I nod slowly, my decision made. "I'll inspect the Wictus Archives first. They're more likely to have something on the Primeval."

Myla taps her cheek. "So you're heading to Acca territory now?"

"That I am."

"It's tempting to skip Purgatory and join you. You know how I enjoy irritating Aldred."

"I'd love it, but we don't have enough time. You must pin down Aldred's plans with Purgatory. If Cissy is uninformed, that may take some doing."

"True." Myla puffs out her bottom lip. It's a blatant ploy for sympathy and attention. It's also stunningly effective.

Tilting my head, I fix Myla with a warm smile. "How about I escort you to the transfer Pulpitum?"

She beams. "You have a deal."

9

MYLA

Lincoln and I head off to the Arx Hall Pulpitum. Fortunately, my guy knows a ton of secret passages inside the palace. Together we sneak through some empty corridors that are made of old wood and filled with cobwebs. Love it. Not only will we arrive at our destination faster, but there's also no risk of running into the Rixa Judgey Old Lady Committee.

As we march along, Lincoln gives my hand a gentle squeeze. "You can ignore Aldred's trials, you know."

"Me? Combat readiness trials? Try keeping me away. Plus, there might be a battle tree involved. Something new for my scrapbooks."

Lincoln laughs. "Only you, Myla."

"Hey, whatever the earl comes up with, I've fought worse." I think back to earlier today and shudder. "I've drunk worse."

"Quite true." Lincoln narrows his eyes. "Lady Bentford gave you saffronia."

"Oh my sweet Hell. That stuff is gross."

"It's not something we offer to those new to thrax culture. Lady Bentford was trying to cause an incident."

I know that tight look on Lincoln's face. "You're debating whether or not to get her in trouble."

"Her family asked me to expand their transport license on the

Incaenda river. Entrapping my fiancée isn't exactly placing them in my favor."

"It's not just Lady Bentford. Most of Octavia's blue haired buddies play the same game. *Dodge ball.*"

Lincoln quirks a brow. "That's a new one."

"Originally it comes from Earth. Two teams throw painfully heavy balls at each other. If you're hit, you're out. Last team standing wins. Make sense?"

"As battle training? No. But I suppose there's a parallel with this game and Mother's friends."

"Yup. Octavia's buddies keep tossing dodge balls-o-manners in my direction. When they hit me, they think I'll cry out. It's like they want me to be hurt, you get it?"

"I do. That's why I'm not inclined to expand Lady Bentford's Incaenda license."

"But they don't hurt me. Ever. They're like dodge *bubbles*, if anything. If you refuse that license, you'll only confirm to Lady Bentford that she ticked me off. Which she didn't."

Lincoln frowns. "I don't know."

"Come on. Who's the expert on irritating people?"

Lincoln chuckles. "Clearly not me."

"Exactly. I've got this." I stop. "Ah, here's the doorway to the Pulpitum." And do I feel a little awesome that I remembered that? Why yes, yes I do. Arx Hall is a mega maze.

Lincoln gives my hand another squeeze. "Before you go, there's another question I've been meaning to ask you."

"Shoot."

"Cissy mentioned you both have a new friend."

Huh. "We do?"

"Yes, someone with an unusual name. Bae Jess."

"I don't remember anyone by that nam—" My mouth snaps shut while my stomach sinks to the very dusty floor. Cissy wasn't talking about a new friend named Bae Jess. My bestie blabbed about BAEJS. Not that I'm embarrassed to be caught having a nickname for Lincoln's junk.

Okay, I'm totally embarrassed.

Lincoln's my first real boyfriend. Sure, we have this Angelbound connection that makes us fated to be together, but it doesn't change the fact that I have next-to-zero in terms of guy-related experience. Maybe the BAEJS thing is super insulting? I don't know.

Plus, Cissy vowed she'd never say a word. We had a pact. There's a principle at work here.

Without my willing them, words tumble from my mouth because, *of course they do.* "Cissy is a loud mouthed traitor. That's all I'm saying."

If I'd been thinking things through, I wouldn't have said anything. But I did. And Lincoln's a hunter. He can tell when there's something to track down and club to death.

Right now, my guy's target is the soon-to-be-infamous Bae Jess.

Pausing, Lincoln pulls me into his arms. His strong hands wind up my back. That feels really nice. Leaning in, Lincoln kisses a line behind my ear. That's even better. Some small part of me knows that Lincoln is just leveraging my inner lust demon to break my will and trick me into blabbing about Bae Jess.

More of me doesn't care. Mostly because my inner lust demon is indeed awake and having a grand old time.

Lincoln goes to work on my ear lobe. *Nibble nibble.*

"Well?" he asks.

"Bae Jess is not a name. It's one of those *each letter stands for a word* things."

"And?" My guy's voice takes on a growly tone that goes right to my girly bits.

"You play dirty."

Nibble nibble. "Always."

And that does it. All my resistance turns to mush. "It's B-A-E-J-S. Body Armor Enhanced Junk Show."

Lincoln freezes. No more nibbling. In fact, I'm not even sure if he's breathing.

This may have been a huge miscalculation. What made me think I could handle a complex relationshippy thing like this one?

"Um, Lincoln?"

"That is amazing. Cissy's getting a gift basket."

Arching backward, I take a better look at my guy. He isn't

working his unreadable face, which is nice. His brows are inching up rather high, though.

"You're shocked," I state.

"Not that such a thought exists in your head, but more that you gave it a name. And with Cissy, no less." He sighs. "Such a shame that I must visit the Wictus Archives now." Lincoln's gaze turns intense. "I want more details."

Okay, so this wasn't such a bad move after all. I keep forgetting how Lincoln likes my lust demon. And the way he's staring at me right now? I'll share details, details, so many details.

"I'll take that under consideration," I sass.

When Lincoln next speaks, his tone carries a bossy edge. "You *will* tell me."

Color me a fan of this conversation. In fact, my inner lust demon does her version of a happy dance. Only one thing left to do. End on a high note.

"Promises, promises," I whisper.

Turning, I sashay out the door, taking care to work my hips salsa-style. My tail gives Lincoln a wave goodbye as I head for my official transport to Purgatory.

Best exit ever.

Or at least, for this week.

LINCOLN

Minutes later, I stand in a maze of wooden shelves crammed with dusty books. *The Wictus Archives.* Servants in yellow tunics stalk about the aisles, all of them wearing the Acca insignia on their chests.

A lanky fellow with wild yellow hair steps up to greet me. "Your Highness, we weren't expecting you."

"This is an unplanned visit, Obadiah."

Side note: How do I know this man's name? I grabbed background on the Wictus Archives before popping by. It's one of my things. Per my research, the folks now on duty will allow me free access, so long as someone rushes off to tell Aldred.

"Did you need any assistance?" asks Obadiah.

"No, thank you."

"If you change your mind, please let me know." Obadiah takes off at a sprint, no doubt to tell Aldred I've arrived. A warm sense of satisfaction balloons in my chest. It's rather nice when my research pans out.

As Obadiah speeds away, a small puff of orange smoke materializes before me. A moment later, Peli appears by my boots. Up close, I can see his wide face, large blue eyes, and fur color that's best described as neon tangerine.

I scan the aisle. There are no Acca servants within viewing

distance, but that doesn't mean they aren't close by. The shelves loom tall while the aisles between them stay rather thin. Undoubtedly, the servants will hear me chatting with myself. Or rather, with my invisible monkey. Still, that won't change what I do next.

"Hello, Peli."

Sure enough, low whispers sound from nearby. *The servants heard that greeting, all right.* And they know there's no one else near me.

"Aren't you going to ignore my existence?" asks Peli.

"You're a trickster. If I do that, it merely gives you an excuse for worse behavior." There is a Trickster sub-class of demons, after all. This is a well-known principle.

"True." Peli bobs on all fours, reminding me of a spring that's coiled too tightly. "But I was looking for an excuse to be tricksy."

"Glad I could foil your plans."

"Oh, I didn't say I wouldn't be tricksy *at all*." Peli holds his pointer fingers a hair apart. "Only a little bit."

After leaning back on his haunches, Peli launches himself halfway across the room, landing atop a particularly tall wall of shelves. The wooden structure wobbles as Peli lands. The impact sets multiple books thunking against each other. A pair of servants wait nearby. I can't see these workers, but there's no missing their worried whispers.

"Did you catch that?" asks one.

"Yes, that shelf is... *moving*," replies another. "I don't see who could've touched it, though."

All this time, Peli lounges atop the structure, his mouth stretching into an overly-wide smile.

This isn't going well. I'm supposed to keep a low profile.

Now Peli leaps across a line of shelves, setting even more of the wall-like structures swaying. The servants gasp. To them, the room is under a kind of supernatural shelf-focused earthquake. Peli chatters with laughter, a noise that only I can hear. With every passing second, the little monkey leaps with more speed and pressure.

I raise my hands, palms forward. "Ukapeli." It's important to use someone's full name when you're about to scold them. "Be careful on those—"

Crash!

A massive wall of books slams onto the floor. Shocked yelps echo about the room. Stepping over, I inspect the damage. The books seem fine. Peli sits atop the messy pile, that over-wide grin still plastered on his face.

"You were saying?" asks Peli.

"Watch the shelves."

"So I did."

A new servant appears at the entrance to our aisle. She's lithe and pale with red hair and wide eyes. I remember her from my research. *Flora.* "Is there a problem here, your Highness?"

"No, all is well."

"Who have you been talking to?"

"Peli."

Flora looks around. "I see no one."

I could deny Peli's existence, but again, that won't help the situation.

"Peli is an invisible orange monkey," I explain.

"Oh. I see."

Let the record show that Flora *does not see.*

Another servant approaches. This one's named Selene. Everything about her is efficient: not too tall or short, thin or heavy, pale or brown. She wears a simple yellow dress. "Excuse us, your Highness. We'll be close by if you and your, uh, friend require assistance."

Both rush away. I give it about five minutes, tops, before the rumors of my decaying sanity and invisible monkey friend are all over Antrum. The Wictus folks are proving to be nothing if not predictable.

"Are you through destroying shelves?" I ask Peli.

"For now."

"Please hold off on any additional funny business. I'm here to do research."

"About the Primeval?"

"Yes. I'm rather concerned that Aldred will unleash unknown evils on Friday."

Peli blinks innocently. "*Aldred* will open the gateway?"

"I stand corrected. Undoubtedly, you'll do the magical opening part."

"True enough." Peli folds his skinny arms over his round torso. "And yet you're still speaking to me. Acknowledging me."

Rocking on my heels, I think this through. Peli does bring up a good point. I've encountered shady characters before. Normally I'm never this friendly.

"Here's the thing," I tell Peli. "I fought my first demon at the ripe old age of six. Over the years, I've developed a feel for true malevolence. I don't sense that in you. You're scheming, but something tells me you've a good purpose in the end."

"Yes." Grief pulls at Peli's features. "My family."

Kneeling, I meet Peli's gaze straight-on. "Protecting your family is noble. Does the Contagion threaten their lives? If so, it explains why you'd expose that evil tree to a room full of demon hunters."

"What, me? Noble?" Peli's face becomes a grinning mask once more. "Don't be daft."

"In other words, I've gotten close to the truth."

Peli raises his arms. A fresh haze of orange magic appears by the monkey's feet. *Another spell.* The mist thins out into a dozen unique tendrils. Peli snaps his fingers. The colored cords speed through the archives, each one heading in a different direction.

Seconds later, the cords snap back. The many colored ropes are now tied to different books. All the volumes land in a neat pile by my feet.

"These hold what you require," says Peli. "Information about the Primeval."

Kneeling down, I scan the top titles.

Interviews With A Battle Lion
Ancient Parallel Worlds
Fairy Tales From The Primeval

"These look perfect," I state. "How useful of you."

"We tricksters like being acknowledged. Your new books?" Peli gestures to the pile by my feet. "Consider them a gift in return for your honesty. A boon made for a bounty paid, that's the Law Primeval."

"So, you only rewarded me because I acknowledged your presence? It wasn't due to the fact that I suspected your noble motivations?"

Peli lifts his chin. "I don't know what you're talking about."

Sure, he doesn't. "Moving on. Would you join me in my chambers while I read? I rather enjoy your company. Plus, you can tell me more about the Primeval."

Peli frowns. A moment ago, the monkey was all sneaky charm. Now, he gives off an air of chilly resolve. "Those books hold all you need to know. I will *say* nothing else."

The way Peli emphasizes the word *say*, it's clear that whatever the monkey plans to reveal about the Primeval, he won't speak it aloud. What does he plan to do, exactly? Show me pictures from the books?

At that moment, Obadiah rushes back in. "Aldred is on his way. You're not to touch anything."

I look down. The stack by my feet are gone. Instead, those volumes are now tied up in a bundle that floats over Peli's head. A thin orange haze surrounds the entire package. The books are invisible to others.

Ha! Love it.

"Am I touching anything?" I ask.

Obadiah scans the floor and walls. The servant looks right through Peli and his hovering book-pile. "Ah, you're empty handed. I didn't expect that."

"If you'll excuse us," I say. "Peli and I have places to be."

"Of course, your Highness… and his pretend monkey."

I march toward the exit. Peli scampers along behind. A steady drumbeat of smashes sound as Peli's invisible packet slams into every shelf along the way. With each mysterious thud, the Acca servants gasp again in fear.

And Peli snickers.

I am starting to like this little fellow very much indeed.

Although I still don't trust him.

MYLA

An hour later, I stand inside the Ryder mansion in Purgatory. The sign before me reads, *Senator Cissy Frederickson.* The muffled tones of my best friend's voice echo through the closed door.

Taking in a long breath, I organize my thoughts. Cissy and I had an agreement about BAEJS. It was secret, yet she blabbed. My inner wrath demon is not happy. And that's the same power which takes down Class A monsters in seven seconds or less, so I need to chill out here.

Inhale.
Exhale.
Inhale.
Exhale.
Calm down, Myla.

Only trouble is, this breathing-stuff isn't working. My nervous system still zings with electric rage.

Eh. Fuck it.

I push open the door so hard, it slams against Cissy's office wall.

There, that felt good.

Inside I find a large square room whose walls are covered with photos of Cissy. There's my bestie with Camilla, AKA my mother, AKA the President of Purgatory. Cis also poses with a ghoul delegation. My friend even shows off a framed selfie with the angelic version of Elvis. *Clutch.*

In each snapshot, Cissy looks lovely with her blonde curls and willowy form. As Purgatory's Senator for Diplomacy, it makes sense that's Cissy's met so many well-known angels, demons, ghouls, thrax, and quasis.

But there's more to it than that.

All quasi-demons have both a tail and a power across one of the seven deadly sins. Cissy's power is envy, so her photo wall serves another purpose. In this case, Purgatory's Senator for Trade (who happens to be our old classmate Paulette) also has a similar photo display in her reception chamber. Cissy won't rest until her wall kicks Paulette's in the dirt and calls it names.

Go, Cissy.

Since we have crap technology here in Purgatory, Cis now sits behind a rather funky steel desk while talking on an old-fashioned rotary phone. She balances the receiver against her shoulder while scribbling on a notepad.

While standing on the threshold to her office, I point at Cissy's nose. "You."

For her part, Cissy twiddles her fingers at me before gesturing to the receiver. The meaning is clear: *She's finishing up a call.* I may be ticked off, but I won't ruin her diplomacy stuff.

"Yes, Ambassador PAX-92," says Cissy smoothly. "Everything will run perfectly tomorrow. The Great Scala looks forward to welcoming your ghouls to Purgatory."

Normally, I'd be curious about what exactly the undeadlies are doing at my Scala Bleugh tomorrow. After all, I worked my ass off to get them kicked out of my homeland in the first place. Not an option. My inner wrath demon is still on a tear. She's not letting go of her rage until we confront this major breach of trust.

"Thank you." After hanging up, Cis leans back in her chair. "What did I do now?"

"Who says you did anything?"

"You're frowning and your eyes are glowing red. Spill, Myla."

"Fine. What's the first rule of Girl Lust Club?"

"What?"

"You know what I mean. Our secret society where we talk about boy stuff."

Cis waves her hand in a motion that means, *close the door already.* "My interns are out there."

I kick the door shut behind me. "Well? I repeat, what's the first rule of Girl Lust Club?"

Cis rolls her eyes. "You don't talk about Girl Lust club."

I stalk up to her desk. "So how does Lincoln know about the Body Armor Enhanced Junk Show?"

"Ooooh." Cis smiles. "I said she was our new friend named Bae Jess. He'll never remember."

Leaning forward, I rest my fists on her desktop. "He remembered."

"Nah. How could he? I talk about Bae Jess in front of Zeke all the time. He doesn't have a clue."

"Zeke is not Lincoln."

A red glint shines in Cissy's eyes. Her envy power is kicking up. You don't screw with another quasi's deadly sin. Sure, Zeke now runs Purgatory's senatorial guard, but that's not the same as being a prince. When you're an envy demon, that stuff matters. Plus, Zeke has other limitations, such as being a douchebag. Don't get me wrong; Zeke's great for Cissy. It's just that, more often than not, he makes my skin crawl.

My bestie's eyes flare a brighter shade of crimson. "Are you saying Zeke is dumb?"

"No." Which is true. My issue is more how Zeke acts smarmy and repulsive. Again, not that Cissy needs to know that. "Lincoln was raised to read a hundred meanings into everything. That's why he honed in on Bae Jess."

"Zeke is trained, too. Back at Purgatory High, Zeke took Advanced Ghoul Servitude, remember? He could tell within two seconds if a ghoul teacher wanted a worm soufflé or a cough syrup cocktail, just by the look on their undead faces. Now that's *smart.*"

Let the record show that there is a ton wrong in that little speech. First of all, we quasis were raised to be what the ghouls called *unpaid multigenerational workers.* Essentially, slaves. Reading ghoul desires isn't exactly an achievement most of my people want to remember.

Second, Cissy's irises now blaze with red light while her golden retriever tail stops wagging.

Total warning signs.

If I push things, Cissy will devolve into all-out *demon mode*. Not a lot of logical thinking goes on when Cissy has an envy fit, and I need some answers about the Trials of Acca. I'll just table the Girl Lust Club convo for later.

"I have an idea." I plunk down onto my favorite egg-shaped chair. Cissy has great taste in funky office furniture. "Let's change the subject."

"We're not talking about Zeke anymore?"

"Nope. What have you heard about the Trials of Acca?"

All the red in Cissy's eyes melts away. My stomach sinks. I've never seen Cissy's envy mode disappear this quickly. Which means she must be experiencing the ultimate envy-killer.

P*ity*.

And since I'm the object of this emotion, that makes me nervous. Even my tail lurches in an odd rhythm.

"You know what?" asks Cissy. "We can talk about Girl Lust Club if you want. Sorry if I screwed up and tattled. I honestly didn't think Lincoln would figure it out."

My skin prickles over. "You're scaring me."

Cissy shakes her head, a movement that sends her golden curls bouncing. After dragging open a desk drawer, Cis pulls out a stack of newspapers. She drums her fingers atop the pile.

"You see, there's been a lot of buzz about your trials over the last twenty four hours. Didn't you hear?"

"I was in Antrum for the last few days. You know how they are about news and technology. Nothing gets through unless it's by royal messenger. Besides, Aldred only announced the trials a few hours ago. How can everyone here already have a clue?"

"Oh, they know all right." Cis sighs. "Aldred announced the trials on last night on Purgatory Live."

"Damn." Everyone watches that show. Purgatory doesn't have cable, so it's one of the few decent programs around. "How did it land?" It's not like Aldred's photogenic. Maybe he got on TV and bombed.

"The response has been..." Cissy glances around her office as if she'll find the words plastered to the ceiling. "Oh crap. I'll just show you the morning papers." She flips a newspaper and reads the headline aloud. *"Great Scala Risks Early Death With New Demon Hunting Obsession."*

"It doesn't say that." I swipe the newspaper from her desk top.

It says that.

"What the ever loving Hell?" I make a lewd finger gesture at the headline. "I fought evil souls in Purgatory's Arena for *years*. How can this even be a question?"

"Well, the quasi population doesn't connect Myla Lewis with being the Great Scala. They see this demon fighting stuff as a fresh risk to moving souls."

"All right. That makes sense. I don't like it, but it makes sense. What else do you have?"

Cis moves on to the next item in the stack. "Here's a good one. *The Great Scala And Fighting Demons: Never Or Never Ever?"*

"Bah. The demon fighting stuff is the only nice part about ruling the thrax. Apart from the Lincoln benefits, obviously."

"Right." Cissy stares at the last newspaper in the pile.

"Okay, none of that stuff is too shocking. What's the pity party about?"

Cissy's eyes go extra-wide. "Who says I'm pitying you?"

"It's me here, Cis. I've known you since you scored your first Burberry bag in second grade. Whatever's on that last newspaper, you know I can handle it."

"Fine." Cissy flips up the last newspaper. *"In Honor Of Purgatory, Earl Adds Igni Test To Trials Of Acca."*

I shrug. "Aldred can add whatever he wants. There's some treaty between Acca and Rixa, blah blah blah. So, the old windbag wants to test my igni in honor of Purgatory. How will that work, exactly?"

"With an..." Cissy inhales a long breath. "Igni Validation."

"Wow. I have no idea what that is."

"I used my spy network to get a copy." She opens another drawer and pulls out a tiny container.

"That's it?" I frown. "A little black box?"

"You got it. The test takes place as part of the Trials of Acca on

Friday. Aldred promised to personally report the results that same night on Purgatory Live. I wouldn't be surprised if he also rented a plane to write *Myla failed* in front of the Pearly Gates, too. That guy really hates your guts."

"It's mutual. The only difference is, I'll win in the end." I lean in closer to the box. "What's inside?"

"Nothing. For the Purgatory test, the box is asked if you can be involved in demon fighting in any way, shape, or form."

"Like a Magic 8 Ball?"

Cissy snaps her fingers. "Exactly. If red igni show up in the box, then you are approved for combat. If not, then you must disavow battle-related stuff forever."

"What total crap." I roll my eyes. "You know there's no such thing as red igni, right?"

"I get that, believe me." Cis pulls more sheets out of her desk. "Still, perception is reality. That's why I did a quick public opinion survey. Sadly, the quasi people got really upset about Aldred's claims about the risk to the Great Scala while fighting demons. 87% of all Purgatory like the Igni Validation test."

"87% can pound salt. That test—" I point to the box "—is never happening."

"I thought you might say that, so I went ahead and asked more questions. There's great news. Aldred also mentioned the Rixa Way on TV. It went over super well. The quasi population want you to adopt what they're calling the Purgatory Path. If you do, then they won't worry about the Igni Validation test."

"The Rixa Way is a nightmare. What's this Purgatory Path?"

"They want you to change how you act and be…" Cissy takes in another dramatic breath. "More goddess like."

"Meaning?"

"Minor stuff." She scans the survey. "You need to hug everyone who asks."

I fold my arms over my chest. "No touchie."

"Build a bunch of temples to yourself."

"Creepy."

"Oh, here's a good one. Buy a flashy wardrobe. The quasis

demand you wear colored scarves, beaded veils, and crystal ball earrings."

"Let me think about that." I tap my chin. "No, no, a thousand times, no."

Cis steps out from behind her desk to kneel beside me. "I know this is hard. But whether it's the Rixa Way or the Purgatory Path… there's a reason this kind of request keeps coming up. People need you to change."

"Come on. You know that won't happen."

"Remember that ghoul saying? *The coffin nail that sticks up gets hammered down.* No one holds out forever. Even you, Myla."

A chill rolls up my back. Cissy's words rattle around my consciousness. *No one holds out forever.*

Sadly, Cis may have a point. Things were different when my world was Mom, Cissy, and the Arena. Now I have whole realms of people telling me to change. First Rixa, now Purgatory, who's next? Over the years, will I really get hammered down?

I shake off the thought. *Bullshit.* This is exactly what everyone wants: me worrying about their Rixa Way or Purgatory Path. All of which is why I'll think about something else.

Namely, going home and hiding out.

A knock sounds at the door. Cissy leaps from her chair and opens it. Zeke stands outside. Like always, his caramel eyes, chiseled features, and messy blonde hair are perfectly matched with a monkey tail.

"Hey, Babykins." Zeke leans to kiss Cissy with his mouth open and tongue a-wagging. I'm part lust demon, and even I think that's over the line. I decide that now is a great time to stare at the ceiling.

Lots of cobwebs. Wow.

Once the *sloppy kiss hello* part is over, Zeke saunters over in my direction. "Myla. Sweetie."

"It's Great Scala Sweetie to you."

Zeke chuckles. "If I didn't know better, I'd think you still had a crush on me."

I stare at the nonexistent watch on my wrist. "Oh, damn. Look at the time. I better get home."

Cissy and Zeke now stare at each other in a way that can only be described as *intense*. As a lust demon, I get where this is going.

"I'll just show myself out," I say. I'm four steps away when a memory appears. *The Scala Bleugh.* I pause. "About tomorrow," I begin. "Did your interns do a prep binder for me again?"

"Yup," replies Cissy. "It's at your parents' place."

Not a lot of guys do a dip-kiss. I'm talking where you swoop your girl into your arms until her hair cascades to the floor, then you lay on a big whopper of a smack. This happens a lot in old black and white movies with humans. And it's the move Zeke does right as I grasp the door handle.

Before I can see or hear too much, I pull the door shut and take off at a jog.

LINCOLN

*L*eaning back in my leather chair, I take in the familiar comfort of my surroundings. My cozy personal library is lined with shelves of leather-bound volumes. A healthy fire blazes in the hearth. For my part, I sit at a round wooden table that's piled high with volumes from the Wictus Archives. Above me, Peli swings from a ceiling sconce.

And no, that is no exaggeration.

Peli's *fixture of choice* is a bowl-like affair that hangs via chains. Usually, the thing burns with angelfire. Today I extinguished the blaze for safety reasons, so it makes a nice pseudo swing for my new orange friend.

Speaking of Peli, the monkey lounges on his back. Stretching, he leans his head over the edge of the bowl-like swing. For a long moment, he eyes me from his upside-down position.

"How goes it with the books?"

"Slowly," I reply. "These are rather dense. And I'm no master of ancient Greek. Latin is more my thing."

"Keep going. What you seek lies on those pages." Peli leans upside-down even further. Now his shoulders are off his little bowl-swing, a position that allows him to stare at the books at a better angle. He's been doing that more and more the last few minutes.

I push my book away. "What?"

"What do you mean, what?"

"Is there a particular volume I should read first?"

"Maybe." Peli smiles. Turns out, Peli has a wide collection of happy faces for various occasions. This one reminds me of the overly-large grin popular on metal monkey toys—the kind you wind up in order to slam cymbals.

In other words, it's unnerving as Hell.

"A boon made for a bounty paid," says Peli. "That's the Law Primeval."

Kicking back, I consider this turn of events. Last time, my so-called *bounty paid* was addressing Peli in front of other thrax who couldn't see him. At the same time, I acknowledged his true—and possibly noble—intentions. Both actions involved an award of recognition on my part.

An idea occurs. "How would you like a title?"

Peli sits upright. The movement makes the entire bowl-sconce swing at an alarming rate. "Like what kind of title?"

"How about…" I purse my lips. "His Royal Emperor of Awesome Orangitude?"

Peli narrows his eyes to slits. "Don't you need to give that that out formally?"

"Quite right." I rise. "Hear ye! Hear ye! I, Lincoln Vidar Osric Aquilus, the High Prince of the Thrax and future King of all Antrum, do hereby award Ukapeli the title of His Royal Emperor of Awesome Orangitude." I fold my arms over my chest. "It is done."

"Perfect. Now there shall be a boon made for a bounty paid."

A moment later, every thread of fur on Peli's body lights up with an orange glow. *Fresh magic.* Over on my table, a volume slips out from the bottom of my book pile. The leather tome flips through the air before landing on its spine and opening to a certain page.

Once again, Peli speaks from his upside down position. "Oh, look. Something for you to read."

"For an emperor, you're quite the sneaky fellow. Not sure I like it."

"Apologies. If you have any alternative sources for information, please go after them. Today is Wednesday. The Trials of Acca are Friday. Better hop to it." He lets out a staccato giggle that reminds me of a snake hissing.

Little bugger thinks I have no alternatives for Primeval info. Which I don't. So I scan the opened page. "This is a spell. And it's in Latin, no less." I glare at Peli. "Who knew there were Latin books in the mix?"

More snake-hiss laughter follows. Peli really is having a ball. "Never trust a trickster. In fact, you shouldn't read that spell aloud. It's very dangerous."

"You've already warned me that reading books and even entering my library were dangerous." Essentially, it's Peli's *trickster way* of saying that something is safe.

Bracing my arms on the tabletop, I speak the spell aloud.

> *Reveal the past*
> *Cast the spell*
> *A boon I require*
> *The bounty paid full well*

Orange smoke pours out from the opened book, filling the room in a haze. When the colored mist vanishes, my library is gone. Instead, I find myself surrounded by an orange jungle.

I step around in a slow circle.

Yes, this is really an orange jungle all right.

Great tangerine-colored leaves dangle from towering palm trees. The scent of musk and decaying leaves fills the air. Two-headed birds flit between the dense undergrowth. Monkeys like Peli swing from the many vines.

One thing is clear. I've been magically transported to the Primeval. To what purpose?

Voices carry through the forest. Stalking through the trees, I follow the sounds and find the speakers.

What I see shocks me to the core.

Before me walks a different version of Peli. No wisdom lines around his large blue eyes. There's even more spring in his movements, if possible. Others surround him, namely his wife and twin children. There's no longer any doubt as to the purpose of this particular spell.

Peli sent me to his past.

13

LINCOLN

Very few magic users can send someone to the past. In fact, the only confirmed instance in the last hundred years took place when Verus, the Queen of the Angels, sent Myla to see her mother's history in Purgatory's Senate. For Verus, casting those spells proved so draining, the Queen of the Angels was forced to rest for hours afterwards.

Now Peli completes a similar feat. *Interesting.*

I follow the small family through the jungle, careful to make as much noise as possible. No one notices me.

That settles it. This is more of an historical recreation rather than an actual passage through time. The former is a less taxing spell, but not by much. For a recreation, the caster must fabricate everything from their own—or someone else's—memories. Not easy.

When I first met him, Peli seemed like a goofy trickster from a strange world. Sure, he cast a gateway. Yet for all I know, that's an easy spell in his homeland. Now I know differently. There is no way recreating the past is a simple task.

Long story short, the more I learn about Peli, the more I realize I have only begun to discover his true identity.

Before me, Young Peli sets his hand on his wife's shoulder. She's a shorter and slimmer version of him. "Please, Nora," he says. "Don't get the twins excited. We don't know what will happen today. I'm not a trained wizard."

"Bah, no one's better at magic than you. Can anyone else cast a gateway? No. And you've trained yourself." Nora pauses. "Where are the twins, anyway?" She cups her long hand by her mouth. "Mlinizi? Walinzi?"

I hadn't noticed it, but the siblings snuck off into the jungle.

"Ugh," groans Young Peli. "I should never have lifted the soul link spell between them. Now it will take even longer to find them."

"Not to worry," counters Nora. "They'll turn up at the Golden Arbor. Trust me."

"We'll see."

Young Peli and Nora step out from the line of orange trees and into a small clearing. In the center of this open area, there towers a massive arbor. I've seen redwood trees on Earth, and this one carries the same majestic dimensions. Eight feet wide. Three stories tall.

And every inch of it shines with gold.

A clear blue sky arches overhead. Now that we're out of the jungle, it's easy to see the gleaming white stone wall that soars in the distance. We've entered some kind of valley surrounded by a mighty cliff.

Waves of recognition move through me. I've seen this tree before. Back in the Royal Gymnasium, Aldred ordered Peli to open a gateway to the Primeval. Within that view, there stood a blackened stump backed by a charred wall of stone.

Here stands that same tree, only now it's full of life. Magic pulses about it.

The Golden Arbor.

Young Peli sits at the tree's base. Nora plunks down beside him. After lifting his hands, Young Peli conjures a small haze of magic to flare across his palms. When the brightness fades, Young Peli holds a small wooden carving. Four faces look from out around the sphere; one for each of his family. The likenesses are perfectly rendered.

"I hope this is enough," whispers Young Peli.

"Nonsense," counters Nora. "I've never seen a finer magical peak for a wizard's staff."

Mlinizi and Walinzi bound out of the forest. "Don't start without us," they cry in unison.

Nora shoots Young Peli a sly look. "Told you." She positions the twins so they sit between their parents. "Now stay silent while your father tests the peak for his wizard's staff."

Mlinizi and Walinzi chatter at once. I can't pick out who is speaking, but I do catch what they say.

"Where's the staff part?"

"He needs to get the peak done first, dummy."

"Then will Poppa become a real wizard?"

"No, he won't."

"Yes, he will."

"It doesn't matter. I have magic, too."

"No, you don't."

"Yes, I do."

"Hush, children," says Nora. "Allow your father to begin the ritual."

Young Peli sets his carving down before the base of the tree. He lifts his arms. Tendrils of orange haze wind around his palms. Fresh magic.

I move in closer, hoping for a better view of the spell. Over the years, I've seen my share of castings. If I had to guess, this is a classic summoning spell. Young Peli will wish to call forth the spirit of the Golden Arbor. Since the object placed on the ground is the peak of a wizard's staff, Young Peli probably wants to know if his future in magic stands a chance.

Although I haven't known Peli long, it's now clear that he carries two unique sides. One is the trickster monkey. The other is a serious wizard. Is this the moment when one path is crushed? And if so, why does Peli wish for me to see that take place?

"Oh, Golden Arbor," states Young Peli. "I come to you to ask for a blessing on the true peak of my wizard's staff. Will you listen to my plea?"

The tree shivers. Golden leaves whisper with the wind. Young Peli grins.

"Thank you for considering me, Golden Arbor." Peli exhales. "To make my case, I shall perform the traditional rite."

Peli lifts his arms once more. A fresh cloud of orange haze appears. The magic flattens out into a map. As the cloud solidifies, the details of the map come into focus. Turns out, the Primeval is a round continent that's divided into four slices, pie-style. At the center sits a round space dominated by a golden tree.

"I summon the power of the Avians, Icythians, Reptilians, and Felines," intones Young Peli. As he speaks each name, a slice of the world lights up. "And most of all, I call upon the energy of my people, the Simians, whose lands hold the Golden Arbor itself." Now the center of the map brightens as well.

I commit the image to memory. At this point, I stand in Simian territory, which sits at the center of the round continent that makes up the Primeval. *Good to know.*

Young Peli continues. "I plead to the Golden Arbor and all lands of the Primeval. My deepest desire is to become a Simian wizard and join my brothers and sisters in channeling magic. Please confirm my future in magic by consecrating the peak of my wizard's staff. With this request, I hereby end the ritual."

Everyone waits.

Nothing happens.

Sweat beads on Young Peli's forehead, he swipes the moisture away with the back of his hand. "I know the trouble." Young Peli looks up to the treetop. "Golden Arbor, I'm unrecognized by Quilliam, our wizard king. All my life, I've been forbidden from court. Yet this month, I've been summoned to his presence. I can only see him if I take with me the consecrated peak to my wizard's staff." Young Peli looks expectantly at the glimmering arbor.

Despite a breeze, there's no rustle of leaves.

This doesn't bode well.

"Please." Young Peli's hands curl into fists. "If you bless my wish to serve as a wizard, I shall protect this land with every scrap of magic in my soul."

At last, the branches of the Golden Arbor sway. A single golden leaf wafts downward, pausing as it touches Young Peli's carving. Golden light flares from the leaf, encircling the peak of his wizard's staff. Magic and energy pulse through the air before the golden leaf vanishes.

Young Peli bows his head. "Thank you, Golden Arbor. I welcome the approval."

Nora elbows him gently. "Told you so."

Orange haze appears on the ground. More magic. The concentration grows heavier until I'm encircled in a haze of power.

Peli's spell must be ending.

Only it doesn't.

Instead of orange haze, I become engulfed in white flames, a blaze that surrounds me but doesn't burn. Angelfire. I see this every time I ignite my baculum sword.

Familiar magic, but it has nothing to do with Peli's spell.

Who's behind this new casting?

LINCOLN

When the white fire vanishes, I find myself standing on the edge of a lush green forest. Trees buckle and sway with the breeze. Stars swirl overhead, the many tiny blinking bodies speeding in coordinated waves. I've seen paintings by the human named Vincent Van Gogh. This scene looks like one of his creations brought to life.

Some part of me screams that this scene should be strange and overwhelming. I brace my stance, waiting for adrenaline to kick in.

That isn't what happens. My breathing slows. If anything, my new surroundings soothe me.

I scan the great expanse of forest before me. About a half-mile ahead, a thin tendril of blue smoke curls up toward the skies.

A memory appears. After my battle training with Rufus, I'd felt a larger and invisible threat looming against me and Myla. At the time, I pictured a forest where smoke curled in the distance, yet I was uncertain if a larger fire would follow.

Now, some kind of magic creates that very a scene.

It can't be coincidence.

A voice echoes through the air. "I soak in power from Peli and his world. Primeval magic works differently in the after-realms. When I've taken in enough energy, I will appear to you."

The voice sounds familiar, yet I can't quite place it.

More white fire bursts up around me. The flames press in, warm as a blanket. When the blaze disappears, I find myself back in my library. I stand in the exact same spot as when the casting began: looking down at the Wictus spell book.

Peli sits upon the tabletop, watching me with his large blue eyes. For a moment, he doesn't seem like the silly trickster who knocked over shelves in Antrum. This is someone who's wise and cunning.

"How long have I been gone?" I ask. There's no need to specify. We both know I'm wondering how long I've been gone from this reality.

"Only a few seconds," says Peli. "What did you think?"

"That was a powerful spell. Why not simply tell me more about the Contagion?"

Peli's mouth presses into a too-firm line. At the same time, his throat convulses with the effort to speak. I've seen this effect in the past.

"You're under a magical aegis not to speak of this, aren't you?"

Peli's throat grinds more furiously. His small hand grips his neck, while his chest heaves. Peli doesn't pull in a breath.

I've seen this before as well. Peli can't breathe. If he doesn't stop trying to fight the spell, he could hurt himself.

"Don't try to answer. When you're ready to share more, simply take me to your past."

Peli sucks in a rough breath. "Thank you."

"Are you all right?"

"Yes." Peli hops about the tabletop while making ooo-ooo noises. The glimmer of the other Peli has vanished.

"May I ask you a question?"

"Ooo-ooo."

"I'll take that as a *yes*. After seeing the Primeval, why send me to a forest?"

Peli falls still. "I didn't."

"Ah, my mistake." I'd suspected this, considering the change in magic. Good to have Peli confirm things, though.

"Many confuse jungles and forests," says Peli. "You need to get out more."

I'd mention my skills as a hunter, but Peli seems to accept the situation *as is*. Somehow, I suspect that news of another magic user tagging onto Peli's spells would make things more confusing, not less.

Best to change the topic.

"Thank you for showing me the Primeval."

"You've much more to learn if you're to protect your people while helping me save mine."

"That raises a good point. You've some plan with Aldred, and my guess is that there's no aegis against chatting about that."

"No, there is not," replies Peli. "Which is why you must rest, my friend."

Peli lifts his hands. A whirl of orange magic appears between his open palms while sending odd shadows across his rounded features.

Peli exhales a long breath. The exhale sends his magic spinning toward me. As the orange mist touches my chest, my head turns fuzzy with the need for sleep.

Seconds later, I pass out.

MYLA

hat a crap day. I need Demon Bars and sleep. In that order.
With that thought in mind, I rush through the Ryder mansion at double speed. If I were a cartoon, fluffy dust clouds would follow behind me. Soon I step out the mansion's front door. A limo awaits.

Hmm. Not sure how I feel about that.

Don't get me wrong. For the first weeks after I became the Great Scala, the limo situation was fun. But now? I'd really rather drive myself, thank you very much. Mostly because—if I'm being totally honest—it helps me let off steam. Professional drivers are totally civil and blah. I'm both a demon and nineteen. Driving like a banshee goes with the territory.

Sadly, my own beloved nasty mobile, the lovely station wagon Betsy, is back at my parents place.

Limo, here I come.

I slide onto the back seat. In no time, I'm at my parents place in Upper Purgatory. Basically, if a haunted gothic mansion got busy with something out of Star Wars, then the resulting bastard baby house would be my parents' mansion. This is what happens when ghouls design things.

Needless to say, I plan to move out ASAP. It's on the list, too. Only unlike saffronia, this is a top ten item.

For now, I hang out in the more space-shippy parts of the mansion and avoid the basement, which is scary as fuck. Another nicer part is my parents' office. That's where I head once I get home. It's a cozy spot with wooden furniture and lots of wall space for Dad to tack up battle plans.

Not that we're at war. My father was General of the angels. Some habits die hard.

When I step in, I find my parents sitting at a small square table. Stacks of paper lie scattered across the top. Both grin as I approach. As always, Mom looks like an older version of me. I'm talking curvy figure, dragonscale tail, and auburn hair. For his part, Dad wears a gray suit and Mister Suave vibe. He has cocoa skin, bright blue eyes, and a jawline so sharp it could cut day-old rump roast (which the ghouls served at Purgatory High and is not unlike eating steel wool with gravy.)

My fam and I say our hellos and share kisses. Once the niceties are over with, I head right for the trouble zone. My conversation with Cissy still bugs me, big time.

"What do you think of this Purgatory Path?" I ask. "It's all over the papers."

"We quasis can be rather bossy," says Mom. "I've been hearing rumblings about this sort of thing for a while now. Nothing to worry about. Everything is *perfectly fine*."

Here's what I think. *Fine* is when you get a run in your pantyhose but it happens by your butt where no one can see. *Fine* is when you step in just a little bit of dog poop with a nice stretch of grass nearby to wipe off the nastiness. *Fine* is when you order diet soda and they add too much ice… but who cares because it's free refills.

All that is fine. Me being forced to alter my entire personality? That's not fine. That's a perfect disaster.

I take a seat at the table. "Be honest with me. Do I really need to change?"

"You're wonderful just as you are," says Dad. He emphasizes the point with one of his million-watt grins. "The rest of the world doesn't matter. In fact, I've half a mind to get on Purgatory Live and tell the quasi population what I *really* think."

I shoot Dad a thumbs up. "I like this plan."

Mom shakes her head. "Xav, we have six new soul processing bills before the senate. We can't get the administration involved in this Purgatory Path scandal."

My eyes widen. "It's a scandal?"

"Just a little one," says Dad. "Everything will be perfectly fine."

There are those two words again. *Perfectly fine*. And I can't help noticing how Dad isn't insisting on the Purgatory Live idea any more. Not that I want my parents to their risk soul processing bills. If Dad went on TV—and then an innocent went to Hell because the bills didn't pass quickly enough— then I'd never forgive myself. Still, I can't help feeling a little mopey about the whole situation.

"We've other matters to discuss." Mom fixes me with what I call her *Mom-idential stare*. It combines an *I run Purgatory* vibe with a clear undercurrent of maternal panic. "We've seen the news. The Trials of Acca take place on Friday. Your father and I are worried about you."

I sniff. "Remember when I got chucked into the Arena for the first time? That was scary. This is a total meh."

My parents share a long look and an exhale. "Good to hear," says Mom. "Because your father and I planned a week-long Purgatory press tour, starting tomorrow. We want to drum up support for these bills."

"That's a good idea." I force a smile. After all, it really *is* a good idea. So why do I feel like I'm six years old again and someone just cancelled my birthday party? Not that my parents need to be standing on the sidelines while I go through some *big nothing* like the Trials of Acca.

But yeah. I want them on the sidelines.

With *Go Myla* signs.

And snacks.

Growing up sucks.

Mom makes her infamous tsk-tsk noise. "You look exhausted." She's in full-blown maternal worry mode now. "Get some sleep, baby."

Which is a super idea.

After all the excitement today at the battle lion lesson, I'm a sleepy mess. I say my goodnights and slump-walk into the kitchen.

This is one of the more high-tech rooms in the house—I'm talking tons of stainless steel along with scary appliances. However, a beautiful sight awaits me there: a box of Demon Bars. And atop that container sits Cissy's binder for tomorrow's Scala Bleugh event.

This is part of my bestie's brilliance, by the way. The binder is thick as a brick, but the extra charge of chocolaty goodness should keep me awake enough to read it all.

Does Cis know me or what?

Hoisting Demon Bars under one arm and the binder beneath the other, I trudge off to my bedroom. If I have to pull an all nighter to read this thing, then that's what I will do. Based on Cissy's call, the ghouls are definitely part of tomorrow's event.

A memory hits me. *Peli.* That little orange stinker said a ghoul was critical for his horror show on Friday. There was something about a skull mark on the ghoul's shoulder, too.

Well, Cissy's interns are nothing if not through. If a ghoul is part of my Scala Bleugh and has a tattoo, then it will be inside this binder. And I can research the whole thing while eating Demon Bars.

Being an adult isn't all bad. I guess.

Within minutes, I've snuggled under the covers and am ready to study. All my Demon Bars sit within grabbing distance. The massive binder lays balanced on my stomach. Determination courses through my veins.

A small pool of orange mist appears on my Wonder Woman comforter. Moments later, Peli appears.

"Hello, Myla."

"Hey, Peli." I rap on the binder with my knuckles. "Know what this is?"

Peli balances on his hind legs. "No."

"It's a big-ass binder made by my friend Cissy's devoted interns." I flip two fingers between his and my eyes. "I see what you're up to."

"Me?"

"You were talking about Purgatory and a certain ghoul earlier today. Now you show up on my favorite DCU comforter right at the very moment I'm about to read about ghoul action at tomorrow's Scala Bleugh. The undeadly you're interested in will be there, yes?"

More blinking follows. "No."

"That's totally a *yes.*" My tail slips out from under the covers. this time, the arrowhead end is balled up for a fist bump, which is exactly what we share. "Nailed it."

"I don't see how this *Bind Her* can help."

"Binder."

Peli inches closer. "Hmm. Is it magic?"

"Kind of. Consider it some organizational magic that's performed with the secret power of unpaid interns. You see, I'll read these pages and figure out who your mystery ghoul is. And once I find him or her, do you know what I will do?"

"Tell me."

"I'll let them roam about free to do cause a disaster on Friday."

"How kind of you."

"Just kidding. Once I find this ghoul—and I will find them—then I will lock up their skull-tattooed ass. In fact, I'll zip them off to Heaven for safe keeping. I'm a supernatural being who can do stuff like that, no problem."

"Suppose I want them back before Friday?" A sneaky look sparks in Peli's blue eyes, but I'm on a roll. I can deal with his trickster ways later.

"Then you can absolutely have them back."

"Good." Peli rubs his hands together in the classic mwah-hah-hah move of all super villains.

"But first, you'll need to share every last thing about the Primeval and your secret schemes involving Aldred." At these words, my tail snakes out again. This time we share a high five. Sometimes I'm so brilliant, I just can't stand it. Also, the sugar high just kicked in. So that's a factor.

"Now, my dear Peli." I say this slowly while rocking my own mwah-hah-hah essence. "What do you think about all that?"

In reply, Peli merely raises his little monkey arms. A wave of orange mist shoots out from his palms and slams right into my face. Magic clogs my lungs. My vision blurs. All sounds dull. Consciousness drains.

Boo.

Peli just hit me with a sleeping spell.

Sneaky monkey.

16

LINCOLN

*W*hack!
Whack!
Whack!

Pounding echoes across my royal suite. Forcing my eyes open, I discover a major change to my circumstances. The last thing I knew, I'd been working in my library. Now I find myself tucked into my own bed. No question who did this, either.

Peli.

According to my grandfather clock, it's now early Thursday morning. Peli must have cast more than a sleeping spell on me. If it had been only that, then I'd have woken up on the library floor, snoozing in a puddle of my own drool. Instead, the monkey magically tucked me into bed.

How do I know this? Orange pajamas. I'm wearing them. Normally, sleepwear plays no role in my nocturnal routine.

Whack!
Whack!
Whack!

Someone's at the door. Undoubtedly, it's Connor. My father's the only one who slams in such a fierce rhythm.

After slipping out of bed, I stroll over to the main door and pull it open. In the hallway outside, I find Connor wearing his kingly best, which means a black tunic and silver crown. *How odd.* I wasn't aware there were any formal ceremonies today. Connor never dons his full kit if he can avoid it.

"Good morning, Father."

"Son."

"What do you need?"

There are two types of *morning poundings* from my father. The first variety is where he barks out a quick order from the hallway and moves on. The second type occurs when Connor shoulders his way into my chambers in order to deliver a long speech.

Sadly, Father pushes past me.

It's *door number two* today.

Speech time.

After closing the door behind us, I take my favorite spot for such occasions. Namely, I lean against a long stretch of wall that overlooks some leather chairs. Father plunks himself into the largest seat and gestures to the one across from him.

"Join me?" he asks.

"No, thank you." Over the years, I've found that sitting down only increases the length of Father's speeches.

"I'll cut to the chase," says Connor. "I hear you've been chatting up an imaginary monkey."

As I suspected, my adventures in the Wictus Archives have been well reported. "Not at the present moment."

Sure enough, a loop of orange mist appears by my feet. A moment later, the haze congeals into the form of Peli himself. He hops on all fours.

"Oh, I love it when I'm the center of attention!"

"What a shock," I deadpan.

Father purses his lips. "Who were you talking to just then?"

"An invisible monkey from the Primeval."

Father nods. "You're under a lot of stress."

I shrug. "Always."

"That's why you're seeing things. Happens to us all. Well, not me personally, but you should be fine. Just don't do anything in public, get more sleep, and everything will simply work itself out."

That can't be the end of his speech. "Any other reason you came by today?"

"As a matter of fact, I wished to discuss the Trial of Acca. That takes place tomorrow, you know."

"I'm aware."

"Seems there's a demon who may come through. A tree creature."

"Also aware."

Father then launches into an extensive history of Acca in general, and Aldred in particular. I tune this part out and start making mental plans instead. I've heard this particular speech before. Countless times.

Specifically, I focus on the best way to catch up with Nat and Baptiste. All those scars on the child's head—combined with Aldred's interest in punching skulls—have me concerned. Baptiste might be harboring a lasting head injury. Not to mention all the other children who may still be at risk.

Father's words break through my thoughts, mostly because he launches the phrase that signifies his speech is almost complete. "All of this boils down to a single fact, my son."

"Go on."

"Aldred wants to kill this tree demon before the crowd tomorrow." Father's eyes crinkle as he gives me his most winning smile. "How hard can that be? It's a damned tree, after all. We need to make him happy."

I fold my arms over my chest. "That is a blisteringly awful idea." I look to Peli. "Anything you'd like to add?"

"No," says Peli. "This is all going according to my plan. I am a very happy monkey."

As for Father, he doesn't realize I was speaking to Peli. "There *is* something I'd like to add, actually. You must keep Myla back while Aldred has his moment. This is *his* kill."

A jolt of defensive energy runs up my spine. I kick off the wall and stalk closer to Father. "Myla is my priority now. If she wishes to step in, she has my full support."

"Sure, sure," says Father quickly. "For her tests, that makes perfect sense."

I scan Father's formal outfit. "What are those tests?"

"I don't know."

"You're dressed to meet nobility the day before the Trials of Acca begin. I suspect the topic of those tests will come up, will they not?"

Father rises quickly. "Well, so long as Myla leaves the tree thing alone, that's all I care about. I best be going."

In other words, father is definitely meeting with the nobles to devise more of Myla's tests for the Trials of Acca. Since most nobility know zero about battle, these tests will likely be of the annoying, non-combat variety.

Peli hops about with joy. "Oh, he's planning tests for the Trials of Acca and not telling you. Secrets, secrets! How tricksy!"

Tilting my head, I think things through. Myla made a good point earlier. Whatever Aldred has planned, it can't be worse than a Class A demon. Still, this is my fiancée we're talking about here. I can't leave anything to chance.

I'll simply have to ask Mother. Alone. Later.

"I take it that's all for this morning." Crossing the room, I open the door again. "Thank you for coming by."

"Best to you."

Once Connor is well and gone, I close the door and round on Peli. "Hello, friend. How about *you* reveal a few secrets? Specifically, I'm still interested in your relationship with Aldred."

"Funny you should ask that," states Peli. He giggles as a fresh cloud of orange smoke fills my reception room.

Another spell.

I should have known.

MYLA

When I wake up Thursday morning, Peli is gone while my Demon Bars remain beside my bed.

Yay.

Meanwhile, Cissy's binder is nowhere to be found.

Not-yay.

Note to self: Don't reveal secret plans to magical monkeys, even if they are small, orange, and harmless-looking.

Kicking off my covers, I take stock of my day.

Negative side: my Scala Bleugh starts in just a few hours. Ghouls are involved.

Positive: There's still half a box of Demon Bars.

Hoisting the *container of yum* under my arm, I head to the kitchen for breakfast. There I chow down and dial Cissy. There's a lot of ringing followed by a long beep. Time for voicemail.

Clearing my throat, I leave a message. "Hey Cis, can your interns rush me another copy of the binder? Thanks!"

Hanging up, I feel pretty good about my bad self. Cissy's interns are the best. This isn't the first time I've asked for last minute binder redelivery. I tend to leave them places, like public restrooms or the back seat of limos. Hence the Demon Bar trick.

With the binder situation in hand, I get my sweet self showered and ready to go.

Now for some Scala Bleugh.

But first, a little happy time for me.

Stepping out the back door, I approach the most beautiful car in the history of ever: Betsy, my beat-up station wagon. I slide behind the steering wheel, turn the ignition, and grin as an ear-splitting boom sounds, followed by a black cloud of odd-smelling smoke.

I pat the dashboard. "Good morning, Betsy."

Tap, tap.

Someone's at my driver side window. *Mom.* I roll the window down. It's a process because the crank's busted. Finally, it's open enough that I can speak.

"Hey."

"What are you doing?" she asks.

"Going to my Scala Bleugh."

Mom waves the smoke away from her mouth. "And you're doing that in Betsy?"

"Yeeeeeeeah?"

Mom looks over her shoulder. "Talk to her, Xav."

My father approaches the car window. The smoke billowing from the tailpipe gets even heavier. Dad coughs into his hand.

"Can you kill the engine for a sec?" asks Dad.

"Sure thing." With a sigh, I turn off the ignition. This is a bummer. Who knows when or if I'll get the engine ignited again? Betsy is a temperamental girl. Once the smoke clears, I refocus on my father. "What's up?"

Dad sighs while shaking his head. I haven't known my father for long—he was imprisoned in Hell for most of my life—but I still know what that particular shake-n-sigh combination means. I'm doing something Dad thinks is nutso.

"Myla, you're now the Great Scala."

"Uh huh."

"You're attending a big event this morning."

"Yup."

Dad gestures to Mom, who stands nearby. "And your mother is now the President of Purgatory."

"Is everything okay with you and Mom? You're both acting really weird."

"You can't drive Betsy anymore," declares Mom. Unfortunately for me, she's using her *this is the hammer coming down* tone. "There's a limo out front."

Dad wraps his arm around Mom's shoulder. "We've also called a tow truck to take Betsy to automotive Heaven. It will be gone by the time you get back."

My mouth falls open. I grip the steering wheel with more force. "No way. I am still a teenager. Having my own car is super critical." I gently pet the dashboard. "I don't want to get rid of Betsy."

"Did you notice the back bumper?" asks Mom.

"It fell off. That's what old cars do—drop their junk on the freeway."

"No," counters Dad. "One of your followers snuck back here and stole it as a holy relic. It's now on display in the First Church of the Great Scala Mother."

I try to process this news. Twice. Total fail.

"The first WHAT of the WHAT?" I get out of the car so quickly, I almost slam the door onto my Mom's kneecaps. "I know that was one of the Purgatory Path things from Cissy's survey, but they already set up a church?"

Dad shrugs. "I'll smite it in my free time."

"Much appreciated, but it's still way inappropriate. Breaking into our driveway? Stealing Betsy's bumper?"

"Does that mean we can send her to car Heaven?" asks Mom. "Betsy's been a good friend. She deserves a rest."

My heart cracks. All those joyful hours with Betsy can't be finished. How many times did I laugh while the tailpipe billowed smoke in some ghoul's face? And what about how Betsy only plays one radio station? Sure, it's polka music, but it's coming from *my* car.

I steel my shoulders. Sadness aside, my parents are right. There's no way I can leave Betsy in the back driveway to get picked over by kooks.

"Fine." I state. "How about we just put her in storage?"

"Not sure that would work," says Dad. "Your storage building is getting pretty full. Soon it will become a target as well."

No storage? Car Heaven? Never!

Anger charges through my nervous system. My tail arcs over my shoulder. *Battle stance.* "You're right, bud," I say to my exceptionally wise tail. "This sucks."

My eyes flare red with demonic rage. I'm vaguely aware of my parents chatting away. The words *demon tirade* come up. I'm not in a place to care.

"This is so unfair," I announce. "The quasi people hated me before. As in, the only person who would speak to me was Cissy—and let's be honest—Cissy rescues moths, so that's not a big vote of confidence. Then I save all of Purgatory from the King of Hell. You'd think the quasis would be like, *yay! Armageddon is gone and Myla's now a demigoddess so let's suck up to her.* But on what page of the *Big Book of Ass Kissing* does it say to steal the bumper off someone's car? Or create churches in their name without permission? Or tell them to live by a Purgatory Path?"

At this point, my rage boils over. I kick something. Hard. Sadly, this *something* is Betsy's driver side door, which I put my foot right though. It makes a satisfying crunch, sure. Still it's not my best plan. Seeing the crumpled side of my favorite car snaps me out of my demonic fury and fast.

"Oh, damn." I frown. "That won't buff out."

"Can we approach her now?" asks Dad.

I round on my father. "Approach me about what?"

Mom pats Dad's forearm. "She's good." My mother then focuses on me. "You shouldn't leave the limo waiting."

"Right. My Scala Bleugh." Taking in a deep breath, I look between my parents. "Can we put Betsy in storage or what?"

"Yes, we most certainly will," says Mom. She's all my mother right now, which I totally appreciate. More and more, I'm related to Camilla the president. I take my Mommy-time where I can get it.

After saying my good-byes, I step around to the mansion's main entrance and slip into my limo. Once inside, I make a fateful decision.

Today I'll rock this Scala Bleugh like a goddess. Forget the Purgatory Path. There's an undeadly somewhere at this event with a skull tattoo and a date with destiny. Because whoever this ghoul is, I will find them.

And there's nothing Peli can do to stop me.

18

LINCOLN

*P*eli cast another spell. Fortunately, this one isn't of the sleeping variety.

One moment, I wait in my reception area, surrounded by orange mist. The next thing I know, I stand inside a large wooden hall with arched ceilings. The walls are lined in a mosaic style, only instead of small tiles, the surface has been stacked with small carvings of monkey faces. I recognize them as the peaks to thousands of wizard staffs.

Young Peli stands along the far wall of the room. That fact alone leaves no room for doubt.

I'm visiting the Primeval again.

And Peli's history.

A long wooden table fills the center of the space. At the head sits a tall monkey with long limbs, orange fur, and a fierce expression. His cheeks flare out with peaks of longer fluff. A wooden crown sits atop his head while a wizard's staff is clasped in his hand. The bottom of the stick presses onto the floor, while the peak is decorated with a small carving of the monkey king's likeness.

Young Peli mentioned this fellow before. This must be Quilliam, the wizard King of the Simians.

Four other humanoids flank either side of the table. I count fish, reptile, lion, and bird. Like the monkey king, all wear crowns and carry wizard staffs. Most wear simple robes.

My interest perks. Back in Antrum, the Contagion announced himself as a wizard. For the first time, I sense myself actually closing in on useful information about the Primeval.

The monkey king raps his knuckles against the tabletop. "I, the wizard Quilliam, King of the Simian Lands, do hereby officially call to order this gathering of the Assembly Primeval. Announce yourselves for quorum."

The fish humanoid speaks first."Wizard Queen Dorsa from the Icythian lands is here." She's got bulbous eyes, pink scales and a halo of fins about her head. Her wizard staff is topped with shells that match her crown.

"Wizard King Nuchal from the Reptilians is here." He's hairless with green textured skin and a wide, frog-style mouth. His staff is topped with a green glass orb. Smaller pieces of green glass decorate his iron crown. While the other regents wear simple wizard robes, King Nuchal sports a frilly shirt and velvet long coat.

Next up comes a lioness with white fur whose staff is topped with a lion's head. She wears a simple golden crown. "Wizard Queen Usawa of the Feline lands is here."

Last to speak is a slim man whose entire body is covered with small blue feathers. He has a small mouth and large blue eyes. The peak to his wizard's staff is a large blue egg, while his crown is made from shards of blue shell. "Wizard King Calamus of the Avians is here."

"Excellent," states Quilliam. His thick eyebrows and pointed teeth give his face a decidedly fierce look. I can't help wondering what how he'd be in battle.

The Icythian queen waves her hand toward Peli. The movement highlights the webbing between her fingers. "Why is that chimpanzee hanging about?"

The Avian king bobs his head in a fast, bird-like rhythm. "Yes, I thought Peli was non-magical and useless."

"None of *us* could bring servants," adds the Reptilian King. His forked tongue flickers over his lips.

Quilliam throws his arms up, bringing them down onto the

tabletop in a movement that would make an angry gorilla proud. "Do you wish to question who I invite into my own halls? Or would you like to set forward your requests for a boon made?"

The Icythian queen goes first. "I suppose we can get to requests. Here is my first. The Icythian feeding waters have grown dirty. We need spells of refreshment."

"Why not clean the waters yourself?" asks Quilliam. "You're the ones who dirty things."

"But your lands contain the Golden Arbor," grumbles the Icythian queen. "You Simians live beside the fount of all magic in the primeval. Why should I waste my scarce powers when your lands hold the Golden Arbor? It isn't fair."

The other wizards agree. All put forward long lists for their lands. The Avians want new colored banners to decorate their villages. As for the Reptilians, the king demands fresh silks so they can properly dress for an upcoming feast. Next the Icythians request that their salmon be enchanted to taste sweeter. And the Felines want new golden beads to weave into their manes.

That's just the first five minutes.

While these long lists are read out, Quilliam pulls out a small block of wood and whittles away. Once the other regents are finished, he carefully sets his creation aside.

"We all know the Law Primeval," states Quilliam. His nostril-holes flare in a movement that clearly says, *I mean business.* "A bounty must be paid for every boon made. To satisfy these lists, I must tap into the power of the Golden Arbor itself."

"No one's ever done that," says Queen Usawa.

"I have the spell all figured out," counters Quilliam. "Give me enough magic, and I'll fulfill your every desire."

Queen Usawa rubs her talons over the top of her golden wizard's staff. "And how do you plan to do that?"

"Simple," answers Quilliam with a grin. "All I need are the peaks from your wizard staffs."

The Reptilian king hisses. "But those peaks contain all the power we've accumulated over the millennia."

Quilliam brushes his fingers over the carving he'd been working on. It's a miniature version of the Golden Arbor. "Your apprentices still have magic. You won't be unprotected."

"No," declares the Feline queen. "It is too much of a risk."

Quilliam kicks back in his chair. "Without those peaks, I don't know when your lists will be completed."

No one move.

Eventually, the Reptilian king removes the glass peak from his wizard's staff and hands it over to Quilliam. The rest of the regents follow suit.

I know this is a vision from the past, but it takes all my control not to shout for them to stop. Great power lures even honest souls along the path to corruption. Quilliam already acts with a manipulative air. I fear his journey into evil will be brief.

Quilliam pulls out a leather satchel and places all his new treasures inside. When he's finished, Quilliam turns around to face Peli.

"You, too. Give me the peak to your wizard's staff."

Young Peli narrows his eyes. For a moment, I wonder if he'll fight a room full of wizards. Instead, Young Peli stretches his face into a silly grin. "Of course."

Lifting his hands, Young Peli summons a small sphere of orange haze. The mist congeals into the form of a round carving. This time, the creation isn't one that shows four faces.

Only one.

No doubt exists in my mind. This isn't the carving that the Golden Arbor consecrated. It's a fake.

Quilliam sets Young Peli's offering into his leather sack. Raising his arms, the Simian wizard summons a fresh cloud of orange smoke. When the mist vanishes, everyone now stands about the Golden Arbor.

The tree looks unchanged from the last time I visited Peli's past. Trunk, branches, and leaves... every part of it glitters with gold. Magic rolls off the thing in waves, making my skin tingle.

Quilliam rubs his hands together, stopping when his palms glow orange. The Simian king approaches the Golden Arbor. Setting his finger against the trunk of the tree, Quilliam draws a line downward. The arbor shivers; then it splits. I've seen my share of operations. This movement resembles skin being sliced open.

I'm no native of the Primeval, but even I can tell this is a bad idea. The other regents gasp or step backward. None try to interfere, even Young Peli.

One by one, Quilliam places the peak of each wizard's staff inside the trunk of the Golden Arbor. As the magical items pass through, a flash of power and light flares within the deep wooden interior.

Blue for Avians.

Green for Reptilians.

Pink for Icythians.

White for Felines.

And finally, a smaller flare of orange appears as Quilliam sets Young Peli's creation inside the tree. *Clever.* Young Peli had the presence of mind to place some magic inside his carving, just not much of it.

All the while, Quilliam keeps his own powers intact. The carving that sits atop his wizard's staff goes nowhere near the Golden Arbor. Essentially, he's asking everyone else to give up their abilities but keeping his own.

This won't end well.

After that, Quilliam then does something I never expected.

He steps inside the tree.

The Simian wizard lifts his right leg and sets it inside the incision on the trunk. Bending over, Quilliam moves to enter the arbor's interior.

My mind blanks with surprise. I've never seen magic like this before.

Once the Simian wizard is fully inside, the wood seals up. This time, I'm reminded of a wound closing. Seconds later, the outer bark returns to being a lovely and unbroken sheath of gold. For a moment, it seems as if nothing about the arbor will change.

Then it does.

The Golden Arbor shivers and creaks. Branches snap. Leaves vanish. Great clouds of smoke surround the entire arbor. A moment later, the tree is gone.

Quilliam is all that's left.

The Simian wizard now appears to be made of gold himself. The only sign of the arbor are the wooden-style swirls on his skin where fur once lay.

"Bow down to me," states Quilliam. "And call me by my new name. The Contagion."

The other regents do as they are told. "Contagion," they all say in unison.

Great branches curl out from the Contagion's back, long and powerful as arms. Four golden limbs reach forward, one for each regent. The branches pause before each wizard; sunlight gleams off their pointed tips.

"Now!" cries the Contagion.

Moving as one, the branches stab all the wizard rulers through their chests. The four regents fall over, dead.

"That was my boon made," says the Contagion. His voice carries the deep creak of tall trees on a windy day. "I gift you death. Your endless requests are now over. All that remains is the destruction of your paltry apprentices."

Young Peli steps forward. "But what if you need more magic in the future? You can't kill the apprentices."

The Contagion tilts his head. The movement sets off a new chorus of creaks. "True." He raises his arms. A swirl of golden magic appears in the air. The haze solidifies into a great circle. I've seen this before.

A gateway.

Once again, the center of the gateway serves as a giant window. A group of Icythians appear within it. All wear the long pink robes that mark them as wizard apprentices. Each carries a small staff in their hands.

The Contagion doesn't say a word. Golden light flashes from behind his back. A fresh knot of branches lurch forward. The long arm-like appendages tear through the gateway, one for each Icythian apprentice. Once more, the ends of those branches stab the apprentices in the shoulder. Golden light flares around the victims.

One second, they are alive and moving.

The next, all the apprentices are frozen into wooden statues of their former selves, complete with the staffs gripped in their hands.

"There," says the Contagion. "Not dead but stored."

"Wisely done," says Young Peli.

"Oh, I'm far from finished."

The Contagion repeats the cycle. The view in the gateway changes. More apprentices appear. Each time, the Contagion transforms them into wood. All lands are wiped out of any wizard kind.

Icythian.

Reptilian.

Avian.

Feline.

Even Simian.

All the while, Young Peli steals closer to the orange jungle.

The freezing continues for what feels like hours. I force myself to watch, but the sight still makes me ill. So many innocents being struck down, perhaps never to be alive again.

Finally, the Contagion lowers his arms. The gateway vanishes. The evil wizard slowly turns about.

"Peli? Where are you?"

No reply.

The Contagion stomps off into the jungle while chanting in a sing-song voice. "Come out, some out, wherever you are!"

I watch Contagion grow smaller in the distance. Worry tightens up my neck and shoulders. After this visit to the past, my biggest question is answered. The Contagion is most definitely a major threat.

Trouble is, everyone in Antrum thinks I'm losing my mind. Stating my invisible orange monkey gave me magical info on Aldred's demon tree won't work here.

Good thing I have other ideas. This isn't over yet.

MYLA

I ride along in the limo, pondering ways to discover Peli's ghoul. Then it happens.

Boing.
Boing.
Boing.

The stretch of leather seat beside me starts to shimmy. It's not a constant thing, more of a pulse. Tilting my head, I inspect the limo. It's not like there's a big sign here saying, *new boingy butt warmers installed*. Still, the strange sensation continues.

Boing.
Boing.
Boing.

An orange haze appears on the seat beside me. Peli materializes. And the little bugger is jumping. *Okay, that explains a lot.*

"Hello, Peli. Give me back my binder." I glare in a way that says, *this is me, not kidding around.*

The little monkey jumps a few more times before replying. "No."

"What do you want for it?"

"There is nothing you can offer that will change my mind. A special ghoul is here today and I will keep that creature's identity a secret."

"Your friend with the mark on their shoulder. Oh, I'll find them all right."

Peli stops jumping. "Doubtful."

The limo rolls to a stop. Thus begins a familiar routine. People cheer outside the tinted windows. Purgatory police form a human barricade so I enter *wherever this is*. Once inside, I'll give a quick speech. Maybe I'll even lure a few igni to fly around, assuming my little magical friends are in the mood. The crowd loves that stuff. Once I'm done, I'll rush back to the limo.

It would be more fun with Betsy, but whatever.

Turning away from Peli, I scan the world outside my window. What I see shocks me speechless.

A few yards away sits a big sign that reads, The Great Scala Memorial Institute for Learning.

And it's on the same spot as my old high school.

I tap the window. "What the Hell is this?"

Balancing on the arm rest, Peli plasters his little monkey hands against the glass. "Looks like your old high school."

"How do you know this stuff?"

"It's like I told you. I'm incredibly magical."

I narrow my eyes. "So you cast an illusion spell?"

"If I made a fake building, it wouldn't be that ugly."

"You've got me there."

The new school is a dark wooden structure accented by skinny windows and long shutters. U-G-L-Y. I screw up my mouth to one side of my face. This reminds me of something, but I can't place just what.

"It looks like four haunted houses got mushed together. A kind of structural goth mosh pit."

"With a nice satellite dish out front," adds Peli.

That's when it hits me. This place reminds me of my parents' mansion. Gothic nightmare meets NASA.

Meaning the ghouls rebuilt my high school. *Ick.*

A gross taste seeps into my mouth. Ghouls are rarely allowed back in Purgatory. The undeadlies must have bought some goodwill by shelling out money for this rebuild.

For a long moment, I can only stare at the sign. "Great Scala Memorial."

"You're not even dead," chirps Peli. "Yet."

"Thanks." I should hate the little bugger, but I can't somehow.

A massive figure steps before my window, blocking my view. The limo door gets yanked open. A wave of cheers fills the air, along with the heavy humidity that says *Welcome to Purgatory*. The figure before me has grey skin, all-black eyes, and pointed teeth. His face looks scrunched-up, like someone grabbed his features and smushed them toward his nose.

"You remind me of someone," I say slowly.

"You recently met my favorite aunt."

"Huh. I haven't met a new ghoul in ages."

"She's not a ghoul. Not now, anyway." He keeps staring at me, waiting for me to catch on. Most times it's pure-blood humans who turn into ghouls, but someone with mixed heritage can also go undeadly when they pass away. For a while, I even thought I was *going ghoul* after I kicked it.

"So who's this relative of yours?" I ask.

"Lady Bentford of Antrum."

"Ooooooh. Her. Yeah." *Talk about awkward.* "And you are?"

"RUL-3. You may call me Rule." All ghouls have letters and numbers for names. It all goes with their love of mindless checklists. "I am Captain of the Thought Police."

My mouth scrunches down to a little 'o' shape. Back when the ghouls ran Purgatory, the Thought Police dictated public opinion. Quasis who complained or protested were made to disappear.

Rule offers me his extremely long-fingered hand. One look and one facts become clear: Someone doesn't believe in nail clippers. Or sub-cuticle maintenance. In fact, a mushroom might be growing under his thumbnail.

No way am I toughing that.

Instead, I self-guide out of the limo. "I'm the Great Scala. You may call me…" I wait dramatically. "The Great Scala."

"Disrespectful," snaps Rule.

I mock-sniffle and tap beneath my eyes. "Oh, the memories. How I love irritating ghouls."

Peli hops out behind me. "This will be fun." He scans the crowd. "My most important ghoul is close, I can tell."

"Care to give any hints, oh small, orange, and irritating?"

Peli grins. "No."

Rule frowns. "Who were you talking to just now?"

"My invisible monkey."

"You are insane." Rule's eyes glow red. "It is as Aunt Bentford said."

"Oh, she doesn't know the half of it." I set my fists on my hips and scan the crowd. There are quasis and ghouls galore here. *Which one is Peli's?* I know a way to find out. Since Herr Ghoul Capitan already thinks I'm unhinged, I might as well use it to my advantage.

I turn to Rule. "My invisible orange friend says there's a new requirement for today."

"I did?" asks Peli.

"He did?" says Rule.

"Absolutely. Every time I meet a new ghoul, they must show me their right shoulder, starting with you."

"Not fair," grumbles Peli.

Rule frowns, but points to his shoulder. Leave it to a ghoul to follow instructions without thinking.

"Not your *covered* shoulder," I state. "Your bare shoulder." I gesture toward the neckline of his ghoul robes. "Just scooch that fabric over a little. If you can hide your dirty nails while you do it, that's a bonus, but not a requirement."

Rule pulls the neckline as requested. Turns out, telling ghouls what to do is rather enjoyable. Stepping closer, I scan for any kind of mark. Peli's ghoul should have a skull tattoo.

But there's nothing. Bummer.

"Great skin," I declare. "Thanks for sharing. Let's check out all the other ghouls now." I gesture across the crowd. "We can set up a conga line situation."

Rule's mouth falls open with surprise. "Aren't you going to enter the new high school? We have all sorts of statues in your likeness."

I wince. "Is that supposed to encourage me to go?"

Rule steps closer. "Listen to me carefully. I just wrote a new Thought Mandate on the virtues of saffronia as extolled by the Great

Scala. It is not yet published. Once the mandate goes out, Auntie and I will l share the profits. And you'll get an easier time tomorrow at the Trials of Acca."

"How interesting."

"Glad we agree," says Rule. "Now you shall enter this school and exclaim the delicious qualities of saffronia." He slams his fist against his open palm. "Today you are my charge. You follow my dictates."

"Dude, I never followed the ghouls when I was a nobody Arena fighter. What makes you think I'll cave in now that I'm the Great Scala?"

"There's an old saying of the ghouls. *The coffin nail that sticks up, gets hammered down.*"

"Yeah, I know that one."

"I'm not alone in wishing changes. All the people of Purgatory loathe your attitude."

"That's totally exaggerating. Plus, I have no time for this. Thanks to Peli here, a crazy earl is opening a gateway to the Primeval tomorrow. A monster tree is involved. That's way more important than selling pee juice."

"I don't know what you're talking about," says Rule.

"You don't need to. I'm monologuing. My point is, I need to find me a ghoul with a skull tattoo on his shoulder and nothing you say or do will stop me."

On a side note, all this standing around is turning the crowd downright rowdy. The mob pushes hard against the barricades and police. That happens a lot. What's new is what they're saying while pressing in.

Hug me, Great Scala!
Wear this scarf!
Bless my bumper!

I haven't even closed the limo door yet, and already there's trouble. This is some kind of personal record. I crook my finger toward Rule. The massive ghoul takes a baby step closer.

"Here's the deal. You line up everyone. I greet them. The ghouls will show me their shoulders."

Peli hops beside me. "That last part is totally optional."

"Quiet, Peli." Let the record show that Peli does not shut up. He stops speaking but keeps making eee-eee noises.

Rule folds his arms over his chest. Since he's wearing ghoul robes, there's a lot of *loopy sleeve swoosh action* that goes into the whole thing. Once he's done, Rule glares at me. "That will never happen. You will smile, announce the delicious qualities of saffronia, and go home."

"Let's get a second opinion on that, shall we?" Closing my eyes, I pull on my inner powers.

Little ones, come to me.

A blast of light sears in to the sky. Hundreds of igni fill the air. Each one is a tiny lightning bolt that hovers in place, glistening and lovely. The crowd falls silent. More and more igni appear. Soon millions of tiny lightning bolts fill the skies in every direction. Damn, they're really motivated today. In my head, their tiny voices echo through my consciousness.

Form a soul column
Protect the Scala
Send the ghoul to Hell

I round on the ghoul captain. "Look, I could send you to Hell right now. Want an eternity of quality time with Armageddon? Just keep giving me lip."

Rule slowly nods. "I'll organize the…"

"Conga line," I finish. In my mind, I send another message.

Thanks, guys. I got it from here.

But the igni are on a tear.

We must send the ghoul away.
Now, now, now!

We've had these fights before, and I know the quickest way to end them.

Who's the Great Scala here?

A moment later, the igni vanish.
Because who's the Great Scala? I'm the Great Scala.

In short order, everyone is lined up. First to appear is the Old Timer, one of my ex-teachers from school. He's still a wrinkly and undead coot who sports one-half of a loopy mustache. He greets me with a huge smile.

"I came to get a picture with my favorite filly."

Major lie.

The Old Timer and I were never buds. Unless you counting forcing someone to make worm soufflé a social outing. I'd correct the Old Timer, but the guy is ancient as dirt and dead to boot. Who cares if he wants to pretend we were friends? Besides, I have more important priorities.

"Pull back your ghoul robes and show me your bare shoulder. Then you can take a picture."

The Old Timer's bushy brows pull together in a show of confusion. Still, he does as asked. The shoulder gets revealed. No mark to speak of. Grr. An older quasi lady with long stringy hair and Polaroid camera takes a snap of us both.

"Thanks and keep moving," I state.

One down. Five thousand to go.

Damn. I'll be here all night.

MYLA

*A*fter hours of speaking the same stuff over and over, particular words stick in brain.

Nice to meet you. Show me your shoulder. Say cheese. Next!

There were ghouls.

So many ghouls.

But none of them with marks.

Ugh.

I'm half asleep as I limp out of my limo and back into my parents' house. That was a lot of pictures with ghouls. And since most undeadlies have the latest technology, it was a lot of selfies with ghouls.

Yes, ghouls all have fancy hand held devices.

Meanwhile, Purgatory doesn't even have cable.

I'm so glad I kicked those undeadlies out.

Speaking of phones, I haul my ass to the kitchen, pick up the receiver from the wall, and rotary dial Cissy's office. She picks up on the first ring.

"Hey, Myla."

"Hi, girlfriend." I always check in after a big event.

"You had quite the Scala Bleugh, huh? Not in the mood to listen to ghoul directions?"

"Hey, I'd have done what that Captain Rule guy wanted, but I've got issues with the Trials of Acca tomorrow."

"So you stripped down thousands of ghouls."

"Eew! I had them show me one shoulder. Who wants to see naked ghouls?"

"That Rule guy published some official paper on how you're out to rape and pillage all the Dark Lands. It seems you started today."

"Gross. Now I need to clean out my brain with bleach."

"We need to counter this."

"I took five thousand selfies with happy ghouls. Let that be my statement."

"This is the Thought Police. That paper *will* be a problem."

"Ghouls are always trouble. They get pissy if their worm soufflé is cold. I ran them out of Purgatory. Do you think they'll ever drop their grudge against me?"

I hear a shuffle of papers on the other side of the line. "Well, quasis have been flipping out and calling my office non-stop. Did the binder help at all?"

Here comes what Dad calls *a crossroads of conscience*. I could lie, but I'm a sucky liar. And even when I'm playing my best unethical game, Cissy can always tell anyway.

So here comes the truth.

"This is going to sound unbelievable, but a monkey stole my binder."

"A monkey. A MONKEY. Did you say a monkey?"

"I did. His name's Peli."

"I just received a pile of selfie pics from tonight's Scala Bleugh. None show a monkey."

"There's a simple reason for that. Peli's invisible."

And because Peli is also annoying, a swirl of orange smoke appears by my feet. A moment later, the orange dude himself appears. He's all smiles. My tail points at his head. Not in an *I'll cut you* way. More of a warning to keep distance. Like me, my tail is still undecided about Peli in general.

"Hellooooooo, Myla!" Peli follows up his greeting with lots of eee-eee noises and jumping around the kitchen countertops. Peli even whips out our silverware drawer and drops it to the floor. What a racket. At least my parents aren't home. They left for their Purgatory tour hours ago.

"What's going on over there?" asks Cissy.

"I told you. Peli."

"The invisible monkey who stole your binder."

"That's the one."

"And you didn't ask me for another one because?"

"I did. Didn't you get the message?"

"No."

"Hold on a sec." I focus on Peli. "Did you erase my message to Cissy?"

Peli rolls his eyes. "Obviously."

That's when it happens. I moved my Demon Bars to the kitchen for breakfast. Now Peli approaches that sacred box while waving his arms around. A haze of orange smoke encircles the container. I glare at Peli for all I'm worth. "If you make my Demon Bars vanish, I will hunt you down." My eyes flare with demon light. "Stop. That. Now."

The orange haze leaves my Demon Bar box. Instead, the colored cloud flies over to encircle Peli. A moment later, the monkey vanishes again. Good riddance to a bad monkey.

I set the receiver against my ear once more. "Sorry about that."

"Do I even want to know what's really happening?"

"Probably not." Now that the Demon Bars are safe, that box looks mighty tempting. I step across the floor, stopping when my tail is in range. "Got else anything for me, Cis?" My tail knows what to do. It spears the box and drags it close enough that I can dive in.

I pat the arrowhead end. "Nice job, boy."

"That Captain Rush wants to watch the Trials of Acca tomorrow. Any issues?"

"I don't know. He's kind of a dick."

"He says he's considering writing a new Thought Police mandate that supports your parents suggestions to change soul processing."

"False. He wants me to say I like drinking pee."

A long pause follows before Cissy speaks again. "Unlike the invisible monkey thing, I totally buy that fact. Ghouls are gross."

"Do you think he'll really publish the mandate?" I ask. "Not the one about pee."

"It's possible. My interns did a profile on him. Sometimes he's actually a good guy. Rule published a mandate last month to encourage ghouls to try the arts. In his opinion, that means playing video games. Still, it's a start."

"Okay. Anything to help fix soul processing. Let Rule in." Cissy's staff are really good at making sure they get the right approvals for transfer central and all that.

"Speaking of your parents," Cissy pauses.

"What?"

"I was thinking about the Trial of Acca tomorrow." She leaves a long pause where I'm supposed to fill in the blank. Which I do, no problem. It's obvious what Cissy's really asking.

"You don't need to go to the Trials of Acca, Cis."

"Are you sure?"

"It's a battle trial in Antrum. I'm not worried."

Yes, there's still the threat of a demon tree, but honestly? I consider that more of a perk than a danger.

"Okay, Myla." Cissy lets out the mother of all yawns. "It's late. Good night, girlfriend."

Hearing Cissy yawn makes every cell in my body scream for rest. That was a lot of ghoul stuff today. "To you, too."

We hang up. A few minutes later, I'm under my sheets and half asleep. That's when a little voice sounds echoes in my mind. It sounds a lot like Peli.

You've no idea what you're in for, do you?

And to be honest, that voice is absolutely right.

LINCOLN

After my visit to the Primeval, I wake up to find Peli has given a repeat performance. Once again, the monkey moved me to my own bed. Lifting my arm, I find that Peli has also placed me in a new set of orange pajamas, only these sport a rubber ducky pattern.

I shake my head. *Peli really is an enjoyable rogue.*

Rolling over, I check my grandfather clock. It's Friday. 2 am. The Trials of Acca take place at 10 am.

My head feels groggy, which is why I don't register the large blue orbs staring at me from the foot of the bed. At least, not for a moment or two. Soon it becomes clear that they're actually a set of luminous blue eyes.

I yawn. "Hello, Peli."

"Did you enjoy your trip to my past?"

"It's enlightening." I yawn. "But still rather vague. I only know the most basic facts about the Primeval." Pulling off my covers, I set my bare feet on the chilly floor.

"Are you off to see Baptiste and Nat?"

For a second, I debate lying to Peli. There's no point, however. *Never trick a trickster.*

"They won't be awake yet," I reply. "I'm off to see Mother. She doesn't sleep much." I crack my neck. "If I'm right, then my parents spent yesterday negotiating the true terms of Myla's so-called Trials of Acca. I must suss out what's coming."

"Let me get this straight." Peli leaps up to land beside me on the mattress. "You don't yet know enough about the Primeval."

"Correct."

"You aren't off to see Nat and Baptiste."

"Right again."

"And you do plan to see your Mother and figure out Aldred's tests for Myla."

"Bingo. I'm also rather groggy. I do wish you'd put some actual rest into your sleep spells. I need to be at my sharpest today."

"Excellent point." Peli gives me his worst grin. I'm talking the one that resembles the tin cymbal monkey. Fresh orange smoke fills the air.

Oh, Hell.

He's at it again.

LINCOLN

Another spell from Peli. This is becoming a theme.

When the magical haze is gone, I find myself standing in the orange jungle that borders on the Golden Arbor. Simian territory. Tangerine-colored trees loom overhead, their wide leaves glistening with rivulets of water. The ground lies spongy beneath my feet. The scent of fresh rain carries on the air.

A figure marches along a nearby path. The Contagion. His skin glistens with gold and is marked by the swirling pattern of wood grain. Quilliam once had downy crests of fur protruding from his cheeks. As the Contagion, that fluff is replaced with golden twigs and tiny leaves.

"Come out, come out wherever you are!" The Contagion's long legs tear up the ground with confidence. His every movement screams, *I'm the baddest thing in this jungle.*

Then, the Contagion steps on a certain spot.

Snap!

Loops of metal encircle his ankles, holding him in place. Fresh magic billows around him.

And it's orange.

Young Peli must have cast this spell.

When the smoke clears, the Contagion stands in a blasted out pit. Turns out, the evil wizard has been transported to the very spot where the Golden Arbor had once stood. Young Peli waits nearby, his face tight with rage.

The Contagion pulls on his leg. He can't break free from his bindings. Based on the lack of magic, the Contagion can't cast either.

"Whatever spell you've placed on this trap, I will end it. Then I will finish you."

"You went after my family," says Young Peli slowly.

"What did you expect? I couldn't find *you*."

"Wrong decision."

Young Peli lifts his hands. Orange light glows from his palms. A wizard's staff appears in his left hand; the carving for his staff's peak materializes in his right. I step closer, seeking a better look. Sure enough, Young Peli has summoned the true peak for his wizard's staff—a carving that shows all four faces of Peli's family .

The Contagion pauses. "What you gave me before… that carving didn't contain all your magic?"

"See for yourself," says Young Peli. He sets the new peak atop his wizard's staff. Instantly, the carving glows.

Young Peli stalks up to the trapped Contagion. "You held me back, hid me from court. I accepted all that. By hurting my family, you tore the heart out of me. Now I'll return the favor."

Young Peli's right hand glows with magic. Little by little, Young Peli curls his fingers into a fist. Time seems to slow as Peli reaches forward, his knuckles brushing against the Contagion's chest.

Then Young Peli punches right through the Contagion's rib cage.

I inhale a shocked breath as Young Peli pulls his hand out from the Contagion's chest. There are some accompanying squish noises which I work hard to ignore. It doesn't work totally. Once Young Peli's hand is free, a new object sits in him palm.

The carved peak from a wizard's staff. It's the original one Young Peli gave to Quilliam. The fake.

I frown, trying to process what I'm seeing. Young Peli just pulled that thing out of the Contagion's rib cage. Damn.

Peli slams his wizard's staff onto the ground. Instantly, a fresh gateway appears. Just as before, the gateway appears as a round and thin circle that seems to hang in the air. Within the window-like center, a familiar scene appears. A vast graveyard stretches off into every direction. Ghouls in black robes parade around the many headstones.

Hold on. Back in Antrum, Peli talked about needing to find a ghoul. Could this be related?

Young Peli slams his staff once more. This time, the glowing carving zooms into the gateway. A minute before, Young Peli had pulled that carving from the Contagion's rib cage. Now it speeds through the gateway, where it slams into the nearest ghoul, striking the undead one on his shoulder.

The targeted ghoul is too far away to see his features clearly. Still, if the undead creature felt the impact of foreign magic, there's no reaction.

The Contagion pales. "What did you do?"

"By the power of the Golden Arbor, this Simian magic became connected to you. If you regain it, you'll eventually figure out how to escape. I can't afford to keep this power in the Primeval. I'm storing it in another realm, where you can't get it at."

Young Peli slams his wizard's staff again. Once more, the scene within the gateway changes. This time, the view shows a battle practice in Heaven. The process repeats. Young Peli pulls out another wizard's peak from the Contagion's chest. This time, it's the blue egg wielded by the Avian wizard. Once removed from the Contagion, the wizard's peak glows with azure light while zooming from Young Peli's palm, passing through the gateway, and slamming into an angel. Again, there's no reaction from the one who receives the magic.

Things happen so quickly, I find it hard to keep up. The Reptilian glass peak enters a demon. The Icythian shell one zooms into a human. And the golden peak of the Felines merges with a thrax.

Five lands for the Primeval.

Five peoples for the after-realms.

Each time one of the peaks enters after-realms, some of the golden sheen leaves the Contagion's body. His skin turns more to bark while his body loses shape. More and more, the Contagion becomes a tree. All along the way, the evil wizard tries every trick in the book to convince Young Peli to stop.

Bribes.

Threats.

Tears.

Nothing works.

In the end, the Contagion stands rooted to the spot where the Golden Arbor once stood. The sight becomes familiar. It's the same one I saw when Aldred showed off the Primeval in Antrum, a few days and a million years ago.

The Contagion is no longer a powerful wizard with golden skin who marches confidently through his orange jungle. Instead, he's a burned out stump that's only six feet tall. No branches arch above him. His skin is a shifting bark of black tar. Gaping holes serve as his eyes. That long gash acts as a mouth.

"You'll leave me here to rot?" asks the Contagion.

"Only until I can kill you," says Young Peli. "Enjoy your prison time. It's my boon to you until I discover a way to end your life."

"Impossible. Now that I've taken in the Golden Arbor, I'm indestructible."

"Not exactly. It's just a matter of uncovering the right magic to destroy you. Don't worry; I'll find it." Young Peli's voice lowers to a growl. "You should never have touched my family."

The Contagion's impossible mouth winds into a smile. "And you never got the peak to my wizard's staff."

"Don't worry. No matter where you hid it, I'll find it. There's only one way to properly hide the peak of a wizard's staff, and you didn't do it." Young Peli pulls the carving off his own staff. The peak transforms from wood into orange light. Young Peli then opens his mouth, takes the power inside, and swallows it whole.

Well, Peli always said he was packed with power. Now I see he meant it literally.

The orange haze surrounds me once more. Another visit to Peli's past is complete.

LINCOLN

Now that I'm engulfed in the orange cloud of Peli's magic, I expect to transport back to the after-realms.

That isn't what happens.

Suddenly, the orange smoke morphs into white flames. More angelfire. Once the blaze dies down, I find myself back at that strange forest with its plastic trees and swirling skies. The same tendril of blue smoke curls up from a single point far in the distance.

Once more, the landscape acts as a magical reminder. A greater threat lurks for me and Myla. But what is it?

A voice sounds again, deep and familiar. "I grow stronger," he says. "Soon we shall meet."

The white flames return, surrounding me in comfort. The blaze grows so fierce, I can no longer see the forest any more. My visit here is ending as well.

With every journey through magic, I hope for more clarity. Yet each time, my vision of the true dangers around me only turns more muddy than ever.

24

LINCOLN

When the white flames vanish, I find myself seated on my bed, in the exact same position I'd taken before Peli cast his most recent spell.

And I am not happy.

"Wasn't that grand? Didn't I tell you all?" Peli spins about in circles. I've seen this *silly trickster* act before. There's no need for a repeat.

It's rather tempting to grab Peli by the tail and chuck the little monkey against the wall. The urge is incredibly inappropriate, considering how Peli isn't attacking. Nevertheless, it's tempting.

It takes conscious effort, but I push my frustration aside and organize my thoughts. At last, I regain enough control to ask a coherent question. "Can the Contagion be freed?"

"Not yet."

"You mentioned checking in on a ghoul in Purgatory."

"Once the peak of a wizard's staff hits you, you gain a marking on your shoulder. For my part, I keep tabs on all my Marked Ones. Or try to. Folks in the after-realms have a nasty habit of dying. When that happens, their mark transfers to whoever is nearest and of the same bloodline. It's rather frustrating."

I recall how the fake peak to Peli's wizard staff still contained some magic. "The ghoul you seek has a mark for Simian magic. The power rests inside their body until you summon it. Before that, the Marked One is oblivious."

"Correct. When it comes to this ghoul, she doesn't know a thing about the Primeval."

"So it's definitely a her."

"Perhaps. I'm a trickster."

"This isn't helping."

Peli stops jumping about. "Trust me, please. I tell you what I can, when I can. Primeval magic mixes strangely with the after-realms. Few tasks here are easy."

"Like telling me the truth in a plain and clear manner." I shake my head. "There must be more you can do."

"Trust me or not. If not, then I leave. Aldred will still have me open that gateway, only it will happen at a place and time beyond your knowledge or control. Is that what you want?"

"Raising the fact that you're scheming with Aldred? that doesn't help your case."

"I'm doing my best for my family and yours." Peli stalks closer. "Now have I your trust, yes or no?"

In this moment, Peli is every inch the powerful wizard in compact form. I sort through everything I've seen of his past. Peli's love for his family... his power to open gateways and fight the Contagion... and his willingness to share at least some information with me.

"Being a ruler means placing bets. I'll wager to trust you."

Peli exhales. "Good news. If you decided to fight me, I'd have been forced to place you in another enchanted sleep for the duration. I rather enjoy your company."

"And I enjoy yours."

"By the way, what convinced you to trust me? Seeing my past?"

I pull at the neckline of my pajamas. "More the rubber ducky PJs. No one truly evil could conjure up something like this."

"I'm glad you like them. You'll be using them once more." Peli spreads his arms wide. A fresh cloud of orange magic fills my bedroom.

And I pass out.

25

MYLA

Friday is here.
　　　　Trials of Acca.
Lady Bentford.
A fighting tree.
Bah.

This is pretty typical stuff for my life, really. I haul my butt out of bed at 6 am. The trials start at 10 and I want to be early. Lincoln and I haven't spoken in what feels like forever. I definitely want to catch up.

Stupid Antrum.

Stupid thrax security making it impossible to talk to my guy.

Yes, I sent some written messages, but Cissy tells me they all got held up at the Purgatory Pulpitum. Antrum's Transfer Central is saying the envelopes have demon spit on them or something.

So sketchy.

And all the more reason to down some Demon bars and get to Antrum fast.

All of which brings me to the present moment. 6:23 am.

I now stand on a round metal platform set into the floor of the main transfer station for Purgatory. The place is dark, save for a grid of white light that covers me.

"Hello?" I call.

"Greetings," says a young guy. He's totally got a shaky voice. Not a good sign. "Who are you?"

"This is Myla Lewis, the Great Scala, requesting transfer into Antrum."

"One minute."

Let the record show that ten minutes pass by.

"Hello again!"

"Greetings. Who are you?"

"We went through this. I'm Myla Lewis. I need you to transfer my ass to Antrum."

"Wait, where are you?"

"Pulpitum VI. Purgatory."

"Right." The guy is panting so much, I can almost picture the sweat rolling down his cheek. "Who is this?"

"For the third time, this is Myla Lewis, your future queen."

"Oh, yes. Of course! We just have a lot of traffic today. Can you believe it?"

"I can. People are coming in for my trials."

Since today may involve demon fighting, I opted to wear my dragonscale fighting suit instead of my Scala robes. Plus, anything other than a dress ticks off the thrax. I'm in the mood to be irritating today.

More minutes pass. I kick at the metal disc beneath my feet. This is the round platform that will haul me to Antrum, when and if transfer Central gets its act together. My tail taps my shoulder in a fast rhythm. It's the equivalent of saying, *are we there yet?*

And my tail raises a good question. Standing around while answering the same questions over and over isn't getting me anywhere. Like Dad always says, *grab the offensive and never let go.*

"Hey," I call. "What's your name?"

"Terence."

"Ter, how long have you worked in Transfer Central?"

"Three days."

That explains a lot. No one asks a newbie to transfer the partially demonic in and out of Antrum. No one outside of Lincoln's mother, that is.

"Did Queen Octavia put you on this duty today?"

"Why, yes. How did you know?"

"Lucky guess." Octavia's scheming to make sure I show up at the last possible second. There must be a reason. Or knowing Octavia, a whole slew of reasons. She'll transfer me when she's good and ready, not before.

I'm all about taking the offensive, except where Lincoln's mother is involved. In these situations, I follow my mother's favorite motto, *discretion is the better part of valor.*

With that saying in mind, I start playing a rousing game of rock, paper, scissors with my tail.

This could take a while.

LINCOLN

This time when I awaken, I'm both rested and wearing pajamas with little monkeys on them.

Ah, Peli.

A few hours remain before the Trials of Acca begin. While I *maybe* trust Peli, I'm still taking precautions.

A lot of them.

Basically, I'll pack the Trials of Acca with as many warriors and magic users as I can find on short notice. And considering I'm the future king of Antrum, I can find quite a lot.

Once the security side of things is set, I have two more tasks to finish before 10 am. First, I must find Mother and see if I can discover what Aldred's trials for Myla will include. Second, I still need to check on Baptiste and the other orphans.

An hour remains do it all.

Not a problem. I've killed more in less time, and those things were breathing.

Slipping out of bed, I quickly get ready for my day. I'm supposed to wear my royal best—meaning crown, leathers and tunic—but that's not happening. Knowing what I do about the Primeval, it's a human-style body armor kind of day. If people don't like it, they can find another prince.

Once I'm set, I make a beeline for Mother. Along the way, I make sure to leave messages for every warrior and magic user worth their salt. All in all, seeking out Octavia becomes quite the journey. I check mother's chambers, Transfer Central, the Royal Archives, and even the secret rooms where she stores notes, pictures, and other intel.

No sign of Mother.

I also make a few half-hearted attempts to find Father. He's secreted himself away as well. No surprise, there.

Ah, well. While it would be better to find out what the noncombat trials of Acca might be, I still hold to Myla's assessment. Nothing can be harder than fighting a Class A demon.

Time to move on to my final task: checking on Baptiste.

To that end, I head over to Nat's preferred training grounds inside a massive purple geode. Once there, I find a familiar square space. Colored light filters through the floors, wall and ceiling. It's so lovely that it can prove incredibly distracting, especially for new recruits. Nat likes it that way, too. He believes warriors must learn early how to focus past their surroundings.

I really do have an exceptional Master at Arms.

Nat and Baptiste are alone in the geode. Both wear loose cotton pants and a black tunic as they run through basic battle poses. I like what I see, and not just because Baptiste has fine reflexes. The dark circles have already lessened beneath the boy's eyes. His skin looks healthier as well, but that might simply be the fact that the kid was able to bathe.

The pair stop as I approach. Nat waves while the boy stands still and at full attention. I wave my Master at Arms over, careful to stand far enough away so we aren't in listening range.

"Morning, Nat." I nod toward Baptiste. "He looks good."

Nat puffs up his chest. He's pleased that I noticed the improvement. "I got him a full physical. He's in good shape. No lasting damage, you know." Nat taps his temple, meaning the royal physicians checked out Baptiste's head as well.

"Good. I'd been concerned about that."

"The boy's been wanting to speak to you ever since the Royal Gymnasium. Not sure if you have time before the Trials of Acca."

"Sure. Call him over."

Nat whistles while raising his fist. It's a basic summons sign. In response, Baptiste jogs up to join our group where the boy stands at perfect attention. It's as if Baptiste has been in the military all his life.

"Permission to speak," states Baptiste.

"Granted," says Nat.

"I wanted to thank you, your Highness."

"Nothing to thank. I can already tell you'll be a great addition to the guard."

"I wish to free my fellow orphans from Aldred," says Baptiste. "Requesting permission to join the mission."

My brows lift. This one has a fire in his belly. "That's Master Nat's mission. Shouldn't he be the one to decide if you qualify to join?"

"Yes, your Highness." Baptiste stares at his bare feet. A sense of disappointment crackles around him like embers from a fire.

I shoot Nat a pointed look. "The Trials of Acca take place this morning." The words are there but unspoken, *do you think Baptiste should go?*

"Considering the place will be packed with warriors, it could be good for Baptiste to observe."

Baptiste beams. "I'd like that. Anything I can do to train or help."

I wag my finger at the boy. "Just stay in the back. At the first sign of trouble, you run."

Baptiste straightens his stance. "That would be my honor."

"Excellent." With my tasks for the morning completed, it's time to head for the Trials of Acca. And, if I'm being honest, the best part of my day approaches as well.

Seeing Myla.

27

MYLA

9:47 am

I'm still in the transfer Pulpitum. I've been standing on this metal disc for so long, I feel like I should set up curtains and a love seat.

At last, Terence pipes up again on the hidden loudspeakers. "Miss Myla?"

"Yup."

"You're approved for transfer now."

"Excellent. Send me off in three, two, one."

Finally, the platform hurtles into the ground. Magma, soil, and random minerals fly past as I speed toward my destination.

The Arx Hall Pulpitum.

Only, that's not where I land.

Instead of a normal platform, I halt in some kind of basement filled with wooden boxes and hidden spiders. Maybe this place is closer to Acca territory, but it's still strange. Normally, there is someone here to greet me and walk me to my destination. Antrum is a maze. It's super-easy to get lost.

I roll my eyes. *Octavia is at it again.* This is yet another stalling tactic. If she wanted me to show up at a certain time, why not just ask me? Not that I would have done it, but at least I'd have a choice.

Whatever. I enter the hallway and pick my way toward the

Sunshine Cavern, which is where the Trials of Acca will take place. It's on Acca territory and dark as Hell, so of course it gets a name that sounds like window cleaning fluid.

Well, if Octavia thinks she can stall me this way, she's totally wrong. Lincoln told me the general direction to the Sunshine Cavern. It can't be that hard to reach.

Turns out, it's *totally* that tough to find.

It takes me for-freaking-ever to find the Sunshine Cavern. By the time I get there, the place is packed. In the crowd, I spy thrax nobles, some ghouls, and even a few angels. The space itself is no great shakes. It's just a huge round cavern with a sloping floor and tons of shadows. The high side of the room makes a natural stage, which is where Aldred has set up a fancypants canopy. It's one of those yellow numbers with fringe dangling around it.

Why do you need a canopy in a cave? I really don't know.

The moment I step foot into the cavern, Octavia pushes her way through the crowd to greet me. We say our hellos and then Lincoln's Mom gets right to it.

"Apologies I made your arrival such a bore."

Well, Octavia certainly gets points for honesty. "What's this about?"

"Your tests." Octavia twists her hands at her waistline. It's a sure sign she's worried. With any luck, Octavia is anxious because I'm about to fight a serious monster. Glad I wore my dragonscale fighting suit.

"What kind of demon am I fighting today?"

"Your trials won't involve demons."

I fold my arms over my chest. "So what's the test?"

"Lady Bentford will give you an Interrogation of Manners. You must respond correctly to her queries or say: *I am humiliated not to know the answer, Mistress.*" She eyes me from head to toe. "Also, you need to wear an actual dress."

Dropping my arms, I take a half step backward. The dress-thing I expected, but the rest of this? Not so much.

"Mistress?" I ask. "As in the she-version of Master? Are there a hidden cameras here? Is this a joke?"

"Lady Bentford does more than brew saffronia. A branch of her family went ghoul."

"Captain Rule." I'd go into the whole story about yesterday but *meh*. "He's around here somewhere."

"Indeed, Rule is in attendance. He still holds great sway in Purgatory. If Rule were to say soul processing needed reform, that could help your parents."

"Mom and Dad say they've got it handled."

"But Lady Bentford could also make the Interrogation of Manners long or short. Just state, *I am humiliated not to know the answer, Mistress*. Do that, and Lady Bentford promises to limit herself to three questions. That is a reasonable test."

The Mistress thing is a total no go. But I've been with Lincoln a little while. Maybe this quiz won't be too bad. I picture the list of questions.

What do thrax do? Fight demons.

What's the High Prince's name? Lincoln.

Who won the Greatest Warrior in Antrum? Me, me, and me.

Excitement sparks in my chest. This could be fun.

"Can I answer these questions?"

"No."

"Give me an example."

"If you insist," says Octavia. "When attending a formal event with all of court in attendance, what is the correct amount of ankle that can be exposed?"

"You're kidding."

"It's a trick question. According to the Rixa Way, you must have your ankles, knees, and shoulders covered at all times."

"Meaning, there's no way I'll answer these questions."

"Not a chance."

"Glad we cleared that up. I'm out of here."

"Please. Is your pride so lofty you can't say a simple phrase three times?"

"No way. You just sprang this on me at the last second, thinking that I'd cave in and do this Mistress Quiz. I understand your friends give you crap about me and the super important Rixa Way. But this is not happening."

Octavia lifts her chin. "We all have to adapt eventually. Look at me today. Do you think I acted in this manner back when I was a lady warrior?"

"Yeah, I totally think you did."

Octavia sighs. *Heh, heh. I totally nailed that one.* "We all must compromise, Myla."

"Hey, I'm compromising. Who isn't sending Aldred to Hell right now? That would be me. And it's because I respect your courts and traditions. Another example. Who didn't spit out the most disgusting drink I ever put in my mouth? Me again. I should be getting a medal here."

The echo of trumpets sounds. "The event is about to begin," says Octavia. "Will you consider my words?"

I pin Lincoln's mother with my most serious stare. "Oh, you can count on it."

LINCOLN

The Sunshine Cavern is packed. Hundreds of thrax nobles fill the huge round cave. I scan the room, cataloguing all the faces. As expected, my warriors and magic users blend in perfectly with the crowd. For his part, Aldred stands beneath an ornate canopy across the cavern.

No sign of Myla, though.

I lean into a fissure on the rock wall. This way, the shadows conceal me while providing a nice view of the entire cavern. At last, I spy Myla speaking with Mother by a side entrance. Octavia must have cornered Myla the moment my girl stepped into the cave.

Not good.

Kicking off the wall, I make a beeline for my fiancée. I try to push forward, but the chamber is packed. In addition, this is a noble crowd, so they're less likely to melt into the shadows as I pass by. If anything, the reverse is true. As I push through, people pull at my tunic, asking questions and demanding favors. I wave them off and keep pressing on. A familiar figure appears.

Octavia.

She must have finished with Myla and sped straight for me. I pause and incline my head. "Mother."

"Son."

"What's all this?" They are three simple words, but a world of meaning lies behind them. The short version says, *I know you're scheming, and I need your true plans.*

Mother straightens the folds of her velvet dress. "Myla won't fight demons today," explains Octavia. "Instead, Lady Bentwood will perform an interrogation of manners."

My eyes widen a fraction. It's a small gesture, but I'm certain Mother sees it. Inside, my soul churns with a heated mixture of outrage and worry. Myla doesn't deserve to be treated this way by any thrax, let alone a noble of my own house. No question what this is really about.

"Myla will never change for you."

Mother sighs. "Everyone adapts eventually."

Lowing my voice, I step closer to Mother. "Do not place yourself between me and Myla. There is no competition. None."

Without saying another word, I step off into the crowd.

At last, I reach my girl. Pulling her into my arms, I hold Myla close. "Hello, lovely," I whisper.

"Hey, you."

"Mother told me about Lady Bentford. It's outrageous."

"Octavia's scheming. It happens."

Leaning back, I get a good look at Myla's face. She doesn't seem upset. While I'm glad that this betrayal isn't bothering my fiancée, it doesn't change the fact that the entire situation is unacceptable.

"You're not doing that Interrogation of Manners."

Myla winks. "Not even a little?"

Some of the heat cools within me. "If you use the opportunity to verbally torture Lady Bentford, then obviously, it's a different story."

"I'll figure something out. By the way, I tried to find that ghoul Peli wanted, but came up with nothing."

"I've other news on the Peli front. Our little orange friend cast some spells on me. I went to the past to learn more about the Primeval."

"Anything good?"

"Not the firm evidence I need to stop today from happening. I did discover that the Contagion is indeed a wizard who's trapped in a tree. He can't move around much."

"And if he does?"

"I have the place packed with warriors and magic users. If the Contagion attacks, we'll be ready."

Across the cavern, Aldred raises his arms. The space quiets. Clearly, the event is about to begin. Tension winds up my spine.

"My thrax!" calls Aldred. "Welcome to the Trials of Acca!" He pauses. Polite clapping echoes through the chamber. I wonder how many folks here have been blackmailed by Aldred.

Virtually all of them, I'd guess.

Speaking of those Aldred is blackmailing, my father isn't in attendance today. Can't say I'm surprised.

The light applause collapses into silence. Aldred continues. "Lady Bentwood will start this session with an Interrogation of Manners. Assisting her will be her guest and relative, Captain Rule from the Dark Lands."

My gaze locks on the ghoul. I hadn't noticed him before in particular. Now I scan him with an extra level of intensity. Sure enough, he looks like an undead Lady Bentford in a long black cloak.

I pitch my voice low, careful so only Myla can hear me. "Are you familiar with this captain?"

Myla nods. "Met him yesterday."

"Is he the one Peli spoke of?" I ask.

Myla shakes her head. "I checked his shoulder. No marks."

My brows lift. "How did you find that out?"

"Not easily. I ended up checking ghoul shoulders for hours last night at the Scala Bleugh." She shivers. "Long story."

Across the cavern, a small orange face pops up over the canopy's top.

Peli.

Grinning, the monkey taps his shoulder. It's almost as if the little guy were listening to me and Myla as we chat. Something to test out.

"Marks," I say.

Sure enough, Peli taps his shoulder again.

Myla narrows her eyes. We don't discuss this topic, but I've no doubt she's with me here.

"Marks, marks, marks," repeats Myla.

Peli taps three times.

"Two things," says Myla. "First. Peli is enjoying this far too much."

"And second," I add. "Peli clearly has a surprise for us when it comes to marks."

Myla frowns. "I hate surprises. Unless I'm the one giving them."

"Agreed."

Across the chamber, Aldred pipes up once more. "After the Interrogation of Manners, I shall perform the Igni Validation test."

That's news to me. "Were you aware of this?" I ask Myla.

"Yeah, Cissy told me all about it. The thing is totally fake and—surprise, surprise—when I fail, I can no longer be involved in combat in any way, shape, or form. Like that will happen."

Aldred waves his across the crowd. The motion reminds me of a carnival barker at a human circus. "And finally, my thrax. We shall end the day with my killing the dreaded tree beast of the Primeval."

At this point, an door beside the canopy swings open. Minstrels step out, playing a happy jig on their lutes.

> *Demon tree*
> *Demon tree*
> *Aldred fighting*
> *Aldred smiting*
> *Demon tree*
> *Demon tree*
> *Tra la la la LA*

Ugh. Aldred really has the worst taste in minstrels.

As the tune continues, Peli hops down from the canopy. As always, everyone else is oblivious to the existence of our small orange friend.

"Uh oh," whispers Myla. "He's on the move."

Seconds later, a wall of orange mist appears before the entire back wall of the cavern. Bands of concern tighten around my chest. Myla and I share a worried look.

"He's not doing what I think he's doing, is he?" she asks.

Across the cavern, the orange haze congeals into a great disc, ten feet high. The minstrels and choir fall silent. No question about it. Everyone can see this part.

A gateway has appeared.

Aldred hustles through the audience to stand before the new and magical addition. "Behold! Another gateway to the Primeval. I decided to open it early."

Total lie, but my nobles buy it completely. For his part, Peli is having the time of his life. The little guy glances our way and winks.

"I'm starting to hate that monkey," grumbles Myla.

"It seems we're hitting the *dangerous tree* portion of the day early," I state.

A loop of orange metal solidifies around the edges of the portal. The center remains filled with the same orange smoke I've come to know so well. The spell isn't finished.

"I don't like this," I state.

"Do we move in?" asks Myla.

"Not yet. It depends what appears in the central window. Rushing up might cause a panic."

Little by little, the view within the gateway comes into clearer focus.

Oh, no.

LINCOLN

The center of the gateway becomes clear as glass. A vista appears inside, revealing the view of a gray wasteland filled with burnt-out trees. In its center looms a tall stump whose bark lives and moves, reminding me of shifting ropes of tar.

The Contagion.

Back in the cavern, I let out a short burst of whistles. That's the cue for my warriors and magic users to usher people to safety.

"No, my thrax!" cries Aldred. "Cease heading for the exits. There is nothing to fear. Besides, I have magically sealed the doors here. No one leaves until my demonstration is complete!"

Myla shoots me a worried look. "Can we break down the doors?"

"My magic users have instructions to try." I scan the back of the cavern. A thin haze of orange magic hangs in the air. My best Striga wizards cast spells by the back wall, yet the exit doors remains closed. "It's not working." I wave my hand through the light haze of Primeval magic that fills the air. The tiny particles shift and dance in the breeze. "Peli said his magic interacts strangely with the after-realms."

"It must be blocking our own casters." Myla frowns. "I bet Peli and Aldred planned this. The earl would know there'd be other magic users around."

A sinking feeling moves inside me. I decided to trust Peli even though I knew the little orange monkey was scheming with the earl. *What have I done?*

I straighten my shoulders and steel my spine. Whatever decisions I made, standing around now won't change them. I take Myla's hand. Her touch grounds me. As king and queen, we'll make thousands of choices. Some will fail. We'll always move forward.

And that's what we do now.

Hand in hand, Myla and I press toward the front of the cavern. All the while, we're careful to weave through the crowd at a steady pace. No need to cause a panic.

Within the gateway, the gooey black tar moves faster. The burned out stump that is the Contagion pulses with energy. Deep holes collapse, forming what look like eyes. A great slash opens for a mouth. The Contagion lets out a roar of rage.

"I am the wizard Contagion! Who disturbs my slumber?"

Aldred steps closer to the gateway. "It is I, Aldred, the great Earl of Acca. I come here to destroy you."

Two thin nostril-holes appear on the Contagion's bark. The lines vibrate as the wizard tree inhales deeply. The Contagion's long mouth curls into an impossibly long smile. "The first Marked One. It's here."

Across the cavern, a figure steps out of the shadows beside the gateway.

Rule.

The ghoul lurches with all the jerky grace of a sleepwalker. A glazed sheen covers his all-black eyes.

Myla pauses. "Can Rule cross through that gateway?"

I picture all the times the Contagion punched through gateways in the Primeval. Each time, his branch-like arms struck a different apprentice with ease.

"Oh, yes," I reply.

Myla's tail pokes a young noblewoman in the side, forcing her out of our path. "Ouch!" She rubs at the spot.

"Your tail has the right idea," I say.

Myla winks. "I love pushy-shovey time."

Forget a steady pace. Myla and I now race toward the gateway. If people get in our way, they're moved.

Ten yards to go until we reach the gateway.

Five yards.

One.

Up ahead, Rule pulls at the neckline of his ghoul robes. The motion exposes an expanse of all-white skin. "I am a Marked One!" Rule cries. "I must reunite with the Contagion!"

Fortunately, Rule is not a Marked One. That would require actually having a skull tattoo. Unfortunately, he's clearly bonkers.

At last, Myla and I reach the gateway. Leaping in unison, we land right between Rule and the gateway's window-like view of the Contagion.

While bracing her legs, Myla presses her hands against Rule's chest. Leaning over, I shove my shoulder against his stomach. Even so, Rule moves closer to the gateway. For a ghoul, he's rather strong.

"You don't want to do this," I warn. "Whatever you think, you don't belong in the Primeval."

Rule inhales. "Can you taste the magic on the air?"

That's a hard thing to do, what with my shoulder lodged against Rule's belly, but I also take in a long breath. I've had enough Primeval magic tossed at my face to know when it's getting heavier. There's no denying the truth. Rule is right.

With every inch we get closer to the gateway, the Primeval magic grows stronger. Not good for our side.

Rule keeps a death grip on the neckline of his ghoul robes. With all his strength, he pushes still closer to the gateway.

"Lincoln!" Shock heightens Myla's tone.

Alarm zooms through my nervous system. I stand up while gripping Rule's shoulders—this way I can keep the ghoul back while seeing Myla face to face.

That's when I witness the problem.

The mark of an orange skull has materialized on Rule's shoulder. With every passing second, the mark grows more defined.

Myla's forehead crumples in confusion. "It just appeared."

"Must be Primeval magic. It reveals what was always there." My mouth thins to an angry line. Not sure who I'm more furious with right now: me or Peli. I should have guessed that the marks wouldn't show without Primeval magic. When I saw Peli handing out the marks, no one in the after-realms reacted to receiving them.

I force in a slow breath. In the end, it doesn't matter what I should have known. Rule is a Marked One. The color symbolizes Simian magic. The skull stands for ghoul kind.

It's a strain to keep Rule back, but Myla and I are getting the hang of it. I scan the cavern. Peli sits atop the canopy again. He wears a half smile while tapping his shoulder.

"I tried to warn you," says Peli. "My marks are tricksy."

How I hate to admit this. Yet in Peli's convoluted trickster way, he really did lob over a few clues.

Damn.

As turns of events go, this is very very bad. Still, there is one good spot here. The Contagion remains stuck in the Primeval. I saw this in the past; the whole point of Peli's spell was to keep the evil wizard contained until he could be destroyed.

Back in the cavern, Aldred raises his voice. "Do not panic merely because a few worriers—" here Aldred glares at me and Myla "—wish to ruin the day."

Inside the gateway, the Contagion inhales once more. "The power of the Marked One. I taste it. Fresh magic. Delicious." The odd face in the tree trunk takes on a look that can only be described as *bliss*.

Myla grimaces. "I've seen that expression before. It's the one I make when chowing down on a Demon Bar."

"Yes," I confirm, careful to keep my tone calm. "The Contagion is taking in new magic."

"So this is about to become a shit show."

"Apparently." I look over to the canopy, ready to demand that Peli stop this disaster. Per usual, the monkey is nowhere in sight.

Within the gateway, the tar-like skin of the Contagion bubbles. This is a different look than I've seen more. In the past, the Contagion's bark shifts, reminding me of shifting colors on a soap bubble.

Now it's on he move.

Little by little, the Contagion seeps into the ground. The movement matches that of a geyser dying out.

"Look now!" Aldred gestures to the gateway. "The Contagion has melted away! I have destroyed it."

The fact that Aldred did nothing to actually demolish the Contagion means zero to the audience. They love a fight and, more importantly, a win. My court breaks out into ear-splitting cheers. Aldred's minstrels strike up again. I whistle more coded orders to my warriors and magic users. The sounds aren't making it past the celebratory din.

Worry tightens every muscle in my body. First, Rule reveals himself as a Marked One. Now, my warriors and magic users are neutralized. The Contagion may have sunk into the ground, but I am not fooled. With every passing second, we get closer to trouble.

Myla and I keep up our efforts to hold Rule in place. Now he stops moving toward the gateway, his shoulders slumped.

"I am a Marked One," moans Rule. "Where is my master?"

Myla pats his shoulder. "The Contagion took like a little *burned out possessed tree* vacation. You're good now."

An odd smell fills the air. It's the scent of burning oil. Looking down, I find black goo pooling by my boots.

"Do you see that?" I ask Myla.

"Eek." She frowns. "Is it some kind of naturally occurring cave thingy?"

"No."

"Good." Myla takes out her baculum and ignites them into a trident made of white flame. "I was worried I wouldn't get to fight today."

Grinning, I pull out my own baculum. With Rule staying put, there's no reason to remain unarmed. I ignite the silver rods into a long sword.

More tar pools on the ground nearby, all of them small points at regular intervals.

"You said that Rule can enter the gateway," says Myla.

"I did."

"Can the Contagion get out?"

"If you'd asked me five minutes ago, I'd have said no. But that was before the Contagion inhaled extra power from Rule and his mark. Now, I'm unsure."

"So these goopy spots on the floor could be the Contagion."

Myla's eyes widen. "Oh, I bet that evil tree monster is looking for Rule."

Meanwhile, the entire cavern retains its party vibe. Nobles cheer. Minstrels play. My magic users cast useless spells while my warriors press against firmly closed doors.

The hairs on the back of my neck stand on end. As a hunter, I can sense when a predator is about to strike. And something's coming right now.

With a great surge of tar, the Contagion surfaces inside the cavern, rising at the very spot where Rule stands. Fast as a whip, the gurgling lines surround the ghoul. For a moment, the burned-out stump of the Contagion looms inside the cavern itself, tall and immobile. Orange light appears behind the shifting lines of bark.

I can't believe it.

The Contagion is consuming Rule.

The cavern falls silent. No more cheering. All dancing stops. A minstrel drops their lute.

Myla and I swing into action. My girl stabs at the Contagion with her trident. I strike at him with my longsword. Sadly, our angelfire seems as limited as my magic users' spells. The baculum weapons don't so much as singe the gooey bark. A face reappears on the tree.

"I am the wizard Contagion!" he cries. "You disturbed my slumber! Now you will pay!"

The audience goes berserk. If I thought there was chaos before, that's nothing compared to what happens now. Everyone rushes for the exits while pushing and screaming their lungs out. Too bad the doors are locked.

"Nothing to worry about!" Aldred cries. A twinge of panic shines in his piggy eyes. "I knew this would happen."

Important note: When it comes to Aldred, saying *I knew this would happen* always translates into *I have no clue what's going on.*

I stalk toward the earl, my baculum sword burning brightly. "Open the doors now or I'll slice your throat."

All the blood seems to drain from Aldred's face. Raising his arms again, Aldred addresses the crowd. "Change of plans! Open everything up!"

Along the back wall, the line of doors pop open. Cries of anguish and fear increase as everyone races through the exits. My guards and magic users try to keep things organized, but when an audience turns into a crazed mob, your options are limited.

"Lincoln!' carries someone over the din. "Over here!"

It's Myla. The Contagion has returned to his gurgling shape. Where once stood massive tree, now a burned-out stump melts into the ground. Within seconds, there is no sign the wizard was here at all.

The Contagion has vanished.

The gateway clouds over with an orange haze. The round structure collapses on itself as if a black hole were at its center.

Peli's gateway disappears as well.

I exhale. If nothing else, the Contagion is gone. That must be good. Turning, I scan the cavern. Even better. The place is clearing out.

Myla stands near the spot where the Contagion last stood. Nat and Baptiste wait beside her with their backs to me, half leaning forward. In all the excitement, I hadn't noticed them before.

My skin chills over.

The pair aren't moving.

I step closer to Nat and Baptiste. Both are frozen solid. I've seen this before. The Contagion transforms enemies into wood instead of flesh and blood. That's exactly what happened to Baptiste and Nat. In their frozen state, both hold metal rods that had been torn from the canopy frame. The pair wield these makeshift weapons as bats. No doubt what happened here.

Nat and Baptiste stepped in to help; the Contagion struck them down.

Myla brushes her fingertips down Nat's arm. "What is this?"

"The Contagion froze them into wood," I explain.

Guilt presses in around me, strong as a vise. I think back to this morning. I was the one who suggested Nat take Baptiste here. Sure, I wanted them to stay in the back, but I should have known better. Nat could never remain on the sidelines if he thought Myla and I were at risk. And Baptiste is the kind of go-getter who would leap in to help as well.

Myla turns to me, her gaze fierce. "Are you thinking what I'm thinking?"

"Oh, yes." I cup my hand by my mouth. "Peli! Open another gateway!"

We're going in.

30

LINCOLN

*P*eli reopens the gateway to the Primeval. This time, the round window shows a forest shrouded in deep shadows. It's not a familiar spot, but I'm not choosey.

Whatever gets me there.

The cavern has emptied out. Even Aldred took off. All that remains is for Myla and I to leave as well.

A pool of orange light appears on the floor nearby. Seconds later, Peli materializes beside me and Myla. He stares at Nat and Baptiste.

"I didn't want them to be hurt," says Peli in a low voice. "It's why I took you to my past. I thought it would help when today came."

"It does help," I confirm. "I now understand why you want the Contagion dead. Kill the caster, destroy the spell."

Peli nods. "The Contagion will never choose to free the apprentices. And my family—" Peli swallows. "He'll never set them loose, either. If we kill the Contagion, we release them all."

I gesture into the darkened forest inside the gateway. "And wherever this place is, it gets us closer to that end?"

"You have my word," says Peli.

I look to Myla. "Jump in on three?"

"My favorite number."

Octavia steps forward. Not sure where she's been lurking this entire time, but that's Mother for you. No doubt, she's also soaked in the entire situation. It's another one of Octavia's gifts.

"Son," she says. "Don't do this. I know you're attached to Nat and Baptiste."

"They're my subjects, same as anyone else."

"If we lose you and Myla, all of Antrum could be in peril. Are Nat and Baptiste truly worth that risk?"

I shake my head. "Would you say the same thing if the Contagion had frozen Aldred?"

A long pause follows. At last, Octavia answers. "It's different with an earl."

"It shouldn't be," I counter.

"No one else makes such distinctions."

"We do," says Myla. "Enough, Octavia. We're going."

"On my mark," says Peli. "Three, two, one!" He jumps into the gateway.

With all the resolve in the world, Myla and I leap in after him.

MYLA

Time was, my honorary older brother Walker shlepped me to Arena games via a ghoul portal. Not gonna lie. I bitched about the barfy feeling I felt while in transit. But ghoul portals have nothing on gateways.

Yow.

The moment I step inside the orange circle, it's as if my body's yanked in all directions at once. Pain tears through my nervous system. And for some reason, inter-realm travel reeks of stinky feet.

After two of the longest minutes of my entire life, it's over. I tumble out of the sky and land in a strange realm.

On my ass.

Looking over, I find Lincoln standing beside me. His face is lined with concern. "Are you all right?"

"Fine." I rise, rubbing my bum. "Too bad dragonscales aren't good padding. You?"

"I'm well."

I step around in a slow circle, trying to process what I'm seeing. To my right, a burned out jungle stretches to the horizon line. Nothing but charred stumps as far as they eye can see.

To my left, there stands a mighty forest. Towering trees with wide, fan-like leaves. And they're all blue.

I squint.

Shake my head.

Blink.

Still blue.

Even more strange, the forest looks like someone cut the edge with a knife. There's no slow transition to the burned out jungle—just a perfect line stretching off into infinity. There's no sign of another living soul, either. Only me, Lincoln and a lot of blue freaking trees.

My mind goes fuzzy as I try to take in the truth. This is the Primeval. An entirely different reality. And we're here.

Now, I knew this little Aldred fiesta would end with some kind of Primeval-related encounter. Yet somehow, I always pictured this other world invading the after-realms, not Lincoln and I transporting to a blue forest.

A small voice in the back of my head reminds me that isn't true. The Primeval did invade the after-realms. My heart cracks as I turn to Lincoln.

"We'll free Nat and Baptiste," I say, my voice hoarse.

"That we will."

My thoughts move on to the other casualty from this morning. "Do you think Rule is suffering? Like being slowly digested or whatever?"

"Doubtful. Trees aren't carnivorous, and the Contagion is mostly plant right now. If I had to guess, I'd say Rules lies in suspended animation."

"But that's a guess." I picture being digested in a tree and shiver. That's some nasty stuff. "Back in the cavern, you said Peli has been shlepping you to the Primeval. I was thinking I could wait to get the full story, but I changed my mind. Care to share?"

Turns out, Lincoln's in the mood to blab. My guy gives me a quick rundown on his trips to Peli's past. I find out how the Primeval is shaped like a pie that's been cut into four equal slices, one for each land. A massive circle sits in the center. That central territory is the jungle where the Golden Arbor once hung out. Good to have the basics.

Lincoln goes on to explain how the Contagion consumed the power of each land and then shut himself inside a tree. Gotta be honest. That's a new one. Peli then ripped out the Contagion's stolen powers—as in literally tore it out of the guy's chest—and tossed magic marks into five lucky winners of the after-realms. Those are the five Marked Ones. Rule was first, and his body contained power from the Simian lands.

Key point: for the Contagion to return to his humanoid (and far more powerful) form, the wizard needs to consume the other Marked Ones too.

"Let me guess," I say after a while. "I don't know much about magic, but I know the order of your spell ingredients is key. Don't toss in the eye of newt before the bat's wing or whatever."

"True."

"Back to my guess. The Contagion must consume the Marked Ones in a particular order. And since the Marked One for the jungle is already gone—" I gesture to the blue forest beside us "—I'm guessing the Marked One for the Avians is now up on the menu."

Lincoln nods. "You're brilliant."

"And lets's not forget my other qualities." Setting my fists on my hips, I pose like a 1940's pin up girl. Humans knew how to appreciate women back then.

Lincoln turns to the forest. "The next Marked One must be somewhere in here."

"Should I ask why Peli just doesn't give us a map, or is it a trickster thing?"

"It's the latter."

"I'd launch into a tirade on the topic, but I'd rather see you do your hunter thing in a blue forest. You can find the next Marked One, right?"

Lincoln winks. "Just watch."

All of a sudden, the entire sky fills with what look like small dots. The points of darkness arch and dive over each other.

"Those look like birds," I state. "A lot of birds."

"Hunt complete," declares Lincoln. "Looks like the Avians found us."

One dot in the sky breaks free and soars down toward our spot. Seconds later, a humanoid bird lands nearby. For a moment, all I can see are his great wings stretching behind him, but those appendages quickly fold behind his back. He tilts her head and steps forward. Up close, I can see how he's covered in tiny blue feathers from head to toe. His large round eyes flicker between me and Lincoln.

"I am Zoar, the Avian King," she says. "You are intruders on our world."

Lincoln starts to work his regal vibe. It involves standing extra tall while talking in an authoritative voice. Works all the time.

"I am Prince Lincoln Vidar Osric Aquilus," says my guy. "And this is Myla. We came here because the Contagion entered our world and froze some of our people into wood."

Zoar moves closer to yours truly. For an uncomfortably long minute, he stares at me from head to toe. "Our women aren't shaped like you."

"Fascinating," I deadpan. "How about we move on to focus on rescuing the frozen people? Spoiler Alert—that involves taking down the Contagion."

Zoar doesn't seen to hear a word I say. Instead, his gaze stays locked on my chest. *Gross.*

"So lovely," says Zoar. That's when the king does the dick move extraordinaire.

He grabs my boob.

And this is not a gentle pat or anything, but a full on clasp.

Here's the situation. Let's say there's an empty platter that holds a single large chocolate donut. The way I'd go after that donut? That's how Zoar clutches my breast.

Now, I'm prepared for death blows. Back stabs. Throat punches. I've just never had someone all-out donut-grab my boob before.

On reflex, I slap his hand away. "No touchie!"

At the same time, my tail arcs, ready to skewer the guy. Before I can make a move, Lincoln has kicked the Avian king's legs out from under him. My guy looms over Zoar. "You heard my fiancée. Do not touch her."

Zoar hoists himself to his feet. "That was a grave error." He lets out a series of high-pitched whistles. "Bring the prison chamber."

A bunch of bird people fly down. If I had to guess, I'd say there about about eight in all. Each one has a long chain clasped in their hands. And those many cords lead to a single destination:

An egg-shaped cage.

Actually, it's more like an egg shaped nest thing, considering how it seems to be made from branches. There's even a hole for crawling in and out.

All in all, there's not a lot of gray area here. Clearly, Zoar is demanding we step inside that cage. I have to be honest. It would be more convincing if he weren't short and covered in feathers. It's just not a good look for being a badass.

Zoar gestures toward the very uncomfortable-looking cage. "Enter and be judged."

Turning to Lincoln, I raise my fist while tilting my head. There's an unspoken question here. *Do we fight?*

Lincoln stares at the Avians surrounding us. I can almost see the battle calculations going on in his head. For a long moment, Lincoln only narrows his eyes. When my guy turns to face me again, all the determination in the world shines in his face. He shakes his head. *No.*

I sigh. "Right. The Marked One." Getting in this cage may be the only way to meet that person.

We climb inside.

32

LINCOLN

As a warrior, I've seen my share of odd battles. For instance, I once fought a mermaid and ended up half-frozen in a glacier. But I've never been strung up inside an egg-shaped cage before.

To kill time, I've been cataloging my surroundings.

Zero.

That's how many Avian guards stand below me, Myla, and our cage. Perhaps they lurk somewhere nearby, but it seems unlikely.

Four.

The number of massive egg-shaped cages hoisted to hang from a tree branch above the clearing below. All the others are empty, aside from the one holding me and Myla.

Six.

The number of hours we've been stuck in this cage.

Fifteen.

The amount of times Myla and I discussed escaping, only to decide that to find the Marked One hidden with the Avians, it's best to play by local rules. And that means waiting for the morning nesting, whatever that is.

Twenty.

The length (in feet) between our cage and the ground.

Fifty-seven.

How many egg-shaped houses handle in the nearby canopy of trees. Of these, only about a dozen appear to be populated.

One hundred thirty two.

That's the number of Avians I've counted so far. So far, all resemble their king, only far thinner. And I'm not talking fashion-skinny either. These folks have ribs sticking out and bony limbs. Someone's not getting enough food. Combine it with the empty nests, and it's clear the Avians have some serious problems.

Myla sits across from me on the cage's curved floor. She fidgets. "These branches are totally sticking in my butt. Who designed these things anyway?"

"I suspect they weren't made for comfort."

"No snacks, either. Good thing I come prepared." Myla unzips her dragonscale fighting suit.

My mouth falls open. "You didn't."

"What? Bring along a Demon Bar? You bet I did. You know how I get when I have low blood sugar."

"That will fix the low blood sugar issue, all right." This is an ongoing point of discussion between me and Myla. Demon Bars are aptly named, I'll leave it at that.

On second thought, I won't. I stretch out my hand. Myla tears open the bar with her teeth. "May I see the wrapper?"

"No way. You're just going to read the ingredients again."

"For a reason. There isn't one ingredient on that list without five syllables, minimum. Think about that. You're putting all sorts of odd chemicals into your body now."

Myla bits into the chocolate concoction. "Mmm, mmm." She chews with exaggerated joy. "If you want some, you'll have to be nice to me."

"Fortunately, I had a big breakfast. Of food."

"Eh, you're just jealous I remembered a snack."

Grinning, I stretch my arms wide. Words aren't necessary. Myla shifts to snuggle against me, her back to my chest. It's glorious.

If I have to be suspended inside an egg cage over a strange village, there's no one I'd rather be trapped with.

33

MYLA

Turns out, it's not easy to sit still.

In an egg prison.

For hours and hours.

At least, I've found a comfy spot cuddling with my back against Lincoln's chest. We spent more time going through all the Peli-related news in detail. I asked questions. Got answers. Now, we're just hanging around and watching the blue forest grow.

It's boring as Hell.

No, I take that back. It's boring as High School. Far worse.

Lincoln twists a lock of my hair through his fingers. That feels really nice. "I've been thinking."

"Let's hear it."

"Did you notice anything odd while traveling through the gateway?"

"My own screaming, that's about it."

His hair-twiddling stops. "I thought I saw Aldred."

I suck in a shocked breath. "Now that you say it, I might have smelled him."

Lincoln chuckles. "Smelled?"

"That man has super stinky feet. I was debating about sending him charcoal inserts for his boots. Anonymously. But I figured that since I'm the only person Aldred interacts with who shops at Purgatory Mart, it might be obvious."

"You should still do it," says Lincoln.

He's such a bad influence on me, I love it.

"Okay, it's on the list." And unlike urine beverages, it's in the top twenty.

"If only I knew for certain whether Aldred followed us." Lincoln drums his fingers on my stomach. It tickles. "What about your igni? Sometimes they have wonderful ideas."

"True." Closing my eyes, I summon my Scala power.

Come to me, little ones.

The igni appear around my hands. Only instead of little lighting bolts of power, they materialize as actual flames around my hands. That burns like a mother.

"Go away, little ones!" I cry. "Vamoose!"

The igni shift to land on Lincoln's hands. My guy doesn't flinch.

"Doesn't that hurt?" I ask.

"No, it's fine. Peli said magic works differently between the afterrelams and the Primeval. This must be part of it."

"Wow, you're so casual. It's not like sentient flames are hanging out on your fingers."

"Oh, I roll with the punches. So are the igni telling you anything?"

"I'll check."

This is the crap part, because interacting with igni usually results in a lot of wince-worthy noises. I close my eyes.

Any insights, little ones?

In a shocking move, I get a coherent answer.

No.

Opening my eyes, I find the igni have vanished again.

"What happened?" asks Lincoln.

"I asked if they knew anything and they said *no*."

"Just no?"

"That's it."

"Oh, my. Magic really does work differently here."

A new voice sounds below. "Do you require assistance?"

Looking down, Lincoln and I find an angel standing beneath the cage. He's on the short side with a thin frame and amber skin.

"We're fine," I say. "I'm Myla and this is Lincoln."

The angel waves in the general area where my just igni appeared. "Take my advice. Whatever that was, don't try your magic here. It won't work the same way."

I'm the kind of girl where if you say, *don't eat that,* then I've got to take a bite. I was happy with the igni experiment being over. But now this angel dude told me not to play around with my magical stuff.

So that's throwing down a gauntlet.

And I never back off a challenge.

Immediately, I pull out my baculum and try to ignite them. Nothing. I suppose it's better than almost singing my eyebrows off like my igni just attempted. Still, a lack of weaponry is a bummer.

"I am Hector," says the angel.

"Nice to meet you," I reply.

A million questions zing through my mind. Is Hector friends with Peli? Does he realize the threat of being a Marked One? And how does he get his angel robes dry cleaned? Dad says that's a lot of drama outside of Heaven. I settle on the easiest query first.

"How did you end up in the Primeval?"

"I was a criminal defense lawyer in human life. You meet all kinds. That's why it wasn't too shocking for my angelic-self to meet an talking orange monkey. Peli was articulate, informed, and invisible to everyone else. He told me to hide in the Primeval, so that's what I did. It's rather nice staying with the Avians, as a matter of fact. Good floor show."

I get stuck on the *floor show* comment. What could that be about? Meanwhile, Lincoln jumps in with another question.

"If it's not too personal," begins Lincoln. "May we ask to see your mark?"

I nod. "Good question."

Hector pulls his robes to the right, revealing a what looks like the tattoo of a blue wing on his shoulder. "It stands for Avian magic in an angel's body. I didn't even know I had it until I got close to the Primeval. Then it appeared."

"Does it hurt?" I ask.

"No," replies Hector. "I can't access the magic inside it at all. It's just… there." He shifts his weight from foot to foot. "Look, I'm not supposed to wait here for long. Here's the situation. You screwed up by attacking the king."

"Hey, now," I say. "He donut-grabbed my boob."

"That doesn't matter," counters Hector. "You're in Avian lands now. You must make things right at the morning nesting. If you're lucky, maybe Zoar will let you return to the after-realms in peace."

"We're not trying to get back to the after-realms," corrects Lincoln. "Not yet, anyway. We're here to destroy the Contagion."

I point at Hector's nose. "And you're in serious danger. The Contagion is after you."

Hector shrugs. "I'm not worried. The Contagion has been trapped at the same spot for hundreds of years."

I make a wincey-face. *This bit of news won't go over well.* "That was before the Contagion consumed his first Marked One. Tree Guy is mobile now. He'll be after you next."

"The Contagion? Mobile?" Hector gestures to the wings on his back. "Not compared to me, he most certainly isn't."

"You must listen to us," declares Lincoln. "We must plan a counter-attack."

Hector steeples his fingers under his chin. Suddenly, I can picture him as a lawyer, doing that pointy-finger move while telling someone they'd be nuts not to accept a plea bargain. "I'm fine as I am."

I throw up my hands. "Come on!"

"This case is officially closed," states Hector.

Based on how Hector's angel eyes are glowing blue, the guy means what he's saying. Without another word, Hector steps into the nearby forest and disappears from view.

"Wow," I state. "That guy is so toast."

"Hopefully not," says Lincoln.

Chatting with Hector got our snuggle positions all screwed up. I tap Lincoln's shoulder.

"Lean back, babe. I need to cuddle if I'm going to get any rest tonight."

Lincoln winks. "As you command."

And even though it's an awkward cage in a foreign land, both Lincoln and I fall asleep rather quickly.

Because cuddling is simply the best.

34

LINCOLN

Once again, I dream of white flame.

Angelfire surrounds my body. Heat warms my skin, but doesn't burn. When the fire dies down, I stand before the same fantasy forest as before. Dark trees sway with plastic movements. A full moon swirls in an impossible sky.

Just as last time, a thin line of blue smoke rises up from the woods. I step into the trees, following a path that leads to a small clearing with a bonfire.

Only it isn't a fire at all.

Someone's here with their back to me. All I see are their wings, which blaze with red flame.

I scan my memories. A number of demons have fiery wings. Why would I transport to meet any of them?

The figure slowly turns. I reach for my baculum, gripping the silver rods in my hands. When the stranger turns, I find it is a man.

He looks a lot like me.

"What's your name?" I ask.

"I am the Guide. Consider me a manifestation of your natural angelic magic. Only now that we're in the Primeval, there's no need for me tag onto Peli's power in order to contact you. Much easier, don't you think?"

"Guide." I turn the word over in my mind. "To where?"

The Guide raises his arms. Blue smoke pours out from his palms, surrounding me. When the haze clears, I'm back in the ballroom at the Ryder mansion. My breath catches.

This is the past. *My past.*

"I'm about to meet Myla face to face for the first time," I state.

"Yes, *we* are."

Past-Myla steps past me in her glorious orange gown, completely oblivious to the fact that the Future Lincoln watches over her. She waits under a balcony. Past Lincoln stands nearby in his tuxedo-clad best.

No question what comes next.

Our first fight.

"You played such the rogue that night," says the Guide.

"I was trying to protect her," I explain. "Aldred saw Myla as a demon to be hunted. I thought that by being rude and callous, I could keep her safe."

"Yet to this day, you never told her why you acted cruelly."

"It didn't matter. I was an ass. I apologized. We've moved on." I watch as the past versions of me and Myla verbally spar. The sight both weighs me down with sadness and lightens my soul with joy.

"You do this to protect her," says the Guide.

I shrug. "Myla sees enough of the anti-demonic side of the thrax. It's the principle of the thing. I take responsibility for the impact of my actions, end of story."

"What would happen if you shared all the details?"

"Not much. Myla's strong."

"Such faith in Myla can be good. It might also become dangerous."

Past Myla storms by me, her tail making a lewd gesture at the previous version of myself. I chuckle.

I so had that coming.

Shaking my head, I force myself to focus on the Guide once more. "Is that why you're here? To make sure I know that my faith in Myla can also be dangerous?"

The Guide nods.

"Do you mean that in terms of defeating the Contagion?" I ask.

"And other things."

The Guide raises his arms again. White flame erupts around us, erasing both my past and the Guide himself. For the rest of my dream, I meander in a world of angelfire, seeing nothing but a blaze around me.

I never do get burned.

35

MYLA

The next morning, I awaken to the sound of voices below our prison egg. I'm still cuddled with my back to Lincoln's chest. He gently kisses my head.

"Sleep well?" he asks.

"Surprisingly. You're very comfy."

"Thank you."

"Have you been up for a while?"

"A few minutes."

I shift so I can stretch my legs and look at the scene below. King Zoar stands beneath our prison egg. About a dozen Avian men surround him.

Yawning, I try to recall details from yesterday. It isn't easy. Mornings aren't my thing.

"What did Hector say again?" I ask. "They're holding a morning breakfast, right?"

"I believe Hector said it was a morning nesting."

"Grr. I was really hoping for food." Lincoln opens his mouth, I hold up my finger. "And if you're about to make another speech about Demon Bars, forget it. I'm hangry."

Lincoln closes his mouth with a very dramatic pop. He then mimes zipping it shut. Saucy guy.

Zoar leans back his head and lets out a long series of screeches. It isn't pleasant, but it has the desired effect. Avian men move to stand in a great circle around him.

"My people!" cries Zoar. "Time for the morning nesting."

At these words, the branches at the bottom of our oval cage open up, sending me and Lincoln tumbling toward the ground. The moment we land on the earth, some birdy minions stand around us, pointing at our chests with spears.

Like that would stop us. Still, Lincoln and I talked about this last night. We want to protect Hector. If that means playing along a little, so be it.

"Good morning, King Zoar," says Lincoln smoothly. I'm really glad he's doing the talking. A hangry Myla is a dangerous Myla.

Zoar sniffs. "You're lucky to be breathing. I've made my decision about both of you. But first, we must nest."

Twenty Avian guys sit in a big circle. At the same time, the same number of Avian ladies come out of the forest. While the guys are pretty blah in terms of feathers, the women have long tails and fancy wings covered with extra fluff. My own tail arches over my shoulder to size up the competition.

I pat the arrowhead end. "They've got nothing on you."

Next follows a lot of dancing and singing. It's pretty screechy, but I force on a smile.

Play along, Myla.

At some point, Hector comes out to stand and the sidelines and clap along. This must be what he meant by the Avians having a *good floor show*. Normally, you've gotta hit Vegas to see this kind of thing.

Zoar claps his hands. "Now nest!"

The ladies sit down, one on each lap of an Avian guy.

"You shall be mated to each other for the next month," announces Zoar. "Cheers and good fortune!" There are a lot of smiles and even a few kisses. It's pretty cute, actually.

Zoar turns to focus on me and Lincoln. "We shall move on to our next order of business."

Hector steps forward. "Your Majesty, I know you may be understandably upset with these two. However, I can assure you that what they did is considered a friendly welcome in the afterrealms."

"Do not worry, Hector," states the King. "I have decided that this pair can make recompense."

I raise my hand. "Will that involve breakfast?"

Zoar steps closer. "A boon made for a bounty paid, that's the Law Primeval."

"I heard. So. Breakfast?"

Zoar keeps talking as if I didn't say a thing. "You've a strong life force. If I were a wizard, I could draw it into myself as magic. A special kind of harvest."

"Okay, Eew."

"Sadly there are no more wizards or apprentices remaining. The Contagion saw to that."

I snap my fingers. "Gee, darn, drat. I always wanted to be harvested."

"Sadly, it is not an option," states Zoar. "Therefore, I make a different request. In exchange for the boon of my forgiveness, the bounty to be paid is that this breasty woman shall mate with me for the next year."

I laugh my ass off. Big belly guffaws and everything. "That's a big *no*. And I won't even comment on the breasty thing."

"This is promising," declares Hector. "Laughter means she is most interested in your offer. At least, that's how I recall it."

I shake my head. "Clearly, you've been dead for a while."

Zoar licks his lips. "Is this true?"

Lincoln moves to stand between me and Zoar. Good idea. I'm starting to wonder if blue feathers are edible.

"Myla and I came here for one reason only. The Contagion is on the move. He has consumed the first Marked One. Hector will be his next target. We must come up with a plan to stop the Contagion and protect Hector."

Zoar waves his hand dismissively. "The Contagion has been trapped for centuries. There is nothing to fear."

"That's how things used to be," I offer. "Then the Contagion consumed himself some Simian magic. Now he can gurgle his ass around, easy peasy."

"Enough," snaps Zoar. "Worrying about the Contagion is a waste of time." He rounds on me yet again. "We must discuss how you'll act during our mating year. Laughing is not acceptable. Neither is pushing my hands away. We Avians have our—"

I hold my hand up, palm forward. "Do not say traditions."

"How did you guess? We even have a name for it."

The hand stays up. "No, you don't."

"We call it the Avian Route."

"You've got to be kidding me. First the Rixa Way. Then the Purgatory Path. Now an Avian Route? What is this? *Pick On Myla Month?*" I elbow Lincoln. "Am I right or am I right?"

Lincoln doesn't reply. His gaze is focused on the forest floor. I know my man. This particular look of his means *hunting mode.*

"What's wrong?" I whisper.

That's when I see it. The ground before us churns in a line across the forest floor. Something moves underground, and it's closing in.

All of a sudden, the earth bursts as a cluster of blackened roots push through the ground. The tar-like appendages dig into the earth like so many arms, pulling up the remaining body up from the darkness. And in this case, that body is one very ticked off tree.

The Contagion is here.

Damn.

LINCOLN

I can't believe it. The Contagion just burst up from the ground like oil a gushing from a well. The tar quickly oozed into the shape of the massive tree. Now, a pair of long branches dangle by its side.

Arms.

After consuming Rule, the Contagion now has arms again.

This bodes ill.

Hector extends his wings and takes to the skies. A desire fills my soul. I have angel wings that appear as part of a certain rare ceremony. They are phantoms, nothing else. But what would it be like if my wings could fly like that?

It takes all my concentration, but I force my mind to focus on the fight at hand. In the heat of battle, odd thoughts can pop into your head. Recently, I had to press away the urge to scream a series of extremely creative and obscene insults at a Viperon demon. In that instance, I was only partially successful.

With all my focus, I watch Hector wings to the skies. It's clear Hector was trained as a warrior after he became an angel. His form is perfect as he speeds away.

I exhale.

Hector has escaped.

Only he doesn't.

What happens next takes place within a few heartbeats. Even so, every millisecond drags by as my mind soaks in each detail.

The Contagion's branches shoot out, long and thin as ropes, and wrap around Hector's feet. The angel fights to stay in flight, but it's a losing proposition. The Contagion is simply too strong. In a whirl of movement, Hector is yanked from the skies. As with Rule, the Contagion opens his trunk-body and drags Hector inside. A flash of blue light shines within the Contagion's interior as the incision closes.

It's all over. Hector is gone.

For my part, I race toward the Contagion, ready to tear out Hector with my bare hands if need be. I don't get more than a few steps before the Contagion sinks into the ground.

Zoar rounds on us, his entire body trembling with rage. "You brought this tar monster upon us!"

Myla points to the hole in the earth. It's the only sign the Contagion was here. "That was not a random tar monster."

I move to stand at Myla's side. "As we warned you, the Contagion arrived."

"Go!" cries Zoar. "Leave before I change my mind and kill you both!"

Myla chuckles. "I'd like to see that. What will you do, peck us to death?"

"GO!"

"Sheesh, what a grouch," grumbles Myla. Together, we hustle off to the forest. In cases like these, it doesn't do to either tarry or run like wild. Best to keep a steady pace that says, *come after me and you'll have trouble*. After a half hour's march under the blue trees, Myla and I pause.

"Riddle me this, Master Hunter," says Myla. "Are they following us?"

I kneel down and set my fingertips against the earth. "No, they're back in their village. Honestly, I suspect they're glad to be rid of us."

A figure drops from the trees, landing right before us.

It's Peli.

"Miss me?" he asks.

It's tempting to roll my eyes. Tempting, but not necessary as Myla beats me to it.

Time to chat with Peli.

37

MYLA

A little recap here.

Lincoln and I just hauled our butts out of bird town. Now who should drop out of a freaking tree to say hello?

Peli.

Even worse, his little round face curls into a shit-eating grin.

"You didn't kill the Contagion that time," says Peli, Monkey Master of the Obvious.

I shrug. "He's pretty speedy for a tree."

"The next Marked One is the demon," states Lincoln. "Can you lead us to where he is?"

"The demon lives with the Reptilians. They're rather skittish. I can guide you somewhere for a proper introduction. They won't try to kill you if I set things up correctly."

"No killing with the intro," I deadpan. "Good to know."

Translation: I'm ticked off at you.

Peli lifts his hands. Orange smoke swirls across his palms. When the haze vanishes, he holds not one, not two, but five Demon Bars.

I slap on my best happy face. "Hello, best friend."

Peli drops the delicious treats to the forest floor before taking to the trees. "Ready or not, here I go!" His orange form takes off into the branches.

Meh. I'm not worried about Peli zooming away. Lincoln can track down anything. Plus, I have more important stuff to contemplate right now.

Come to Momma, Demon Bars.

Leaning down, I scoop up my sweet treasures, then turn to Lincoln. "Want one?"

"I'm fine." He pulls some natural funk from a nearby bush. The thing looks pretty picked over.

"Are you sure that's safe?"

"I saw the Avians eating these seeds before."

"Who knew they ate?" Those folks looked skeleton-skinny.

Lincoln gestures to another mini-tree standing nearby. "I also noticed their water source. That fern has cup-like leaves which hold condensation… if you should get thirsty after your sugar high."

"Wow, you were a busy boy last night."

"I didn't sleep well."

For my guy, saying *I didn't sleep well* is a big deal. It's the equivalent of me having a ten minute tirade. I take a break from worshipping my Demon Bars to closely inspect Lincoln's face. He doesn't look particularly tired, but my guy is great at hiding stuff.

"What's wrong?" I ask.

"I've been seeing a version of myself as a Guide in my dreams. I seem to be attempting to provide self-advice about how to destroy the Contagion… as well as possibly avoid another disaster."

"There's another-*nother* disaster coming?"

"Perhaps. Hence the poor sleep."

Stepping up, I set my palm against Lincoln's cheek. He leans into my touch. "Here's what going to happen. We'll chop up this Contagion into little evil—yet useless—matchstick-sized chunks of enchanted tree. Then we'll face the another-*nother* thing."

"Matchstick-sized." The ghost of a smile rounds Lincoln's mouth. "How specific."

"Hey, that's how I roll."

Lincoln sets his own palm against my own. "Thank you, Myla."

"Any time. Pep talks are always free."

Lincoln kisses the center of my palm. "We better catch up to Peli.

So that's precisely what we do.

38

LINCOLN

*W*hat a trail.

Following Peli through the woods proves rather interesting. Sometimes, he leaves a clear line of broken leaves and footprints to follow. In other instances, it takes all my tracking skill to determine his direction.

As in everything, Peli can't help being a trickster.

Which brings me to the present moment. There's no mistaking the chilly edge to the air. Night will fall soon. Myla and I follow Peli's trail across the forest floor. Pale blue trees tower overhead. A few lonely beams of dying sunlight cut through the canopy, casting odd patterns onto the ground.

Then it all ends.

Once again, the landscape changes with the precision of a ruler. The indigo forest cuts off to be replaced by a vast desert of emerald sand. This isn't a wasteland such as the place where we landed. Instead, the rolling dunes are perfectly sculpted into an undulating landscape that appears almost too beautiful to be real. My skins prickles over at the sight.

A familiar string of eee-eee noises sound from the branches above. With a thud, Peli falls leaps from a nearby tree to land beside me and Myla.

Peli stretches his arms wide. "Behold the Reptilian lands."

"Are they expecting us?" I ask.

"Not exactly," says Peli with a grin.

"Which means *no*," counters Myla.

"They'll be here soon in order to hold a little ceremony. Happens every month. I'll introduce you to their king. You'll ask to protect their Marked One. They'll ask for a trade."

I know this routine. "Boon made for a bounty paid."

"Precisely," states Peli.

Myla holds up her finger. "For the record, this trade thing is BS. Lincoln and I are here to protect their buddy the demon. The Reptilians should be paying us, not the other way around."

Peli ticks his finger from side to side. It's a *no, no, no* move if I ever saw one. "The Reptilians are keeping a demon named Spivey among them. He's not one of their own. They don't particularly care if the Contagion consumes Spivey and moves on. They know that the wizard must take in more Marked Ones before becoming a serious threat."

"That's totally short sighted," says Myla.

Peli throws up his hands. "It's the Law Primeval."

"So how do we convince the Reptilians to take us seriously?" Myla asks.

Peli does a back flip followed by more eee-eee noises. "That's your problem."

"Nice, Peli," deadpans Myla.

While they talk, I scan the horizon line. No sign of anyone in any direction. "How long before the Reptilians arrive?"

"Some time in the day or so. You're welcome to make camp on the forest floor." A sneaky gleam shines in Peli's eyes as he says these words.

I've only known Peli for a few days, yet I'm familiar enough with the little monkey to realize one thing.

We should *not* make camp on the ground.

Myla has the same idea. She pats a nearby tree trunk. "I don't see why we should reinvent the wheel here. The Avians live in trees. I've seen zero creatures with nests on the forest floor."

My heart warms with a heady mixture of affection and pride.

Myla has visited few woods in her lifetime, yet that insight was one many senior trackers might have missed.

Leaning back on my heels, I scan the trees above. "The higher branches are stout and relatively flat. That's about as comfortable as trees get. Plus, we'll also have a better view from up there."

Myla nods. "We'll see the Reptilians coming."

"You're no fun!" In a great display, Peli hops around while screeching. He even bites his tail. Myla and I share a dry look. This may take a minute.

At last, Peli stops. "The moon dreamers come out tonight. I was rather looking forward to you meeting them."

"Moon dreamers," I say slowly. "What a sweet name."

"And you know what that means." Myla rolls her eyes. "Only badass predators get cutesy names."

"Spoilsport." Peli lifts up his rounded chin and scales the nearest tree. With an extra chorus of screeching, he takes off into the forest.

"Should we go after him?" asks Myla.

"Not necessary," I reply. "I suspect he needs to cause trouble at regular intervals. If we chase after him, he'll only lead us into some kind of problem." Stepping out from the line of trees, I inspect the sands nearest the forest line. "These were regularly dug up and replaced."

"Really?"

"There's an unnatural line in the dunes."

Squinting, Myla stares at the area I pointed out. After a moment, she shakes her head. "I'll take your word for it. Peli said there was a ritual here. Maybe that's part of it."

Myla and I share a quick glance followed by a small nod. Without further discussion, we scale up the closest tree we can find. In short order, we each find a decent branch and settle in with our backs against the trunk and our legs kicked forward.

Or rather, I settle in.

Myla fidgets on the branch above.

"Once again, I am somewhere that's not designed for butts." She rubs her upper thigh. "I'll have bruises."

"And?" I know my girl. Her rant isn't over.

"I'm hungry again."

"That's the sugar leaving your system. Five Demon Bars in a row is a lot for anyone."

"Oh, I don't know about that." I can't see Myla, but there's no mistaking the sound of a smile in her voice.

And so we settle in for the night.

MYLA

My tail sways below me.
Swish.
Swish.
Swish.

It's like the tick-tock of a clock, marking the passage of empty time. Around me, the forest lies silent. Gentle breezes rustle the nearby leaves. Clouds obscure the moon. It all adds up to one conclusion.

This is one lonely branch.

Using my tail as a kind of anchor, I stick the arrowhead end into the branch beneath my feet. Stepping forward, I swing forward until I stand upside-down and nose-to-nose with Lincoln.

"Hey," I say.

Lincoln grins. "Hey."

"Want company?"

He kisses the tip of my nose. "I'd love it."

I do an awesome somersault flip and land so my back rests against Lincoln's chest once more. This is rapidly becoming a trend.

Lincoln wraps his arms around my waist. Leaning forward, my guy kisses up the column of my neck.

Mmmm. This is getting fun.

Screech!

An unearthly sound echoes through the forest. The sound zooms right down my spine, setting off alarm bells throughout my nervous system. I shiver in surprise.

"What was THAT?" I ask.

"It appears the moon dreamers have arrived," announces Lincoln.

Glancing down, I see the ground shift. The sight reminds me of a slow-moving river. The clouds roll past the moon, allowing beams to shine upon the forest floor.

What I see is nasty.

The ground is covered in bugs. And not just regular bugs, mind you. These are some kind of hybrid with an ant's body and spider legs. Each one is large as a baseball.

A foul taste creeps into my mouth. "Freaking Peli," I state. "If we'd slept on the ground, those would have crawled all over us. That thing —" I point to a particularly big bug "—could have skittered across my mouth."

"The moon dreamers probably would have stripped us down as well. They're leaving a swath of cleared forest behind them."

"Classic Peli. Nothing painful, unless you count standing naked in a strange forest as pain."

Down on the forest floor, a glimmer of color catches my eye. On their backs, the insects carry bits of leaves and other tiny junk. Yet what stood out to me so clearly? One bug carries a small scrap of yellow fabric. Being that everything here is blue, that color shines out like a spotlight. Even more surprising, the shade of yellow is particular to Antrum.

The yellow of Acca.

But how would a bug from the Primeval get a scrap of Acca fabric?

A small voice in the back of my head says that Aldred did indeed follow us into the Primeval. That's when the flash of yellow disappears. Maybe I imagined it. For a while, it's all I can do to stare at the moon dreamers. I never see the flash of yellow again. Searching becomes a bore.

Eventually, I do settle against Lincoln's back. My guy's regular breathing tells me he's fallen asleep. It takes some time, but I finally catch some rest as well.

40

LINCOLN

Once more, I dream of angelfire.

I'm surrounded by an inferno of white flame. When the blaze dies down, I find that I now stand in the clearing of that unusual forest once more. The Guide awaits me. Again, he appears as my perfect doppelganger, save for the fiery wings on his back.

"You have wings as well," he states.

It's an odd way to start a conversation. "They show my inner nature. It's for show only." It's also part of a very private ceremony, but that's nothing I wish to discuss right now.

While wing facts are fascinating, they aren't what's truly crucial right now. Ever since my last dream, I've been thinking about the Guide. Indeed, there is one key question I wish to ask.

"You're part of my soul, aren't you?" I ask.

The Guide nods. "I am to lead you to battle the larger danger."

Perhaps I've been spending too much time with my fiancée, but I simply must ask the question. "Why not simply tell me what the risk is?"

"If I did that, the words wouldn't have meaning." He takes a pointed step backward. "Until we meet again."

The dream ends.

My questions remain.

What's this great hidden threat behind it all? And why can't I see it directly? I know the magic of the Primeval is affecting things in odd ways, but I've no idea how. That said, I do know one thing.

The answers simply must appear before it's too late.

LINCOLN

I awaken to the gentlest tremble on the tree branch beneath me. Early sunlight brightens the forest as I scan all around. Nothing seems amiss.

Interesting.

Whatever causes the movement, it isn't coming from nearby. Setting my palms against the branch, I soak in the staccato rhythm. It takes me a moment, but I place the tremor.

Footsteps.

Someone's marching this way.

Based on the depth of the reverberation, this is quite a large group. I scan the horizon.

No sign of anyone approaching. *Yet.*

Minutes pass. The shaking grows more violent.

Myla wakes up. "What? Hey? Who?"

I kiss her cheek. "Good morning."

She slaps her palms against the branch. "What's up with the tree?"

"The problem comes from the ground. We'll have company soon."

A greenish line finally appears on the horizon. Soon the group comes close enough to determine who approaches: a great crowd of humanoid reptiles. Just as I saw in my visions with Peli, they have green textured skin and dress in elaborate clothes. Their outfits seem more appropriate for Marie Antoinette and Versailles than a desert.

The men wear long coats with short pants and heeled boots. The ladies sport foot-high wigs and dresses that jut out three feet on either side.

And I thought being stuck in the middle ages was bad.

The only Reptilians not dressed up are the great beasts which lumber along the front line of the group. They are truly large with streamlined bodies and bat-style wings. Myla gestures toward them.

"Those look like..." Myla snaps her fingers. "What are those flying dinosaurs called again?"

"Pterodactyls," I state.

"That's it."

"Actually, they're not dinosaurs. They're archosaurs."

Myla shoots me the side eye. "Sometimes, I just want to punch you in the junk."

"But then you'd have no BAEJS."

Myla groans. "I am never living that down, am I?"

"Nope."

The group pauses a short distance from the forest's edge. The Pterodactyls lurch forward. Using their massive taloned feet, they scoop up the emerald sands, depositing their quarry in great piles to the side.

"You called it," says Myla. "They're digging up the very spot you pointed out before."

I frown. "But for what?"

After digging out a shallow pit, the Pterodactyls flap their mighty wings, blowing away a final layer of sand. What they reveal is a surprise.

It's a collection of statues.

A jolt of realization moves through me. These aren't just any statues. These are the Reptilian apprentices who were frozen by the Contagion. Earthly reptiles bury their eggs to keep them warm and safe. The Reptilians in the Primeval are doing the same with their frozen loved ones.

One by one, Reptilians step into the pit, find a loved one, and brush their fingers down the statue's frozen face. The world seems to pause as the ritual continues. Myla and I have focused on finding the

Contagion. Meanwhile, these poor souls have lived with the loss and pain brought on by that awful wizard.

Even so, these Reptilians can't hang out forever. We must make contact before they go. According to Peli, we'll need an introduction first. I look around again. This is the place where our small monkey friend could help.

Peli is still gone.

Can't say I'm surprised.

MYLA

That Reptilians are here and Peli has ghosted us.
Classic.
And I wouldn't eat any of the funk Lincoln scrounged up, so I am craving another Demon Bar like it's my job.

One figure steps up to the edge of the pit and bows his head. Unlike everyone else, this guy has red skin, tiny horns, and a long and pointy tail.

"That would be our demon," I whisper. "Peli said he was named Spivey."

"Genus?"

"Standard Red. Can't tell the subtype, though. Stealth, maybe?"

"It's unclear. Whatever he is, it's a fairly calm genus. They don't attack unless desperate. Perhaps we can reason with him."

Spivey lifts his head before stepping back to the fringes of the crowd. In fact, Spivey hangs out rather close to the forest line.

Could be useful.

"So." I tap my chin. "How do we contact the Reptilians without a formal introduction? Peli said we needed one."

"Hold on a moment."

Lincoln does that thing where he kneels and touches the ground—or in this case, the branch—and concentrates like a mutha. When my guy focuses on me again, he whispers three words.

"Others are coming."

The entire tree rumbles. Someone is definitely heading this way, and it's not the Reptilians. Following Lincoln's line of vision, I detect a yellow blob moving across the dark desert.

The group comes into better focus.

I blink.

Pinch myself.

Blink again.

All thoughts of Demon Bars fade from my consciousness.

Aldred is here.

Lincoln shakes his head. "I thought I detected him when we first crossed over."

"Last night, I thought the moon dreamers carried some Acca stuff. Guess I was right."

Quelle bummer. Trumpets blare from Aldred's group, followed by the plinky-plink of lute players. What, did this guy bring along bulldozers, too? I'm no expert hunter and even I can detect these guys.

"Any ideas?" asks Lincoln. He's a long term planning man. I'm stronger in off-the-cuff situations.

"Let's see." I purse my lips. "Maybe we split up. I go north and chat up the demon. If I work my mojo, perhaps we can get an introduction that way." I squint at Aldred's group. "Team Aldred parked themselves by the woods south of here. Think you can use your super hunter skills? Get some reconnaissance going?"

"Absolutely," replies Lincoln. "The earl wouldn't enter the Primeval without both a plan and Rufus. That old lion and I go way back. I'll gather some intelligence easily."

"Meet back here when we're done?"

"You got it."

My guy and I share a fist-bump before jumping down from our branch. We've both got some serious sneaking to do.

LINCOLN

I slip through the woods. As I speed along, I can't help but notice how all the seed trees stand spindly and bare, their leaves picked over. If I weren't so familiar with the wilds, I wouldn't have found anything to eat.

A memory appears. When Peli took me to the past, all the peoples of the Primeval seemed healthy and well-fed. That isn't the case any more, at least with the Avians. *Something to consider.*

With every step through the woods, the racket of Aldred's camp grows louder. There's the clang of pans, whinny of horses, and even a new lute tune.

I roll my eyes. Minstrels. Only Aldred.

Moving quietly, I pass the main camp. Rufus wouldn't want to be near so many noises and smells. He'll choose the high ground and keep sentry.

Sure enough, I spy the old lion sitting atop a boulder, far away from the main group. He's not wearing his armor, but there's no missing the battle-ready edge to how Rufus scans the desert. Ever since leaving Myla, I've been careful to ensure foliage separates me from the wind. Now I step out to the perfect spot for the breeze to catch my scent.

And I wait.

For his part, Rufus sits Sphynx-like on his rock, paws forward and belly against the stone. With the vista of emerald sand behind him, the lion looks more like a painting than a living creature. That won't last. The very moment my scent reaches him, a shudder rolls down Rufus' spine.

Cupping my hand by my mouth, I let out the classic whistle that signals the start of our matches.

Rufus' gaze locks on my direction. He rises up onto all fours and stretches, before leaping off the rock. If I didn't know the lion, I'd think he was just off for a meaningless walk.

There's no missing the glint in Rufus' eyes, though. Or the way his muscles bunch with every step. My friend is on high alert.

Rufus pads into the forest and heads right to my spot. He eyes me from head to toe.

"You're alive."

"That I am."

"You may scratch my mane, if you wish." For Rufus, this is a the emotional equivalent of jumping up and down while screeching with joy.

"It is my honor." Stepping closer, I rub my fingers just behind Rufus' ears. It's a favorite spot.

"I worried you were dead." Rufus inhales. "I scent Myla on you as well."

"We're both here." I drop my hand. Rufus isn't one to like a lot of touching.

Rufus scans around us. "No one is nearby. We can speak freely."

"When did you cross over to the Primeval?"

"Right after you left," replies Rufus. "We've been marching for days. I've met my people along the way. Unofficially, of course. They slip up to camp at night while everyone else is drinking and singing."

"And were they welcoming?"

"No," says Rufus. "They were starving." He bares his teeth in anger. "It isn't right, Felines without food."

"I saw the same thing with the Avians. I'm sorry, Rufus."

"I stole some meat from Aldred's larder and handed it over. I've never seen such lions. Their rib cages show through their pelts. Patches of fur have fallen off." Rufus' voice lowers to a growl. "And it's all the Contagion's doing. He turned the best of the pack to stone.

There's no leadership. No one to set hunts. And precious little game remains, even if they tried to catch it."

"Myla and I are here to destroy the Contagion. Kill the caster, end the spell. It will release those he froze, both here and in the after-realms."

Rufus scratches at the ground with his claws. "Aldred wants to do the killing. Yet he's no warrior."

"What do you know of the earl's plans?"

"We're to find the thrax Marked One who lives in the Feline lands. Once we have him under our protection, we'll make our way to the Golden Arbor, or what's left of it. Aldred will set up camp there."

I nod slowly, thinking this through. "So Aldred wants to use use the thrax Marked One as bait in order to lure in the Contagion. The Golden Arbor is where Peli cast the spell to crate the Marked Ones in the first place. It makes sense as the best place for Aldred to destroy the Contagion."

"It won't come to that," states Rufus. "You and Myla will end the Contagion long before he reaches the fifth and final Marked One."

"That's the plan."

"Rufus!" Aldred's voice carries on the wind. "RUFUS!"

"You'd better go. We'll meet up soon."

"Be safe," growls Rufus. "Kill quickly." With silent moves, Rufus takes off toward the camp.

As I watch Rufus leave, my thoughts wind back to my childhood. Mother and I used to play a thrax game called Remembrix. You stacked up small slats of wood, and for each tiny plank, there was a fact to recall. The game ended when the stack fell over or one player couldn't recite everything that had been built up so far.

At this moment, it's as if I stand before a Remembrix stack that towers far above my head. There are so many things to keep track of, especially with all these messages from the Guide thrown in as well. Some key fact is bound to be lost.

I only hope that the omission doesn't bring everything crashing down.

MYLA

I'm not a *hide behind the tree* kind of girl.

I'm more of the *kick first and ask questions later* type.

Still, here I am, lurking behind a blue trunk in a random universe, waiting for a chance to catch someone's attention. In this case, the *someone* is a demon named Spivey who could be the definition of what's called the *Standard Red*.

Backwards knees? check.

Cloven feet? Check.

Shaggy body, pointy face, and little horn-buds on his head? Check, check, and check.

This guy even has a long and pointy tail. Totally rat-like without any dragonscales or pointy end, though. Not that I have a better tail or anything.

But yeah, I totally have a better tail.

Turns out, hiding behind a tree trunk gives a girl time to contemplate these things.

All this while, my demon target has been chatting up a small group of Reptilians. Now Spivey steps towards the forest. And based on how he's gripping his groin? Someone needs a potty break.

This will be gross, but I can work with it.

After entering the woods, Spivey relieves himself on a nearby tree. I wait until he's almost ready for the tap when I clear my throat.

Spivey resets himself (thankfully that fur hides a lot) and turns in my direction.

I sashay out from the line of trees. "Hello, fellow demon." To back up the point, I make sure my eyes flare red.

"You... you're from the after-realms."

"Yup. I'm Myla."

"They call me Spivey." He scrapes his hands down his face. "I'm so glad you're here. This place is horrible. Everyone is so mean to me."

Hells Bells. Now I know his sub type. This guy is a Whinus.

Which is a problem. I can handle rage, envy, lust... pretty much all your deadly sins. But whining drives me batty. The less time I spend with Spivey, the better.

"Look, I need an introduction to the Reptilian King. Two introductions, actually. My warrior friend is off on a mission now." I don't mention how Lincoln is a demon hunter because, *duh.*

"You want an introduction to King Salientian? He's meanest to me of all. His Royal Stinginess won't give me extra insects for my collection. How cruel is that? I need entertainment, considering how I'm living with a bunch of reptiles."

There is so much strange in that story, I won't even acknowledge it.

"Great. Cool. Bugs. Now let's just do the introduction thing with the thing." I don't wait for a reply. I grab his wrist (not the one he was just using for potty time) and drag Spivey out of the forest. "Time to meet King Salientian!"

"Now you're being mean, too. Ow, that hurts my wrist!"

No question who the king is, either. He's the reptile guy who's helpfully wearing a big-ass crown. Salientian stands in a small circle with other reptiles in long coats and overly tall heels. I step up with Spivey in tow.

Salientian is on the short side with big bug eyes and a wide frog-style mouth. He stares at my hair.

Hair?

Hair.

Whatever. He's got pingpong balls for eyes. Maybe he's looking across the way at something else. What do I know about Reptilian vision?

"I am Myla, a demon from the after-realms, just like Spivey."

Salientian's long froggy tongue flicks out. "Have you a formal introduction to be here? The consequences for approaching royalty without one is death."

"You know, my friend here was just about to mention that." I stare at Spivey while rolling my hand in circles, encouraging him to start talking.

A long silence follows where Spivey says zero.

"Spivey," I urge. "Help a fellow demon out here." My tail swoops over to prod Spivey's elbow. *Totally appreciate the back-up.*

Spivey groans. "You're putting a lot of pressure on me. This is really hard."

Salientian just keeps staring at my hair, which I suppose is better than making more death threats. Still, we can't just stand around forever.

"How about I sum up? Spivey and I are buddies and he wants to make a formal whatever so we're all good."

Salientian turns to Spivey. "Is this true?"

Spivey lets out a long-suffering sigh. "It is. She's been super draining to deal with, but yes, Myla and her warrior friend have my introduction to join our court for a few weeks."

"Court? Weeks? No." I hold my hands up, palms forward. "Look, this needs to move fast. The Contagion is loose. As in the guy is moving around now. Trouble. His next target is Spivey here. Long story short, my warrior buddy and I want to use your Sir Whines-A-Lot as bait, lure the Contagion out into the open, and then end your little tree wizard problem, once and for all."

"Yet you have no weapons," says the Salientian.

My tail juts forward to point at the Reptilian kings' heart. I pat the arrowhead end. "He didn't know about you, bud." Using my pointer finger, I *boop* my tail's pointy end. That always cheers it up.

With my tail happy, I refocus on Salientian. "To answer your question, some weapons would be great." My tail points right at my nose. It's getting ticked off. "What? Just as a back up. You know you're my first line of defense."

Salientian rocks on his heels. "You wish a rather large boon to be made. What bounty will you pay?"

"Come on. My friend, Lincoln, and I are offering to do you a solid. What's with the sacrifices?"

"Lincoln?" asks Spivey. "Isn't that a traditional thrax name?"

I point in the opposite direction. "Oh my, is that a huge and unusual insect?" Sure enough, Spivey runs off after a non-existent bug. *He he.*

If Salientian noticed the thrax comment, he doesn't respond to it. "I have decided," declares the king. "Myla and Lincoln are approved to enter my court for one week. We shall discuss things in more detail over the next seven days."

"What? No! The Contagion is mobile now. He's slithering underground and grabbing people with his slimy roots and stuff. This isn't a *let's go hang in court for a week and chit chat* sort of situation."

Salientian whistles. Everyone heads back across the desert.

Guess that's a *no*. Effective, too.

One of the big Pterodactyl types lumbers up to me. Raising its front leg, it curls its talon like a swing. I've dealt with enough dragons to know this gesture.

Come aboard.

For the second time, someone's trying to carry me around. At least with this instance, there are no egg-shaped prisons involved.

I shake my head. "Appreciate the offer, but I'm not going anywhere without Lincoln. I can meet you up wherever. Just give me the coordinates."

"Not acceptable." That's a voice behind me. Turning around, I find Salientian.

"You're pretty stealthy. Is that something you train for?"

Not my best conversation opener, but I want to get Salientian talking about something *other* than traveling by Pterodactyl Airlines. I've seen my share of human horror movies. Only a dumbass goes off with the random Reptilian people and leaves her battle partner behind.

"You must depart now," says Salientian. "Or I shall rescind the approved introduction to my court. And you know what that means."

I crook my finger at him. "Bring it on."

45

LINCOLN

After chatting up Rufus, I head back to meet up with Myla. Strolling through the forest gives me a moment to process everything I learned about Aldred's plans.

Then I see Myla, a Pterodactyl, and a Reptilian wearing a crown. That could be the start of a bad joke, but my girl is crooking her finger at the king. I've seen this move before. She's itching for a fight.

I take off at a run.

Once I break through the forest line, I call out to Myla. "Over here!"

She lowers her hand, which is a good sign. I rush to her side.

"You," says the king. "You're Lincoln."

"His name's Salientian," says Myla.

"Prince Lincoln Vidar Osric Aquilus, pleased to meet you." I bow slightly at the waist.

"You smell of lion," says Salientian. This doesn't seem to be winning me any good graces. "My spies have been tracking one of their number. Fat and slow moving. Has lots of after-realmers with him, too."

"They are off to visit the Felines." *Which is true.* I don't add the bit about picking up the thrax Marked One.

"This situation makes you two far more interesting. I should like to discuss the after-realmers." Salientian raises his hand, and there's no missing the long talons of his fingernails. "I officially accept your introduction to court. Again."

I bow again, because it seemed to be a winning move last time. "Thank you."

"It will be an interesting week," adds Salientian.

I look to Myla, my brows raised. "Week?"

"Yup." She pops the last *P* on yup.

Letting out a loud squawk, the Pterodactyl stomps his front claw against the sand. Some of the other Pterodactyls take to the skies. Salientian saunters off be carried away himself.

I offer Myla my hand. "Shall we?"

"Let's."

Reptilian lands, here we come.

46

LINCOLN

Moments later, I balance on the bottom curve of the Pterodactyl's claw as it carries me over undulating sheets of emerald sand. Myla stands beside me. The vague scent of charcoal hangs in the air. Wind roars in my ears. The morning sun sears onto my skin. Below, the desert resembles a green ocean that somehow froze. Curling dunes line up like waves heading toward an unseen shore, yet never moving any closer.

The image arrests me. A frozen sea is similar to me and Myla in this moment. We move toward a goal, yet at the same time, we're stuck with no progress.

I watch the sands speed beneath me and consider our situation. These Reptilians simply must take the threat of the Contagion seriously. There aren't an unlimited number of chances to stop this monster.

The Pterodactyl wings toward a great sinkhole. Having lived my life underground, I've seen my share of such formations. Our Pterodactyl swoops over the great gap in the desert floor. With a giant caw, it sets me and Myla loose.

That's a kick of adrenaline.

Myla and I tumble through the air. Sunlight vanishes as we pass through the great gap in the desert floor. Perfect darkness engulfs us both. The barest glint of a cave floor appears below.

We're nearing the ground.

Twenty yards.

Ten.

Five.

I land in a crouch. Myla is not so fortunate.

"Not a great week for my ass," she quips. Rubbing her backside, she rises.

Myla wouldn't be sassing if she were truly hurt. Still, it's best to make sure. "Everything all right?"

"Peachy." Myla steps around in a slow circle, soaking in our new surroundings.

Again, the advantage of underground living comes into play. "If I had to guess, this is a back entrance to their cave system."

Myla shrugs. "Just looks like a big old cavern to me."

I gesture to the base of the walls. "There are large backpacks lined up here, and they're dusty. Safety ladders wind up the walls to the surface. We do this in Antrum. It's a failsafe in case folks need to evacuate in a hurry."

"Makes sense." Myla turns once more and pauses. "Oh, and here's a dead giveaway." She gestures to the far wall. "Behold, the big-ass wooden thing."

Sure enough, a massive arch has been set into the wall. A huge slab of wood blocks up the space beneath. And in that plank sits a small rectangular door.

It swings open.

Salientian steps through, along with a small group of courtiers. It's odd that he doesn't have any ladies in his immediate clique. I'm used to Octavia being ever-present.

"Welcome to the new Reptilian homeland," states Salientian.

"New?" asks Myla. "What happened to your old one?"

"Nothing happened," answers Salientian quickly. "The desert palace still exists. It simply became boring after the Contagion lured the apprentices out."

"Oooh." Myla's eyes widen with sympathy. "The desert palace was for the wizards."

"No, the underground palace is simply better." Salientian beams. "We live a rather unusual lifestyle. I hope it won't shock."

"Can't wait to see it," I state. *Which is true.* I'm unaware of any other peoples who live underground. This will be an education.

We follow Salientian through the small door. An elaborate palace greets us on the other side. There are checkerboard floors, glittering chandeliers, and large paintings in elaborate frames. All of them are colored in different shades of green.

"It's all right to be stunned," says Salientian. "No one else in the Primeval lives such a civilized existence."

Just as outside, everyone here is dressed to drink champagne with Marie Antoinette. The ladies sport huge dresses and massive wigs. The men have long velvet coats with frilly shirts underneath.

"You've both been rather quiet," says Salientian. "What do you think?"

Myla steps around in a low circle. "There may be something about living underground and the need to overdress."

I nod. "Good point."

"Be that as it may," says Salientian. "You may now change and rest. Soon we shall feast and discuss things in more detail."

"Anything more specific for us on that?" asks Myla. "*Soon* is a little vague."

I step to Myla's side. *All the better to show our united front on this topic.* "Agreed. We must go after Contagion now."

Salientian chuckles. "Please. The Contagion can't touch us here. Why do you think we live below ground?"

I think back to the sink hole. "This settlement isn't that deep below the surface. You need to be miles below for enemies to stay out."

Salientian hisses. "We are the most secure land in the Primeval."

"No," I counter. "This place is a death trap." Salientian bares his pointed teeth.

Myla moves to stand between me and the king. "Usually, it's my job to piss people off. My guy here is a newbie."

"What did you say?" asks Salientian. "Speak plainly."

"We'll just do whatever you want right now." She accents that point by twiddling her hair. It's a classic move from her *I'm so innocent routine* during fights in Purgatory's Arena. Makes opponents drop their guard.

Sure enough, the move works on Salientian, although it's in a slightly different way than in the Arena. He stares in rapture at Myla's wavy locks. "Your hair is crimson. Everything here is green." He shakes his head, as if snapping himself out of a dream. "Go to your rooms and await orders."

A servant with a massive green wig steps up. "This way," she announces.

"We'll follow," I state.

And I mean it. *For now.*

MYLA

The green reptile chick with the puffy wig leads us to our chambers. The moment the door swings open, I make my proclamation.

"This is some over-the-top stuff."

After closing the door, my guy gives the room a once-over as well. "I've never seen anything to match this, and I visit many places on demon patrol."

I decide to transform myself into *chamber tour hostess* for the occasion. I swing my arms wide, gesturing across the space. "First of all, we have the green-ness. I'm no expert on colors, but there's your emerald color, moss shade, the particular light green of that sauce that goes on rolly tacos at restaurants…"

"Mole verde," says Lincoln, because that's my guy. "Anything else?"

"I'm out of green things. If Cissy were here, she'd list for an hour. Moving on." I step over to the wall. "Now these curtains are interesting." I pull the fabric back. "But there's nothing behind them but glass with a nice view of dirt because we're underground."

"Not deep enough underground," quips Lincoln.

"True." I shake out the curtains in question. "And look how long these go. What is that, two, three feet over the floor?"

"Thirty-eight inches," says Lincoln. I could ask how my guy

knows that, but it probably involves math and/or science. More fun to keep complaining about the curtains.

"What happens when you vacuum and suck up part of the curtain? This is totally useless." I tap my chin. "Not that they have vacuums here, but you get the idea."

Lincoln grins. He loves it when I go off on random junk. "Testify."

I set my fists on my hips and continue my survey. "The carved wooden furniture could be cool, but it's all painted green and decorated with frogs and whatnot." I spy a dining room table area. "Hold on! Food!"

Like a tornado to a trailer park, I rush over to the very large ceramic bowl on the table. A matching cover sits atop the dish. Looping my fingers around on the top handle, I close my eyes, and take in a long breath.

"Now we conclude our episode of Myla Bitches About Random Stuff with some questions. What could be inside this thing? Brownies, cookies, or brownie cookie lava cake?"

"You might be setting your hopes up a little high," deadpans Lincoln.

"Shhh. I'm having my time for me."

I lift the cover from the bowl. Inside, there's a surprise.

Bugs.

Dead.

And a lot of them.

I slap the cover back on and take a big step backward. "There are moon dreamers in there. Like big nasty ones." The horror sinks in. "They breaded and deep fried them *with their shells on*. What kind of monsters are these Reptilians?"

Lincoln cracks a smile. "I'd guess moon dreamers are a good source of protein."

"Sure. Take their side." I stare at the covered bowl and sigh. Brownies weren't a requirement. A donut could have worked. "That is a big bummer."

Lincoln steps up and cups my face in his hands. "When was the last time you really slept?"

At the mention of the word *slept*, I yawn my face off. "A while ago? Not that you aren't snuggly, but I don't think I've been snoozing as much as I think I have. Definitely less than *I* think that *you* think that *I* think I have." I crumple up my face, wondering if that made sense. Probably not.

"How about we both get some shut-eye? The bed here looks rather comfortable. I don't think you're hungry so much as tired."

"What makes you say that?"

"Your disappointment factor. All-out rage is your true mental state when in need of sustenance."

"Good point."

We strip off our clothes and slip into bed. Once we're snuggled under the sheets, Lincoln updates me on his chat with Rufus, but I don't catch all the details. Mostly because he falls asleep half way through.

Seconds later, I'm zonked out right beside him. Although I do still drape myself over his side. My guy is really cuddly.

LINCOLN

For once, I don't dream of the Guide.

Instead my night visions have me wandering about the Reptilian palace, searching for Myla. At times, I hear her voice or catch the swish of her tail around a corner. In classic dream-like fashion, I can never quite catch up to her.

Hours stream by.

The search continues.

Monotonous.

Unending.

There are no visions of my past.

No cryptic messages about the future.

Although I'm asleep, some part of my consciousness analyzes this night vision. As my dream-self seeks out Myla, that other part realizes one fact.

There's still more at risk here than I realize.

I must see the Guide again.

MYLA

*D*amn, but I have some funky-ass dreams.

In my night visions, I'm twelve again and getting ready for another day at Purgatory Middle School HJ-261. Mom takes a brush to my hair, pulling and tugging, all in a vain attempt to get the tangles out. Since it's a dream, this goes on for way longer than it needs to.

I give Mom's hand a gentle tap.

Fine, I smack it hard because this is Dream Mom and she's really yanking hard. My scalp feels like its on fire.

One smack hits air. The second connects with scaly skin. A high-pitched yelp sounds.

That can't be right.

My brain is still drowsy with sleep, though, so who knows? I might be hearing things. Opening my eyes, I find that my side of the bed is surrounded by six Reptilian ladies in enormous gowns. The closest one has her webbed fingers around a lock of my hair.

Lincoln sits upright beside me, a look of pure malice shining in his mismatched eyes. He speaks the next two words slowly. "Back off."

In my opinion, these Reptilians only pretend not to understand slang when it's useful for them. Because Lady Grabs-A-Lot understands exactly what Lincoln means. Releasing my hair, she steps away.

"What are you doing here?" asks Lincoln.

"The feast begins soon," replies Grabs-A-Lot. "We wondered if Miss Myla needed any help with her hair."

"My hair," I repeat.

"Of course," says Grabs-A-Lot. "You've such pretty red hair. And everything here is green."

"No," declares Lincoln. And there's a whole lot of malice crammed in that word.

"But—"

Lincoln gets up, totally naked, to cross the room and open the main door. "Out."

I can't tell if the ladies are blushing, what with their scaly green faces and all. But I'm pretty sure they are.

And I get it. There's a reason BAEJS is a thing.

Grabs-A-Lot is last through the door. "The feast starts any minute, simply open the door and someone will take you to the—"

SLAM.

Lincoln kicked the door shut before Grabs-A-Lot could finish.

"They have no right coming in here without announcing themselves." Lincoln's hands ball into fists. "And I was so dead asleep, I didn't even hear them. That's not like me."

I slide out of bed and grab my dragonscale fighting suit. The thing is getting a little rank, but it's not like I have a lot of choices right now.

"Eyes on the prize," I state. "We need to get our game faces on. Salientian must realize the threat from the Contagion."

"You're right. Game faces." Lincoln cracks his neck. "The process probably begins by getting clothed."

My stomach rumbles. Now that I'm rested, my hunger is coming back with a vengeance.

Salientian better be reasonable or I won't be responsible for what happens next.

A hangry Myla is a dangerous Myla.

50

LINCOLN

Myla and I enter the feasting hall. It's another space very much like our chambers, only far larger. Once again, there's a lot of green everything as well as questionable use of window treatments. Sadly, the meal consists of more deep fried moon dreamers.

Myla sets her napkin over her bug bowl. I don't blame her.

"I'll just sit here," says Myla. "That way, I can work hard on not killing anyone."

"Excellent plan," I state. "I'll speak with Spivey." I nod toward a far corner of the feasting hall where the demon in question paws at the wallpaper.

"Good luck."

When it comes to Whinus demons, your best bet is to be direct and quick. That's why I make a beeline for Spivey's spot.

"Greetings, Spivey."

"Ugh." Spivey drops his hands from the wallpaper. "I almost caught a spider. You frightened it away."

"I'm here to discuss your safety. Myla told you the Contagion is free and consuming those who store his power. As a Marked One, you're the next target."

"That mark so ugly, too." Spivey lifts up a flap of fur, showing off the image of a demon's face just below his shoulder. "Every morning, I must brush everything *just so* to cover it up."

"There are greater things at work here. The Contagion is on his way. You need protection. Even if you aren't worried, perhaps you don't mind Myla and I protecting you?"

"I need all the help I can get. No one talks to me. People avoid me. If you're my personal guard, will you help me find more insects?"

"Focus, Spivey. Myla and I want to guard you. Where can we obtain some weapons?"

"Didn't you see them in the cavern where you ent—" Spivey clears his throat. "How would I know anything about weapons? They don't tell me anything. I'm so lonely except for my bug collection. It's hard to get good insects, too. The Reptilians eat them all. You don't have any pins with you, do you?"

That was a lot of Spivey speaking without breathing. "Pins?"

"For sticking the bugs to my wall. It's very had to get after-realm style pins around here."

"No, I'm fresh out."

"What a shame. Nothing ever goes right for me."

My thoughts tick through Spivey's revelation about weapons and that cavern. Where could those weapons be? That's when I realize the truth.

The backpacks.

I saw rows of them along the cavern floor. Those packs must carry small weapons. Perhaps Myla and I can revisit that spot after the feast and load up. It's a good first step.

"Don't bother me anymore," says Spivey. "I'm fine here with the Reptilians. Why do you keep acting like there's some kind of problem? It's very upsetting." He sets his hands on his belly. "My bowels are churning."

I indulge in a little fantasy of punching Spivey in the throat. *Satisfying.*

"Salientian should care," I begin. "Other realms are short on food. Doesn't that concern you here? If the Reptilians could regain your magic users, perhaps that would be helpful."

"Bah, we've enough underground stores to last for years. Dried toads, pickled cactus, vats of fresh water… we're all set. Let the other lands fend for themselves."

"Eventually, those stores will run out. You know that, right?"

"Why do you keep pestering me with questions? It's giving me a migraine." Spivey points back to the feasting table. "Ah, the king has risen from his seat. Now you'll find out what he really wants."

Spivey brushes his palms, setting his curved talons clacking against each other. He rushes back to the main feasting table.

What an annoying creature.

After indulging in one more punching fantasy starring Spivey, I march back to my own seat at the feast. With every step closer, my warrior sense goes on a higher level of alert.

Something's about to happen, and it won't be good.

MYLA

*E*veryone ignores me, which is good. Then lady Grabs-A-Lot stops by.

"You're not eating your meal," she says.

My eyes blaze demon red. "No."

When Grabs-A-Lot next speaks, there's a quiver to her voice. "I'll just leave you alone now."

"That would be safest."

Not sure how long I sit there and try not to hurt anyone, but at some point, Lincoln returns.

"Salientian is about to speak," my guy says gently.

The feasting hall is silent. Everyone seems to be staring at me. "What?" I snap.

Salientian stands at the head of the table. Maybe he's been there for a while. Hard to say. My focus is a little all over the place right now.

The king gestures in my direction. "I'll say it again. You may fight the Contagion, but I wish something in return from the girl."

Lincoln takes my hand. "Try not to kill anyone."

My stomach rumbles. "No guarantees."

Salientian gestures toward me. "Are you willing to follow the Law Primeval? A boon made for a bounty paid?"

I point to my face. "Not mating anyone."

"What?" Salientian chuckles. Since he's Reptilian, it comes out as more of an ack-ack-ack noise. "No, that's ridiculous."

I shoot him a thumbs-up. "Good call."

"I was more focused more on your hair."

On reflex, I pat my head. "My hair?"

"We've never seen that shade before. Everything here is green. I should like to make a wig from it."

I speak to Lincoln from the side of my mouth. "Did he just say wig?"

"He did," confirms my guy.

"You do not seem pleased," states Salientian. "Are you soul bound to another? If so, we'll need to summon them forth at the same time in order to cut their hair. It's a simple process, really"

I look to Lincoln. "What is he talking about?"

"I saw this with Peli. It's where you get linked to another person with Primeval magic."

"Well?" asks Salientian.

"There are no Primeval spells on me. Honestly, I'm still stuck on your original ask here. Did you say hair?"

"If you wish our help, that will be the price." Salientian snaps his fingers. "Servants! Now!"

Reptilians step toward me, all of them holding their Sweeney Todd style razor blades high. Lady Grabs-A-Lot leads the group.

Ugh. That's what they were doing in our bedroom—sizing up my hair for a wig.

Rising, I point right at Grabs-A-Lot. "Ho, there!"

In a bad move for her own safety, Grabs-A-Lot slows down, but doesn't actually stop.

"Here's the deal," I continue. "I haven't eaten in a while. Do you know what that does to someone like me? Not good stuff. So back off with the razors and answer a simple question first. *What do you eat around here that's not bugs?* I need a decent snack and some time to think. After that, we can not-cut my hair and figure out how to kill the Contagion. In that order."

Nice work, me. That was a very mature and clear set of statements. Everyone remains vertical. No one's bleeding.

Salientian lets out a long hiss. "This is taking too long." He points at me. "I offer you a boon made for a bounty paid. You must accept it without question."

"Oh, I'm questioning!" I cry. "Why do you need *anything* when we —" I gesture between me and Lincoln, just to make things clear "— are doing *you* a favor?"

"I said, no questions." Salientian raises his chin. "Certain actions are unacceptable in the presence of royalty. That's the cradle of our lifestyle. It's what we call the Reptile's Nest. You're disturbing that."

Frustration and hunger boil inside me. This isn't going well. "You mean capital R-reptile, capital N-nest, I'm guessing?"

"Yes," answers Salientian. "The Reptile's Nest is an ancient code of conduct and and you're tearing it apart with your unreasonable attitude. Not that I'm surprised. The Avians said you brought in a tar monster to destroy their village."

"That was the Contagion!" I yell.

"No," snaps Salientian. "It was a creature made of moving black oil."

"That *is* the Contagion," states Lincoln. "The old wizard is changing as he consumes new Marked Ones."

Do I love how my guy has my back? You bet, I do.

CRACK!

Long breaks form along the ceiling. Black goop oozes through the jagged fissures. The scent of death and rot fills the air.

All the Reptilians freeze. Not me.

"Is that what I think it is?" I ask Lincoln.

"Yes."

"Thank fuck." My tail arcs over my shoulder. Battle stance. "If I can't eat, at least I can kill something."

With one great leap, I land atop the dinner table. Dishes clatter and Reptilians stay frozen in fear. Battle excitement thrums through me.

The Contagion is on his way? *Yes.*

52

LINCOLN

*T*ar-covered branches tear through the roof of the feasting hall. Chunks of stone break loose and tumble down, smashing up plates and snapping apart tables.

"What kind of monster is this?" cries Salientian.

A newly formed hole yawns in the rock ceiling. More branches curl out from the opening, spreading out across the rock like so many arms. A voice echoes out of the darkness.

"I am the wizard Contagion!"

Salientian rounds on me and Myla. "A tar monster is invading. You've brought this creature upon us."

Myla points to the ceiling. "Hey, the thing already said it's name. The Contagion. Con. Tag. Ion."

Salientian slaps his webbed hands atop his skull. "We have been betrayed!"

Fresh chunks of stone drop to the floor. The tar-covered branches reach out farther.

"Everyone," cries Salientian. "Make for the escape tunnels!"

Moving in unison, the slimy branches swoop down. The many appendages have one goal.

Spivey.

Fast as a whip, the hefty cords wrap up Spivey from head to toe, then drag him into the freshly-made hole in the stone ceiling. No question about it. The Contagion is growing faster and more powerful.

It all happens so quickly, Spivey doesn't even have a chance to cry out.

53

MYLA

*B*oom!
    Boom!
Boom!

Great chunks of rock tumble from the ceiling, shattering the fancy wooden floor into kindling. Reptilians screech and run in all directions.

I have to hand it to Salientian. Dude is calm in a crisis.

"Remember the evacuation protocol!" calls Salientian. "Find your nest mates. Make for the main escape tunnel. It's the most fortified."

The Reptilians instantly calm. Boulders still crash around them, but they organize into groups and speed off in a single direction.

Salientian points to me and Lincoln. "Follow us."

Lincoln nods. "We'll be with you."

I know how my guy thinks. He'll want to help people escape and round up any stragglers.

Salientian grins, and the move shows off his pointy teeth. "Once we're above ground, I'll personally flay the skin from both of you. That's the bounty paid for bringing this destruction upon my people."

"Flaying. Got it." I look to Lincoln. "Know how to escape the way we came in?"

"Absolutely."

Turning, Lincoln and I run in the opposite direction from the rest of the Reptilians. In my peripheral vision, I catch Salientian watching us go, his head shaking slowly. The king so thinks we're about to die.

He might not be wrong.

More chunks of stone break free from the ceiling. The air fills with a heavy mixture of grit and dust. My pulse speeds. All my focus narrows to the path ahead.

At last, I spy the archway where we originally entered.

Snap!

The wall above the arch splits in a dozen places at once, tearing the fancy wallpaper into lumps. Beneath the arch, the wooden panel buckles and splinters. Sweat beads along my spine as Lincoln and I reach the door.

Locked.

Not an issue. Lincoln and I have been in similar situations before. Both of us set our weight onto our left legs while kicking forward with our right. The door bursts open.

Low rumbles sound as the rock wall finally collapses, the deep notes accented with the staccato crackle of the wood breaking apart.

We race forward.

The moment Lincoln and I pass through the doorway, the entire wall behind us implodes with the loudest boom yet. My ears ring with the impact.

We race into the cavern. This one is a little more stable considering how there's no ceiling above us. That's one bonus of being a massive sinkhole, I guess. Even so, that will only buys us a few minutes.

High pitched pings sound as one by one, the ladders snap from the wall. Lengths of metal slam onto the nearby ground. Out of six ladder paths to the surface, only one remains standing.

This is getting dicey.

Lincoln and I race toward the final ladder. Along the way, we grab a pair of dusty backpacks from the floor.

Then we climb upward.

All around us, the walls are an odd thatch of broken ladder segments. The rock around us shifts, sending fresh bands of metal breaking loose. Bolts zing free with all the power of a bullet from a gun before slamming into the walls nearby. One scrapes my shoulder.

My dragonscale suit holds, but for how long?

The world collapses into the simple actions of climbing as fast as possible. Lincoln reaches the top first. Turning about, he offers me his hand.

All Hell breaks loose.

Or more accurately, the ladder.

One moment, I stand on a metal slat. The next, there's nothing but air beneath me. Reaching forward, I hook my fingertips with Lincoln's. The ladder tumbles free below me. My hold with Lincoln slips.

No, no, no.

Lincoln reaches his free hand forward. My tail arches up, the arrowhead end slapping firmly against Lincoln's palm. With this new double grip, Lincoln hauls me onto the desert floor. Sunlight floods my vision, making it hard to focus.

I flip onto my back and catch my breath.

"Let's—" *pant, pant* "—never do that again."

All Hell breaks loose, part two.

The desert floor slides toward the sinkhole. For a moment, my mind blanks wth shock. Then it hits me. The caverns underneath us are collapsing. If the Reptilians lived miles below the surface, then it might not be a big deal.

But they don't.

And it is.

All around us, the ground careens toward the sinkhole, reminding me of sand in an hourglass. I try to stand and get my footing. No dice. I keep sliding toward the sinkhole once again.

Fuck fuck fuckity FUCK fuck.

54

LINCOLN

The desert pulls me and Myla inexorably downward. This must be what a beam of light would experience when ensnared by a black hole.

My pulse thuds against my rib cage. Gripping Myla's hand, I race away from the tumbling sands.

It isn't easy.

My legs burn with the effort. Sweat streams into my eyes. I focus on two things—moving forward and keeping my hand firmly with Myla's.

It seems to take forever, but eventually Myla and I move past the impact area of the cave in. We collapse onto the sands, gasping for breath. Nearby, more of the desert slides away with an ominous hiss.

Heat makes me lightheaded. My pale skin burns under the unforgiving sun. I want to lay here and sleep.

That's not an option.

We must get moving.

Sitting up, I swing off my backpack and dig inside. Say what you want about the Reptilians, they know how to pack for emergencies.

Myla stays sprawled on the sands, reminding me of a starfish that washed ashore. "What have we won?"

I put on my best game show host voice. "Inside bag number one, we have a dagger and holster."

"Sweet."

I dig deeper. "Also, a map."

"Even better."

I pull out a jar. Myla turns to me, her right brow quirked. "Is that food, by chance?"

After twisting off the lid, I examine the contents. "Pickled cactus." I pull out a chunk and pop it in my mouth. "Tastes like chicken."

"Really?"

"No, but it wasn't a bug in a former life." I pull out another jar and jiggle it a motion that says, *want one?*

Myla raises her hand. "I'm game."

I toss Myla the container, she opens and eats. "How is it?" I ask.

"Like old cardboard that got soaked in embalming fluid." Myla fishes her canteen from her own pack. While pinching her nose, Myla chews with her mouth open. Once she gets a bite down, she guzzles the water. The process continues.

Chew, swallow, water, repeat.

My girl hasn't eaten anything vaguely nutritious in a while. Even though Myla's a demon, she can't consume the equivalent of chemically treated air and not have it back up eventually. Once I'm certain she's taken enough of a meal, I spread out the map and get a closer look. Takes me a bit to get my bearings.

Myla moves to sit beside me. "The next Marked One is a human who lives with the Icythians. Any ideas?"

"The Icythians only have one major city. If they're like the other lands, then they'll keep their Marked One there." I tap a spot on the map. "This is it. Finn Quay."

Myla lets out a low whistle. "They live on a beach. Much better than underground. No offense."

"None taken." I scan the area we've crossed so far and make some quick calculations. "Finn Quay is about a day's march from here. If we head out now, we should be there by tomorrow morning."

Myla points to another section of map. "There's a bunch of pink on the map between us and the quay."

"That's arctic tundra."

"Fun." Myla hoists herself up to stand. Gripping the straps of her backpack, she stares out toward the route we must take.

My heart swells with awe. We've both been through a lot but Myla's gotten an extra dose of unwanted attention, what with being asked to sacrifice her hair and mate with a random bird man. Even so, she's up and ready to go.

My woman.

Something itches at the back of my mind. For a moment, I see a flash of the lush green woods where the Guide awaits me. The thought strikes me.

Another threat remains, and you're missing it.

Still, we take off across the desert. With every step, I sense soundless voices screaming in my direction, warning me of impending doom. For now, there's nothing to be done.

All I can do is to move forward.

LINCOLN

We soon reach the edge of Icythian territory. Before us stretches a chilly tundra, all of it formed in various shades of pink. Like before, a blade-like line separates this new slice of the Primeval from the last.

And what a territory it is.

Pale pink pine trees stand covered in picture-perfect swirls of coral-shaded snow. Small fuchsia birds hop along the branches. A fox-like creature, pink and with four tails, scampers across the ground.

It's stunning.

And yet, I can't wait to get home.

My thoughts return to Antrum. Baptiste and Nat are still frozen. No way can we return without having ended the Contagion and set everyone free.

Anything else is simply unacceptable.

I choose a safe spot in a small clearing, pull off my pack, and begin to sort through supplies for setting up camp. Once more, the Reptilians have stocked things well. I find metal bowls and utensils, as well as thin blankets that stretch into tents or can be used a sleeping bags.

I don't find matches though. "Myla, can you please summon a few igni?"

Myla frowns. "Why would you…" She spies the pile of untouched wood and nods. "Sure thing."

My girl closes her eyes. A second later, a dozen tiny flames appear near her hands. The igni have arrived. Again, they appear as fire in the Primeval.

"Go get him," orders Myla.

The tiny flames whip across the clearing to land on my fingertips. I hold up my hand, marveling at the sight. "Care to help me make camp?" I ask the igni.

The little flames flare more brightly, which I take to mean *yes*. I rest my fingertips atop the wood pile. Instantly, the camp fire bursts to life.

I hold up my hands once more. "Thank you." The igni flames shimmy as if caught in a breeze. After that, they vanish. I look to Myla. "As igni interactions go, that was relatively simple."

"I know, right? If only they were so easy to control in the afterrealms."

With the fire blazing away, I focus on setting up our tent. Meanwhile Myla heads off to fill the canteens in a fresh water pool we spied along our journey. Turns out, the tents are a little odd, but eventually I figure them out. Once that's done, it's easy to follow Myla's path through the snow. The trail heads directly for a small pool of fresh blue water.

There I see Myla.

Naked.

Washing her hair.

The sight immediately heats my blood. My breath catches. She's a vision.

Myla glances at me over her shoulder. "I found these pink berry things that act like soap. I already cleaned out my fighting suit."

Words escape me. It's all I can do to strip my body armor and enter the water.

"You want to get clean, too?" asks Myla.

Not for the first time, it strikes me how Myla has no idea how gorgeous she is. Men, women, demons, angels… everyone is thunderstruck by her. It's more than being lovely, although Myla is certainly that. Energy pulses through her.

"Let me help you," says Myla. She dips underwater to rinse off her own hair. When Myla surfaces again, it's one of the most erotic things I've ever seen.

Every cell in my body wants to take her, right here. But my first time having sex with Myla won't be in a random jungle on a strange world. That said, there's no reason we both can't enjoy ourselves.

Thin branches hang over the pool. Myla pulls fresh berries from them before wading over in my direction. My body tenses with desire. I've half a mind to grab her and plunder her mouth, but that's too fast.

Anticipation. It makes everything more intense.

Myla slowly rubs the berries across my chest, arms, and back. She's thorough everywhere, touching and teasing. I return the favor. Just at our most intense moment, I kiss her deeply. Our bare bodies press. The play of our tongues turns rough.

That's when a whirl of orange smoke hovers in the air nearby. One second, Myla and I are enjoying a intimate moment. The next? Peli appears in the air, his body curled up cannon-ball style.

Splash!

Peli careens into the water, sending spray everywhere. His head surfaces a moment later.

"Hello, you two," he says with that half-crazed grin. "How I love a nice swim."

Myla ducks down until she's neck deep in the water. "You have a gift for bad timing."

"But I conjured Demon Bars. They're back at the camp."

Myla narrows her eyes. "Now I love you *and* hate you."

Peli flips onto his back and paddles around the pool. The little monkey has a talent for splashing.

Beneath the water, I set my hand on the base of Myla's spine, guiding her back to the water's edge.

"We'll see you back at camp," I tell Peli.

"I'm making dinner," he calls.

I shake my head and smile.

Cheeky monkey.

56

MYLA

With *sexy swimming time* cut short, I move onto the next best thing.

Demon Bars.

In short order, Lincoln and I sit around our little campfire, wrapped in blankets from our backpacks. I've got mine over my shoulders. Lincoln has his wrapped about his waist, kilt style. I shuck Demon Bars from their wrapper like they're fresh ears of corn. A small pile of shiny paper soon builds up between my bare feet.

Before us, Peli stands by the fire as he works over a cauldron. He claims it's dinner, but I'm not taking any chances—which is why I tear open the next Demon Bar in my queue. Nearby, our clothes hang on a branch by the flames. Clean stuff and a full stomach. Things are looking up.

One area where everything is far less than perfect, though: *privacy*. While we were swimming, Peli conjured his own orange tent right next to ours. If I were a different lust demon, I'd be able to get busy with a magical orange monkey nearby. Not my bag.

Peli sips the cauldron goop from a wooden spoon. "Perfect." He turns to us. "Ready?"

Lincoln hands me a bowl and spoon—more handy items from the backpacks. It isn't easy, but I force myself to set aside my last uneaten half of Demon Bar.

Peli spoons stew into bowls. I down a bite. It's spicy vegetables and broth. *Pretty good.*

Peli waits nearby. "How is it?"

"Yummy," I say with a smile.

While letting out a long sigh, Peli sits down beside us. "So," begins our little monkey. "Tell me everything that happened."

Lincoln and I take turns, talking about the Reptilians, Spivey, and the Contagion. Peli listens intently. For a time, I see the guy Lincoln talked about from his visions: Peli, the powerful wizard and future leader. Versus, you know, the trickster and pain in my butt.

Peli drums his fingers on his knees. "You've lived underground." He looks to Lincoln. "What will become of the Reptilians?"

"They'll escape, but they'll never return to that particular area again."

Peli shakes his head. "What a shame."

"I'm not so sure about that," I counter. "The Reptilians spent their time hiding out and hoarding stuff. Now they'll have to deal with the same problems as everyone else."

Peli stares more deeply into the fire. "True," he says. "That could be useful, when the time comes."

There's no question what Peli means about the *time coming*. That would be the hour when the Contagion is gone. It says a lot about Peli, the way he's planning for the future of his world.

"What can you tell us about the Icythians?" asks Lincoln.

"They're rather clever for fish," says Peli. "You may find an easy ally with them." Peli rises.

"Are you leaving?" I ask.

Peli doesn't answer, which is a *yes.*

"Where have you been running off to?" I ask.

"The same place I visit now," answers Peli. "There are things I need to do which you can not be part of yet."

Orange smoke curls up around Peli's body. Colored light flashes around his small form.

A moment later, Peli is gone.

"One thing I'll say," I quip. "Peli is consistent in his inconsistency."

A weight settles onto my shoulders. After so much running and excitement, I haven't really had a moment to think. Now that we're in a break, the world seems to press in around me. I watch the flames bite into the log pile. It's familiar. Something inside me is burning down as well.

Lincoln wraps his arm around my shoulder. "What's wrong?"

"You told me about the wizards from the other realms. How they pestered the Contagion. He was strongest, so they asked him to do every little thing."

Now that I've started talking, I can't stop. "All these rules," I continue. "The Rixa Way. The Purgatory Path. The Avian Route. The Reptilian Nest. I can see it, you know?"

"See what?"

"How the wizard snapped. Why he decided to stop dealing with what everyone else wanted and just take for himself. It's shitty and now he's a freaking tree, but I get it. Is that weird?"

"No," Lincoln says gently. "Everyone has limits."

"Cissy said something like that." My voice breaks.

Lincoln pulls me onto his lap. "What did Cissy say?"

"That no one can hold out forever. She reminded me of the ghoul saying, *the coffin nail that sticks up gets hammered down*."

"Oh, Myla. What can I do to help?"

"Just what we're doing now."

There's so much more to tell, but I can't find the words. My soul feels hollowed out. Every nerve ending shot. I'm used to fighting enemies on the Arena floor. Not this constant barrage against the essence of who I am. First it happened in the after-realms, now it takes place here as well.

I lean my head against Lincoln's shoulder. For a few minutes, we watch the fire burn down. Neither of us speaks. Lincoln rubs my back in soothing circles. It helps.

Eventually, the fire is nothing but embers. At some point, I'm aware of Lincoln carrying me to our tent. The last thing I sense is Lincoln's body next to mine as I fall into a deep sleep.

LINCOLN

It takes me a while drift off. The conversation with Myla has me concerned, to say the least. Still, there are so many other things to worry about. The Contagion tops the list, but nearby there's Nat and Baptiste, the other Marked Ones, and whatever it is that Aldred's really up to.

When I do fall asleep, I dream of white fire. The flames quickly vanish, leaving me in the same fantasy forest from my previous dreams. I approach the line of blue smoke that curls above the treetops.

When I reach the clearing, my Guide is nowhere to be seen. A different figure stands facing the fire. It's a woman. Although her back is facing me, I can tell how her gown hails from the House of Rixa. Betrothal jewels—earrings, tiara, and a diamond ring—all glimmer in the firelight.

I step closer. "Myla?"

The figure turns around. It's Lady Bentford. This dream is always surreal, but now it takes on an even more plastic quality. The woman's face seems too long. Her mismatched eyes bulge in odd ways.

"Hello, my love," says Lady Bentford.

I frown. "Where is Myla?"

"What do you mean? I'm Myla."

Something pulls at my boots. Looking down, I find the forest floor fills up with the same tar I saw back in Antrum. It's a sign of the Contagion. Fast as a heartbeat, the black ooze rises to my knees.

Danger.

Yet where is Myla?

My pulse speeds as I race through the pull of tar, searching for my Angelbound love in every cluster of trees.

Once more, I never do find her.

LINCOLN

The next day bring more marching through brightly colored tundra. Along the way, Peli points out which paths include new sink holes or old predators. With every change, Peli suggests we follow a slightly different and longer path.

If it means avoiding the sink hole situation again, then I'm all for it.

It's nightfall by the time we reach a bluff overlooking the ocean. The beach stretches before us, a streak of pink sand before a bright blue sea.

Finn Quay.

Humanoid fish saunter across the sands. The setting sun highlights the webbing between their arms and bodies. A halo of fins surround their heads. The women wear flowing white gowns, the men sport loose pants. All have overlapping scales the color of coral. Too many appear as thin as the Avians, with skeletal bodies and sunken eyes.

Some Icythians sit about a bonfire. Others enter or leave the surf. Still more sit beneath half-shell tents that point toward the ocean.

"You understand the plan?" asks Peli.

"We both do," I state.

Peli only reviewed this scheme about a dozen times on the trek over. We're to stand within twenty yards of the bonfire. Peli knows the Icythian queen. She'll recognize us when she's ready.

For their part, the Icythians act as if three strangers haven't just marched to their beach. The exception is the human in their group. She glares at our group as if we're enemies to be sliced through with pure joy. It reminds me of the thrax in my mother's house, Gurith. The human looks similar as well, with her muscular body, leather armor, and braided blonde hair.

Classic Viking.

An Icythian woman steps toward us across the sands. Unlike the others, her dress is woven through with gold. Her bulbous eyes also carry a pink tinge, unlike the all-black of the rest of the Icythians.

That must be her. Queen Caudal.

She approaches Peli and smiles. "Greetings, my friend."

Peli falls to one knee. "It is always a joy to see you, your Majesty."

"Come join us at the bonfire." Caudal gestures to me and Myla. "Bring your friends. We've been expecting you."

We all take a seat around the blaze. Peli introduces us; Caudal asks questions about the after-realms. The human, Elyse, watches the interaction from a few yards away, her fingers toying with the hilt of her longsword.

I like her.

Once Peli finishes, the queen makes her pronouncement. "We realize the threat from the Contagion. The Icythians are happy to help."

Myla pumps her fist in the air. "Yes! We were starting to wonder if everyone in the Primeval was a little HEH-heh, if you know what I mean."

"Of course, we shall assist you. Our warriors are experienced and this human is a valued member of our community." Caudal turns to Elyse. "Isn't that true?"

Elyse goes into fighting stance. "Viking. Kill."

Caudal smiles, a movement that makes her overly large lips stretch half-way around her head. "As you can see, Elyse is a warrior. That's why she's so valued by our people."

"Viking, kill, kill, kill," grumbles Elyse.

"Where can we obtain more weapons?" I ask.

"There are other things to discuss first," says Caudal.

Myla groans. "Here it comes."

"Our waters are depleted. Our little ones go hungry. We cannot assist you without gaining something in return." Caudal gestures to Myla. "I'd like you to make a sacrifice."

"So you need food?" asks Myla. "Peli here can conjure something."

"They can not consume my magic," says Peli. "It is a benefit of your being from the after-realms."

"Okay." Myla purses her lips, thinking. "So maybe Lincoln and I find you something to eat. Can you down the same seeds as Avians?"

"You've a powerful life force," continues Caudal. It's like she didn't hear Myla's question. *Not a good sign.* "Here in the Primeval, it translates into magic. In the old days, wizards would siphon that off for a bounty paid."

Myla narrows her eyes. "But all the wizards are gone."

"Sadly, yes." Caudal sighs. Every line of her body seems to weigh down with genuine sorrow.

I'm reminded of the pain all these people share. How each land lost many loved ones when they were frozen. It's a weight everyone here carries, invisible and omnipresent.

Caudal lifts her chin. "Therefore, I've another request for a bounty paid." She returns her focus to Myla.

Here it comes, indeed.

MYLA

There were warning signs.

So many warning signs.

I've been through this before with the Reptilians and Avians. Both peoples had an odd level of focus on yours truly.

Not that I'm a little competitive bitch.

I'm a BIG competitive bitch.

This feels like losing, and *me no likey*.

I step closer to Caudal. "Ho ho hoooooold there! Before you say another word, please take a look at my guy here." I make a sweeping gesture toward Lincoln.

"Ouch," deadpans my guy.

"Not that we'll ever go through with *this bounty paid thing* for either of us, but it seems like someone—" here I point to my face for emphasis "—keeps getting picked on. I just want to be make sure we're equally offered as possible participants."

"You're extraordinarily competitive. You know that?"

I wink. "You love it."

Lincoln's eyes sparkle with mischief. "Do your best. Or worst."

Turning, I refocus on Caudal. "Here's the thing. Lincoln here is a prince."

Lincoln raises his hand. "I am."

"That means he has prince hair."

The Queen looks to Peli, her brow-scales lifted. Peli shrugs. I'm losing my audience here.

I make another, grander gesture toward my guy. "He has prince arms."

Caudal now whispers to Peli. Our little orange buddy does that *chuckle thing* where he chatters his teeth in subdued laughter. They've clearly moved onto topics are that aren't what I'm talking about.

Time to take this to the next level.

"He has a prince junk."

"She even gave it a name," adds Lincoln.

At those final words, the entire beach instantly falls silent. There's nothing but cawing birds, the rush of surf, and every googly fish eye locked on me.

My guy shoots me a sly grin. This is indeed a competition and Lincoln just won there. Bastard knows it, too.

Caudal focuses on Lincoln. "What does she call your so-called junk, pray tell?"

"B-A-E-J-S," answers Lincoln.

"How very odd," says Caudal. "B-A-E-J-S. Whatever could that mean?"

Things are about to get ugly.

Correction. *UgliER.*

"You know what?" I ask. "Forget it. What's your bounty paid?"

Caudal straightens her stance. "It is hereby decreed that the Icythians shall give Peli's friends full support for protecting our friend, Elyse, from the Contagion. And in return…" The Queen pauses dramatically.

I roll my eyes. "Out with it."

"In return, you shall give us your tail."

"Say what?" I ask.

At this point, my tail perks up to arc over my shoulder. Normally, it adores being the center of attention. This time, though? Not so much.

Even so, I can't believe what I'm hearing. "My tail. You blah blah blah about the hungry kids, but what you want is to chop off my tail. Is that right?"

"Of course." Caudal says this so sweetly, it's not like she asked to cut off a freaking body part. "My people don't have tails. We should like to study it and see if it can be added to my person. Perhaps sewn on."

Rage courses through me. My eyes flare red. "Why not ask to chop off my arm?"

Caudal sniffs. "I already have arms." She lifts her own as evidence. "Are you soul bound to another perhaps? Then we could have two tails."

"We went through this before with the Reptilians. The answer is *no*. I am not soul bound."

Caudal beams. "Excellent. Bring forth the surgeon."

Something inside me cracks. It's the thin shell of resistance that stops me from losing my temper, twenty-four-seven. My eyes flare red while my mind derails into a haze of rage. I focus the anger into words. At this point, it's the best I can do.

"This is a disaster," I cry. "I'm talking *bad perm the first day of school* kind of problem." I stare up at the sky. "And you guys seemed so reasonable."

"We're not guys," corrects Caudal. "We're Icythians."

"She's tirading," explains Lincoln. "Just give her a minute."

I hear them talking, but it's as if the words take place in an echo chamber on another beach. "My guy and I have our own lives back in another realm. It's not easy. Folks back home want to fake-test my superpowers, if I don't pass, then I can't kill things."

"I can vouch for that," says Peli solemnly.

"And that doesn't even cover the dead-eyed old ladies who want me to drink urine. Actual stuff that tastes like pee, I tell you!"

"That, I've got nothing," adds Peli.

"Plus, don't even get me started on the quasis! They want me to insta-accept every hug out there. That's just disgusting and not only from a germ point of view. The quasis have issues with *over hugging*. You know what I'm talking about? Lean and hug, people. Do not press your boobs and junk onto me. I just don't want to know." I jog in place. "Hoo. Hooooo." *That's a two-hoo tirade.* "I'm good now."

Lincoln gives me a golfer's clap. "Lean and hug, that's a new one."

"Thank you."

"Ah," says Caudal. "Does that mean you're ready to give us your tail now?"

If I felt that I'd cracked before, now I full-on snap out of my shell and emerge a major rage monster. "I have had it. I'm so done trying to help you with Elsie."

"Her name is Elyse," corrects Caudal.

"Kill, kill," says Elyse.

"Look. My tail is a sacred part of me. And if that's what you need here? Then the ground can just shimmy-shimmy-shake until that slimy tar-covered Wizard of Goopopolis pops up to chomp down on Viking Kill Kill Kill Girl."

Suddenly, a low rumble fills the air. The beach beneath my feet trembles. Birds screech and fly away. The crowd falls deathly silent. A line erupts in the sand, its direction heading right for our group. I freeze, every nerve ending in my body on alert. Lincoln and I have seen this before.

The Contagion is coming.

Dang.

60

LINCOLN

Myla's words seem to hang in the air.

The ground can just shimmy-shimmy-shake until that slimy tar-covered Wizard of Goopopolis pops up to chomp down on Viking Kill Kill Kill Girl.

My thoughts race through every time we've encountered the Contagion before. It's always taken the monster a few minutes to actually break through to the surface. Assuming the Contagion hasn't gotten much stronger, we should have enough time to escape. We just need to grab Elyse and go before the Contagion shows up.

It can work here.

Only, it doesn't.

The sands by the camp fire blast apart, sending fiery bits of log flying in all directions. Ropes of tarred branches reach out from the new pit in the beach, spreading across the sands while hauling out the full bulk of the Contagion's tree form.

This monster has gotten larger. And stronger.

There's a moment where I soak in the latest incarnation of our tree-bound wizard. He's now ten yards in diameter, covered in writhing cords of black tar. The peak of his charred out body now soars at least four stories above the beach, while his face—with holes for eyes and a slash for a mouth—now appear in dimensions that would make a giant quiver with fear.

Fast as a whip, six branches grab Elyse, winding around her from head to foot. Shock prickles across my skin. The Contagion never moved this quickly before. Another branch tears a line down its own trunk-belly, opening up a massive incision. The rope-like arms yank Elyse from the sands and pull her inside.

Pink light flares from inside the Contagion's trunk. Shock and worry tar through my nervous system.

It happened again.

The Contagion consumed Elyse.

Taking out my dagger, I toss it at the Contagion's trunk. The blade sinks into the gooey surface, only the vanish within the monster's body. I have have one more blade remaining.

With a great whoosh, the Contagion drops back into the ground.

A long pause follows. The air turns heavy with shock and rage. All heads swing toward Myla. Bulbous eyes glare at her with murderous intent. I scan the nearest escape routes.

Myla raises her hands, palms forward, in a move that says, *not my fault*.

"Just a lucky guess, I swear. I had no idea Evil Greasy Treebeard would consume Viking Kill Kill Kill Girl right this very second. Honestly."

Meanwhile, Myla's tail expresses a far different attitude. It bobs happily in a rhythm that's clearly *nyah nyah nyah NYAH nyah*.

Caudal points at Myla. "The Avians were right. You brought a strange tar monster into our homes. How could you?"

"Not a tar monster," corrects Myla. "That was the Contagion."

The Icythians pull weapons from sheaths beneath their wide scales. Dozens of blades now gleam in the dying sunlight. All of them are point toward one target.

My Myla.

Not an option.

I've one dagger left. Pulling the weapon from its holster, I raise the blade high. Peli hops over to stand beside me and Myla.

"Time to run," states Peli. And the tone he uses says, *this isn't a question, it's an order*.

Peli raises his arms. Orange smoke pours out from his hands, clouding over the beach. He turns to me and Myla. "That will slow them down." Next Peli runs on all fours toward the pink tundra, all while chanting out a single word. "Go, go, go!"

Myla and I do just that.

MYLA

Lincoln, Peli, and I run all out for at least a half hour. There's no sign of the Icythians following us. Even so, I remain wary. Those googly-eyed bastards looked ready to kill.

Eventually, we reach a clearing with high ground and stop. Spend enough time in the wilds, and you know a good place for a break when you see it. Here, nothing will fall from a branch to bite our heads off. And with the high ground, we can see any pursuers coming at a distance.

Peli hops on his back legs while saying ooo-ooo before making an announcement. "That was a disaster." He points at me. "And they totally blamed you. Those Icythians will loathe you forever."

I shoot him a deadpan stare. "You think?"

"Back on the beach, what spell did you cast on the Icythians?" asks Lincoln. "That was the largest cloud of magic I've seen from you."

"Confusion spell," replies Peli. "If it worked, they won't see which way we went or remember to follow."

"*If* it worked?" I repeat. "All your spells succeed."

Peli kicks at the snowy ground. "I'm not a true wizard."

I frown, thinking this through. Lincoln shared Peli's self-image issues, but the little guy is always such a pain in the ass, I didn't really see it before. After all, I'm a pain in the ass and I've never had confidence problems.

Well, not before I became Great Scala and Future Queen.

But I digress.

Back to Peli.

Someone did a major number on Peli for this little monkey to think he's anything but amazing. Kneeling down, I take care to look Peli directly in the eyes. "You're the best wizard I've ever seen. All your spells ring true."

Peli draws an arc in the snow with his toe. "You must not have met many wizards."

My tail juts out to pat Peli's shoulder. "Whatever," I state. "We think you kick ass."

"Thank you," says Peli, and it's as if the two words are torn from him.

"There's only one more Marked One remaining," announces Lincoln. "The thrax will be with Aldred by now. All of them are heading to the original site of the Golden Arbor."

"They'll arrive by tomorrow afternoon," adds Peli. "I should think at about one o'clock."

I set my fist on my hip. Lincoln knew Aldred planned to end up at the Golden Arbor, but not *any specific time*. Peli's been hanging out with Aldred again.

Tricky monkey.

"That's awfully specific, Peli. Did you cast a seeing spell to know what Aldred's timetable?"

Peli snaps his fingers. "Yes, that's exactly what I did. I cast a spell to see the future and divine Aldred's plans."

"You're a crappy liar," I tell Peli. "I should know. I suck at it, too."

"You opened the original gateway for Aldred," adds Lincoln. "The pair of you have been working together all along. It's time to come clean."

Peli folds his arms over his chest. "Absolutely not. You can take my guidance or try to reach the Golden Arbor on your own. My plans and reasons are always secret."

Lincoln and I share a long look. I can guess what my guy is

wondering, because the same questions are ricocheting through my mind.

Can we trust Peli?

Is this a huge trap?

If we leave the little monkey behind, what are our chances?

No matter what the question, the answer seems to return to the same fact. Following Peli is a terrible choice, until you consider trying the same thing without him.

I shrug. Lincoln nods. That's about as long of a conversation that we need on the topic.

"All right," I say to Peli. "Lead on."

And let's hope this isn't the worst decision, ever.

LINCOLN

*P*eli's stalling.

There are faster paths we can take to reach the Golden Arbor. I do have a map, after all. And whenever I ask why we're taking a longer trek, Peli replies with rather questionable answers.

There may be snow snakes on that path.

People get struck by lightning on that route all the time.

Ghosts. Lots of ghosts.

As Myla pointed out, Peli is a rather horrible liar. For whatever reason, our orange friend wishes to arrive closer to nightfall, and I'm in no position to disagree.

Besides, I've been in situations like this one. If this were a card game, Peli would be revealing his hand. He thinks there is some benefit to arriving late. If I reveal I suspect he's up to something, then Peli may do more to hide his true intentions.

And I do suspect he's up to something.

Best to let Peli feel comfortable, and hope the little fellow mistakenly reveals his true arrangements with Aldred.

It's almost nighttime by the time we reach a spot to make camp. The place we choose lies a safe distance from a cliff's edge. Here the pink tundra of the Icythians ends with an abrupt drop. Down below is nothing but burned out hulks of trees.

That was Peli's land, once. Great redwood-style arbors had towered here as they reached for the skies. Now it's a graveyard of charcoal and memory.

Which brings me to the present moment. Peli, Myla, and I all stand at the cliff's edge, looking down upon the devastation below.

"I'm sorry this happened to your people," I say solemnly.

"I was never one of them really. You know that." Peli's mouth thins to an angry line. "The Contagion only brought me in at the end to try and drain my power for the final Marked One." Grief and pain seep from Peli, filling the air around us.

"That may have been how the Contagion treated you," says Myla. "That doesn't mean it's who you are."

Peli chuckles, but there's no humor in it. "Aldred will be here tomorrow afternoon," states Peli. "We should set up camp for the night."

"And?" I ask.

Peli blinks up at me, his blue eyes luminous in the dying light. "What do you mean?"

"We've been meandering across the countryside to arrive at this spot by nightfall. It's not the optimal place to make camp. There's higher ground on the other side of the cliff."

"How would you know?" asks Peli.

"We walked past it," I reply. "Remember?" I step closer. "Just once, tell us what your real plan is. Myla and I will decide what to do."

Peli flips his bottom lip back and forth beneath his upper one. Clearly, he's debating here.

"Come on, Peli," urges Myla. "Tell us."

Peli sighs. "It's you, Myla. There's something nearby that I would like to show you. Alone."

Defensive energy runs through my nervous system. "What will you do to Myla?"

"Nothing. What I wish to show her is personal." Peli lifts his chin. "It concerns family matters." His voice warbles as he speaks those last words.

Peli's speech breaks down my defenses a little. But only slightly. "I still don't like the idea of you dragging off Myla alone. You're a powerful magician and self-described trickster."

"Hey." Myla locks her gaze with mine. "This'll be fine."

And I know what Myla means here. Peli's tricks have all been in fun. When things get serious, our orange friend always looks out for our safety. And Myla's a strong warrior. I don't worry that anything could take her down. It's more the principle of the thing. I don't like open questions when it comes to my woman.

Still, we need answers of another kind—meaning Aldred and the Contagion. Perhaps Peli's about to give some intel to Myla. That's not something we can afford to pass up.

I focus on Peli. "Don't be long or I'll track you down."

Peli laughs.

Myla doesn't.

"Lincoln's not kidding, my little orange buddy."

And Myla's absolutely right.

MYLA

Peli leads me to the cliff's edge which connects the Icythian tundra to the Simian wasteland. A wooden ladder lies embedded into the cliff wall. *Huh.* I haven't had the best of experience with ladders lately.

"You want me to climb down that?" I ask.

"Of course."

"How secure would you say it is, on a scale of one to ten?"

Peli purses his thin mouth. The movement makes his lips stand out an full inch. It's a view I never really get used to. "I'd give it a six."

I bob my head, considering. "Better than five. I'm in."

We scale down the ladder. More than once, I curse the fact that I agreed when this is clearly a *three* on the safety scale. The wood isn't bolted to anything most of the time. Some steps are totally rotted through. The entire experience definitely stress-tests my ability to produce adrenaline.

At last, we reach the solid ground. *Whew.* Peli pulls away some dried branches from the base of the cliff wall. What he reveals is s shocker.

A tiny door.

"This is why we made camp here." Peli pulls the handle. The door swings open with a long squeak. "Come along. I should like to show you what's inside."

Entering is easy for Peli. The door's not Myla-sized, though, so I have to crawl through. Not sure what I expected would be inside, though.

Not this.

A small living room greets me. Every surface gleams. Fresh flowers sit atop the kitchen table. A figure sits on the ground nearby.

It's a woman.

Or rather, it's a carving of a woman. She's a monkey like Peli, and she's crouching over something. Every inch of my body feels numb. My mind blanks.

With uneven steps, I move toward the wooden figure. The woman holds twins on her laps. The children cling to their mother.

Peli moves to stand beside me. "The Contagion came here and froze them. My wife is named Nora. The twins are Mlinzi and Walinzi."

All the anguish in the world shines in Peli's blue eyes. I try to imagine having Lincoln frozen somewhere for *who knows how long*. Can't.

"Why were they frozen?" I ask. "Lincoln told me there were other victims in the Primeval, but they were all apprentices."

"The Contagion wanted to hurt me, plain and simple." Peli steps closer to his unmoving family. "From the moment I found them frozen, I vowed to free them while killing the Contagion. He'd never willingly set them loose, you see. And if you kill the caster, you kill the spell."

A realization appears. "This is where you've been." I scan the gleaming surfaces and fresh flowers. "When you've been disappearing, you return home and care for them."

Peli nods. "I had to. I've been away for so long."

"Why?"

"For centuries, I've been in the after-realms, searching for the Marked Ones. My original spell wasn't too specific. And if a current Marked One dies, then the power moves to the nearest person of the same lineage. So when I've found a Marked One, then I would send them back to the Primeval for safe keeping. The ghoul was last on my list."

"That's why you said you were looking for a ghoul back when we first met."

"True. Yet I wasn't searching the after-realms only for the ghoul. I also needed a magical source strong enough to destroy the Contagion." Peli sighs. "Imagine my joy when I learned about a new and incredibly powerful Great Scala."

"Hey, if you need me to kill something, I'm all about that. You don't have to drag me anywhere." I mime writing in the air. "Sign me up."

"It won't be easy."

I narrow my eyes. This is rapidly sounding like a crap deal. No wonder Peli dragged me out for show and tell. "What are you asking me to do here?"

"You must give the Contagion some of your life force. You're angel, demon and human. Here in the Primeval, that's powerful magic."

I frown. "And how will that kill the Contagion, exactly?"

"The Contagion doesn't know how I built my spell for the Marked Ones. That evil wizard thinks he can take in any magic. But he can't. Your energy has no tie to the Primeval."

I nod, processing this news. "Because I'm not a Marked One?"

"Correct. And one the Contagion consumes your power, it will eat him alive."

"That's rather graphic. Not that I care about how the Contagion buys it. The guy deserves what he gets at this point. My question is, once the Contagion is destroyed, what happens to me?"

"The energy you give him will be gone, but you'll still be alive. Only more... sedated."

"Riiiiight. That doesn't sound like fun."

Peli grips my wrist. "Think of my family. There are so many others out there, too. Your igni will be freed once your life force is gone. The after-realms will still function. Please, just promise me you'll think about it."

I stare at Peli, open mouthed, and I don't say no right away.

That scares me quite a bit.

"Let's get back to camp," I say at last.

And when we arrive, I don't tell Lincoln how I never actually said *no* to Peli.

That frightens me even more.

64

LINCOLN

For hours, I lay beneath our blankets and try to sleep.

Not happening.

My thoughts whirl through everything Myla told me about her visit to Peli's home. I'd be outraged that someone would ask Myla for her very life force, but I also know what it means to truly love a woman.

All in all, I can't blame Peli for trying.

Shifting under the blankets, I stare out the tent's exit flap to the vista beyond. From this high ground, I can make out the edge of the cliff wall, as well as the great expanse of stars glimmering over everything. Myla curls against my side, the gentle rhythm of her breathing a comfort. Even so, it isn't until the sky begins to lighten that I actually fall asleep.

There isn't much rest, though.

My dreams fill with white fire. Once more, the flames surround me without burning. Before, I'd felt wary of this nocturnal journey.

Now, my soul trembles with anticipation.

I'm a man who memorizes schedules, names, and strategies. Things just don't fall to the wayside, especially when I've deemed them important. And yet? There's an open question of what trouble lurks beyond the Contagion.

If I can find the Guide again, perhaps I can get some answers.

The white flames die down. I find myself at the edge of the same surreal forest. I follow the familiar path to the clearing and small campfire. This time, the Guide is waiting. Once again, he looks like me, only with fiery wings.

"I need to understand why you're here," I state.

The Guide nods and lifts his arms. Blue smoke rolls out from his palms, surrounding me in a magical haze. When the colored cloud is gone, I find myself back in history.

My personal history.

I stand in the stables of Purgatory. It's just after Myla fought arachnoid demon. She'd gotten infected with its poison and fell ill. I tried to help her, but I wasn't sure if it was enough. Now I stand, watching over a previous version of myself as I cradle Myla's body in my arms.

The Guide stands beside me. "Do you remember what you promised here?"

"Yes," I say. "Myla was dying. I decided nothing was more important than us. Whatever happened, I would follow my heart and keep her in my life."

"And what do you face now?" asks the Guide.

"The Contagion," I state. Yet even as the words leave my mouth, I know they aren't the full truth. "Isn't that right?"

"Yes. And no." The Guide shakes his head. "There is also a bigger threat to you both."

"I realize that. I simply can't see what it is."

"That is the problem."

There are a dozen things I'd like to say in this moment. Most of them revolve around pushing the Guide for more details on the true threat to me and Myla. Only there isn't time. A combination of white flame and blue smoke surrounds me.

The dream ends.

I open my eyes to find Myla still asleep. Dawn has just risen. At last, it's time face Aldred and the Contagion, once and for all. Normally, I savor the thrill of a future battle.

This time, I can't stop the sense of dread that fills my bones.

65

MYLA

Lincoln, Peli and I march over to the burned out pit that once held the so-called Golden Arbor. No matter what lands we visit, they all talk about this freaking tree with reverent tones.

I thought that was I got closer, maybe I'd pick up the vibe.

Not exactly.

It's a nasty old black pit, that's all. The Contagion took over the tree and marched off, end of story.

Woo hoo.

Things don't get better as time passes. The sun rises in a cloudy sky. It's a Purgatory kind of day. Back home, the most we ever see is the halo of a sun behind a light gray cloud. The whole Purgatory vibe isn't helping this, either.

Lincoln and I share a dry look. Both of us raise our brows with an unspoken question. *How long do we wait?*

After all, I wouldn't put it past Aldred to just make us stand around like losers.

Peli scans our faces. "You need to be patient. Aldred will arrive soon."

I poke at the pit's edge with my boot. "What about you, Evil Greasy Treebeard? Care to bubble up make an appearance?"

The pit does zero.

Oh, well.

The soft trill of lute music carries on the air. It's a sound I've heard before.

Aldred's minstrels.

I pinch the bridge of my nose. "Don't tell me Aldred brought his back-up band."

"Only one of them," explains Peli. "He wanted to make an entrance."

"Of course," quips Lincoln.

The good news is that we're done waiting. The crap side of things is that Aldred is clearly on his way.

It's showtime, and in more ways than one.

66

LINCOLN

The plinking tones of a lute echo across the wasteland. A single minstrel's voice sounds.

Alllldred
Nothing but Alllldred
All-All-Aldred

I tap my chin, trying to remember. "I believe I've heard that song before."

Myla's opens her mouth in dramatic surprise. "That's the theme to Star Wars. It's only the most famous song in the history of ever. Aldred added new lyrics."

"Star Wars? You mean the movie with the space puppets?"

"Sha! We walked about this. Those have a name. Wookies."

"Right." I do so love needling her on this topic. And at this point, I believe we both relish the distraction. "The wookie space puppets."

"I don't know why I try to educate you on the basics of modern culture. Star Wars is a super-important movie."

Peli picks bits of lint from his fur. "I've never heard of Star Wars. And I've spent hundreds of years in the after-realms. On the other hand, consider the Bayeux Tapestry. Now *that's* culture."

"See?" I wink. "Peli agrees with me."

Myla rolls her eyes. "Can we please focus on killing the Contagion right now? Otherwise, I'll make you watch all the Star Wars prequel movies."

"Heaven forbid."

I'm not being dramatic, either. Myla has started this unfortunate *prequel viewing experience* a few times. So far, I've been able to derail her. Mostly, I use sex.

Aldred approaches. Four men in yellow uniforms hold a fabric canopy above his head. The minstrel skips along beside him, replaying the same tune. Rufus lopes along in the back of the group. An older man with a grizzled face, gray hair and a lean body rides upon the lion's back.

Aldred pauses before us. "Greetings, my friends. Lincoln and Myla, you both look judgmental as usual."

"We forgot our minstrel," sasses Myla. "Puts us in a bad mood."

"Obviously," retorts Aldred. "And Peli, you brought them both here, just as we planned." Aldred tilts his head, waiting.

Seconds pass. The older man riding Rufus looks especially confused. The minstrel yawns.

"What?" asks Myla.

"Aren't you shocked that Peli and I are in league together?" asks Aldred.

"Not in the slightest," I reply.

"Come now, not even a little bit?"

"Not even this much." I hold my thumb and forefinger so they almost touch. I gesture toward Rufus and his passenger. "Why don't you introduce us?"

"If you insist," huffs Aldred. He's really disappointed that his Peli surprise was no surprise. *Perfect.*

Myla raises her hand. "Insisting here."

Aldred gestures to the very old man in a new Acca tunic. "Meet Hereweald. He's a thrax and the final Marked One."

Hereweald grins, a movement that shows off his gummy toothlessness. "I six huuunnned-an-four."

"What?" asks Myla.

"Hereweald says he's six hundred and four years old," explains Rufus.

"An I wanna drink," adds Hereweald. "Primeeeeeval ale!"

"That means it's whiskey time," says Rufus. "Check my side pouch, Hereweald."

What follows next is a lot of Hereweald almost-not-quite falling off Rufus while trying to pull out a bottle.

"Are you certain that's a good idea?" I ask. "It's over a hundred degrees outside and that's a very old thrax."

Rufus smacks his lips. "At six hundred and four, Hereweald can do whatever he wants."

"Good point." Myla nods. "Guy seems happy."

Hereweald uncorks the bottle and chugs. That must be a half-gallon of booze the guy downs. In some ways, it really is an achievement.

Aldred saunters to Hereweald's side. "Remember how we talked about performing a magic trick for our new friends? It's time for that now." The earl helps Hereweald to the ground.

"Maaaaaagic." Hereweald finishes off the rest of his bottle and tosses it into the wastelands. The container smashes against a nearby tree stump.

With Hereweald leaning against Aldred, the pair march across the burned-out ground, pausing before the darkened pit that marks the original place for the Golden Arbor.

Aldred gives the thrax a gentle shake. "Show them your mark, Hereweald."

Hereweald pulls the neckline of his tunic, showing off the mark on his shoulder. This time, it's a yellow shield.

"Thank you, Hereweald." Aldred shifts his arm behind Hereweald's back. A snick sounds. The elder thrax's face slumps over, his mouth dribbling blood.

"What?" Myla gasps. "Did you just kill Old Drunk Medieval Grandpa? What is wrong with you?"

"Patience," cautions Aldred.

The mark on Hereweald's shoulder vanishes. Aldred releases his hold on the old man, allowing Hereweald to slump to the ground, dead.

Aldred pulls at the neckline of his own tunic. The shield mark now glows on his own shoulder. "The magic trick complete. Peli told me how his spell worked. The mark goes to the nearest one of like bloodline. Thrax to thrax." Aldred scans our faces closely. "You still don't know what I'm *really* planning, do you?"

Myla and I stay silent.

Sadly, I fear Aldred's true schemes are still a mystery. And I've the sinking feeling that's about to cause a Primeval-sized world of trouble.

MYLA

There's an old dead thrax and the ground and the heavy scent of alcohol in the air. Unbelievable. Who kills a medieval dude who's whatever-hundreds of years old?

Aldred does, that's who.

Even worse, the old thrax guy has a very clear dagger in his back. Blood pools around the wound. That's not an honest death, thrax wise. There's a reason it's an insult to call someone a *back stabber*. It's just a shitty kill.

Fury tightens my limbs. I point at the dead thrax. "You murdered one of your own people, Aldred. We need to talk about this."

Aldred rolls his eyes. My rage demon roars inside me. Electric jolts of anger charge through my nervous system.

Aldred using an eye roll *to me* as an actual response to getting hassled about stabbing an old dude in the back? I may have wanted to kill Aldred before. That's nothing compared to the level of loathing I feel in this moment.

Aldred snaps his fingers. "Peli, clean up the mess and summon the Contagion."

My fury makes it hard for me to follow what happens next. Peli summons some orange cloud thing that makes Hereweald disappear. Lincoln says something about what a crap idea it is to bring the evil tar monster here at this point.

Those words snap me out of my rage funk. *Did I just hear what I thought I heard?*

I round on Lincoln. "Let me get this straight. Aldred is bringing the Contagion here? Now?"

"Unfortunately," says Lincoln. My guy fingers the dagger strapped to his thigh.

Meanwhile, Peli summons another big old blob of orange air goop. I debate about smashing the little monkey to the ground, killing Aldred, or both.

Then the image of Peli's frozen family appears in my mind.

No question about it. When it comes to magic, Peli is a rock star. And that monkey adores his family. Whatever is happening now, I have to believe it's for the best of everyone.

And if it isn't? Then I can start flattening and killing.

The freaky orange air slop congeals into one big ass tree stump. With a nasty face and arms.

The Contagion has arrived.

On his tar-trunk face, the Contagion's scooped-out eyes narrow while his mega mouth curls into a sinister grin. "Just the people I want to see. Thank you, Peli."

Peli bares his teeth at the Contagion. "I didn't do this for you."

"That makes no difference," booms the Contagion. "You still brought me what I want. Enemies to destroy." The hollowed out eyes swing in my direction. "And new life force to consume."

Sure, Peli said that if the Contagion consumed my life force, then evil Treebeard might explode. But so will a big chunk of me. There's a lot to try before considering that route.

The Contagion isn't waiting, though.

The tar-covered stands of bark churn more quickly on the Contagion's trunk. Cords stretch out into long branches that reach for me. Pointed fingers drip dark goop as they get nearer.

If Peli has another plan, now would be a great time for it to start.

I look to Lincoln. The dagger stays gripped tightly in his fist. He and I spoke about Peli a lot last night. We're agreed. Peli gets a chance until he doesn't. Time is running out.

The branches get within five yards.

Three yards.

One.

"Stop!" cries Aldred.

In a major shock, the Contagion actually freezes in place. Looking at Aldred, it's obvious what's happening here.

The earl holds a round wooden carving of a monkey's head. I suck in a shocked breath.

I know what that is.

The peak to a wizard's staff.

Quilliam's staff.

Lincoln and I discussed this as well. We figured the original peak to Quilliam's staff just got lost somewhere along the line. Looks like Aldred found it. And right now, that carving glows with orange light.

It's giving Aldred the power to control Quilliam, and therefore the Contagion.

Peli slowly crawls toward Aldred. "Where did you get that?"

Aldred smirks. "I have my secrets, even from you, little monkey."

Peli halts in place, his eyes wide with shock. "I'd no idea."

This is super crap news. Peli's big plan was for me to my life force so we could blow up the Contagion. Now Aldred basically has a magical remote control for evil Treebeard. Things are going to Hell.

"Now." Aldred really drags out that single syllable. "Do you finally see my full plan?"

Lincoln and I share a look that encapsulates a sad mixture of insight and resignation. Because *yes*, the full plan is clear at last.

"You don't want to kill the Contagion," says Lincoln.

"You want to become him," I add.

Aldred nods.

Sometimes, it sucks being right.

LINCOLN

I tighten my grip on my dagger. Now that Aldred has the Contagion in his power, a battle is almost certainly coming.

Chances are, it won't be one I expect.

Aldred turns to Myla and grins. "While I'm at it, I should gather up as much magic as possible, don't you think? It's simply a matter of efficiency." Aldred snaps his fingers. "Peli, cast the spell we discussed."

Peli hops backward. "That casting was for the Contagion, not you."

"Change of plans. Cast the spell... unless you want me to ask the Contagion to cast it. He has all the magic he needs to do so, doesn't he?"

"Yes." Peli says that word with all the excitement of accepting an invitation to a funeral. "I will cast it for you."

Peli lifts his palms. A fresh haze of orange magic appears above his hands. When the power vanishes, Peli holds a new carving. The creation is identical to the others that I've seen for the peak of a wizard's staff, but with one key difference.

This carving shows Myla's face.

I round on Aldred. "It's not enough to have the Contagion's power, you want Myla's too?"

"Don't blame me," says Aldred. "Peli was the one who explained everything. Why should I stop short of all the magic I can get? Especially when it will be so satisfying to watch you suffer as Myla does my bidding at last?"

All rational thought flees my head. I race after Aldred, my dagger raised. Aldred doesn't so much as move into fighting stance.

"Contagion," cries Aldred. "Pin him down."

Fast as lightning, the branches that reached for Myla move again. I'm not six steps toward Aldred when they slam into me, knocking me onto my back. Branches sharp as daggers pierce my shoulders and thighs, tearing through my body armor.

Pain radiates from the puncture wounds. Warm blood trickles down my shoulders and legs. I struggle to move. Even the barest flinches cause agony to burn through me.

"I didn't mean to be so literal," says Aldred. "But that was rather effective."

Myla rushes to kneel at my side. She pulls at the branches, trying to jar them loose. They don't budge.

Rufus rushes forward, claws and teeth bared. "Set my friend free!"

A fresh branch bursts from the Contagion's side. The tar-covered limb slams against the lion's skull, knocking him out cold.

Poor Rufus.

Myla takes my dagger and hacks at the tar-like surface. The blade has no affect.

Aldred steps closer. "Don't fret yourself, Myla darling. Give Peli your consent, and he'll cast a quick spell. Your life energy will enter that peak for a new wizard's staff. I'll eventually add it to my new self, just as Quilliam added to his original glory. Your body will still be alive, and I'll free Lincoln. Isn't that a sensible course of action?"

I wait for Myla threaten bodily harm to Peli, Aldred, or both. She doesn't. Instead, Myla's blue eyes line with tears as she hacks away at the Contagion. Her tail gets into the mix as well. Nothing causes so much as a scratch.

"Aww," says Aldred in a low voice. "I've seen you struggle, my sweet. Everyone will be better off if you agree. You know that, don't you? I've already pledged to protect Lincoln. My promise extends to your family as well. And just think—you'll bring back so many lives."

Myla stops hacking away. Despite the pain, a chill runs over my skin.

Myla is actually considering this.

"No," I whisper. "Don't."

Myla doesn't reply. In fact, she doesn't even meet my gaze.

"Come now," says Aldred. "It's the Rixa Way. Don't be selfish with your powers. Give them over. Protect those you love."

Myla drops the dagger.

Oh, no.

MYLA

I stare at my palms. My hands drip with goop from the Contagion. I haven't so much as made the thing flinch, let alone let Lincoln free. There's no way to end this. I'm in a strange world with odd powers.

Aldred waves his hand at the Contagion. "Clarify the threat for her."

A fresh branch oozes out from the Contagion's side. The slimy appendage speeds across the clearing, stopping when the knife-like end hovers just above Lincoln's eye. My mind washes clean with panic.

"Agree to Peli's spell," says Aldred in a sweet voice. "I will protect Lincoln and your loved ones. You'll still be alive. It's the best offer you'll get."

I try to meet Lincoln's gaze. *Total fail.*

"Myla, look at me," says my guy.

I can't. If I do, I'll lose my nerve. And I have to be strong here.

"Peli told me about this spell," I say in a low voice. "I'll live through it and free others."

"It's not an option, Myla." Lincoln takes in a long breath. Every line in his body seems to firm with resolution. "You see, I now understand what the Guide wants me to do."

"I can fix this, Lincoln."

"No, *we* can end this. Trust me."

The pull of his gaze is too strong. Lifting my chin, I look right into Lincoln's mismatched irises. In this moment, there really is only one choice. It's the same one that's always existed.

When I next speak, I place all my heart into three simple words. "I trust you."

LINCOLN

*P*ain bites into my shoulders and legs. Gritting my teeth, I focus past the hurt. There's no ignoring the lines of misery etched on Myla's face, though.

Her suffering must end. Now.

I slightly arch my head toward Aldred. It's the most I can manage, given that there's a knife-sharp stick hovering just above my eyeball.

"If I gave you my strength, would you leave Myla alone?" I ask.

For Aldred's part, he pretends not to hear the question at all. Even so, there's no missing the interested gleam in his button eyes. "What power could you possibly have here?"

"Ask Peli," I reply. "Your ally has been hiding things from you."

Here's where my plan hits a crossroads. If Peli really is in league with Aldred, then the monkey wizard will admit I've got nothing in terms of power in the Primeval.

Aldred rounds on Peli. "Is this true?"

What follows next is a lot of hopping around and screeching. It's a virtuoso performance of raw animal fear.

"Answer me!" cries Aldred.

Peli stops. Shivers. Nods. "Yes, it's true."

One thing about greed. It quickly becomes a fog that clouds your judgement. Aldred doesn't actually need any more power than he has today. What he craves is the thrill of taking something. Of winning.

Honestly, the man needs a hobby.

Aldred stalks closer to me. "In that case, I want your energy as well."

"If I give it willingly, do I have your assurance that Myla will be safe?"

Aldred slaps on a simpering smile. "Of course, I'll leave your demon girl alone."

Which is an absolute lie. Not that I'll say anything. When Aldred thinks he's outsmarting me, he's much easier to manipulate.

Myla flashes Aldred an angry look. "Still have a name here, dickhead. Myyyyyylaaaaaaa."

I can't help but grin. Nice to see my girl's sass returning. She'd been far too quiet through this entire exchange.

Peli bobs on all fours. "Give me a moment. This is a tricksy spell."

That's what Peli says, but I know what's truly taking extra time here. Peli has no idea what to cast. Fortunately, all my visions from the Guide are now crystal clear.

"It shouldn't take too long," I tell Peli. "After all, you're just casting the same the spell you did on Mlinzi and Walinzi."

"Who are those two?" asks Aldred.

"Some locals Peli and I met on your travels." I can be a rather smooth liar, if I do say so myself.

Peli's blue eyes widen so much, they dominate his small round face. "Yes. You're right. That won't take long."

Lifting his hands, Peli summons a fresh haze of magic to hover above his palms. The small orange cloud stretches, turning into a long cord that reaches out to both me and Aldred.

As the bright line of magic closer, I start to question my scheme here. Linking with Aldred's soul? That won't be pleasant. Or safe.

All the while, Aldred stares at the cord of power with a look that's the very definition of the word *gloating*. The earl has worked very hard for this moment. Clearly, he's savoring it.

Magic brushes against my neck. The touch is soft as raindrops. For a moment, all my pain fades.

The spell enters my body.

Instantly, I sense the blackened soul that is Aldred. *Ambition, malice, and so much greed.* The man is all craving and no contentment.

I pull on my inner sense of control and press Aldred's self into a far corner of my consciousness. Even so, his presence remains, like an old and open wound. For the purposes of Primeval magic, we are the same person now.

Disgusting but—in this situation, anyway—the only possible way to save Myla.

When I next speak, I place an extra ring of authority to my voice. "Contagion, release me."

Aldred huffs out a sarcastic breath. "That won't work, Lincoln."

Yet the branches in my body shiver. Then they snap back. I'm now free again.

Aldred stares at me, his face slack with shock. "How did you do that?"

"I'll tell you." Pressing the pain aside, I hop to stand and lurch over to Aldred. Once we're inches apart, I do what I've wanted to for ages.

I punch Aldred in the head. Hard.

The earl falls over with all the grace of a sack of potatoes. Rifling in the earl's tunic, I search for the monkey head carving. The action takes my attention away from the Contagion.

The evil wizard uses this moment to strike.

Black sludge oozes around me. Like the other Marked Ones, I'm now being consumed. Dark branches yank the wizard's peak from Aldred's tunic, pulling it inside the Contagion's body. More tar encases Aldred as well.

The slime quickly rises up around me. Ankles. Knees. Chest. My thoughts whirl. Adrenaline courses through my veins. This move by the Contagion was unexpected, but not necessarily unwanted.

A chance remains.

Myla senses it, too. "How do I kill this thing?"

"Once I'm inside, send me fire."

The dark ooze covers my head.

MYLA

My inner wrath demon rages inside me, claws bared and fangs ready. There's a simple reason why.

That tree monster just freaking digested my future husband.

Not okay.

Sadly, I've already seen what happens when I try to battle the Contagion directly. Not a whole Hell of a lot.

Stupid Primeval.

Stupid powers.

Peli shuffles closer. "What will you do?'

Lincoln's final ask reverberates through my head.

"Once I'm inside, send me fire."

No question what that particular request means. My igni have been dancing over Lincoln's skin ever since we arrived in the Primeval.

"This," I reply. Closing my eyes, I summon my igni.

Come to me, little ones.

It's always a crap shoot if my igni will show up. And if they do, what happens next can be unpredictable. But today, my little ones appear right away. A dozen tiny flames materialize on my palms. It's like playing catch with lit matches.

"Ouch, ouch, ouch!" On reflex, I shake my hands. "Go help Lincoln."

The igni zoom from my hands and slam against the Contagion's trunk. The sight isn't as odd as it could be. The Contagion is no longer sporting his creepy bark face, so it just seems like I'm trying to burn down a really gross tree.

Hiss.

Hiss.

Hiss.

As each flame hits the gooey bark, the slimy surface extinguishes the little blaze. The good news is, it doesn't hurt my igni. They just bounce back and hover in the air. But the bad part here is obvious.

Lincoln is inside that thing.

My igni need to reach him.

I round on Peli. "Open up the Contagion."

Peli shivers. "I can't."

"There must be a spell you can try."

"There are many, and I did try them for years. That's why I had to find you."

Peli's words echo through my mind.

That's why I had to find you.

An idea appears. It's totally whacky and a major long shot, but since when have I had good odds?

"Do you still have that carving of me?"

Peli lifts his palm. A miniature cloud of orange magic materializes above his palm. The haze vanishes to reveal the carving of yours truly that Peli offered up before.

"It's too late," says Peli. "The Contagion has consumed both Lincoln and Aldred."

"I'm not talking about draining me here," I retort. "Just put a little of my mojo on that thing. All I need is to break up that goo bark."

Peli turns the round carving over in his hands. "That could work."

"Damn right, it could. So start siphoning off some Myla sass and let's get this party started."

Peli lifts his free hand. A fresh tendril of orange power whips off his palm and zooms across the wasteland. A second later, the cord connects with my rib cage, right above my heart.

Damn. That hurts like a mother.

A pulse of red energy moves out from my chest, across the magical cord, and right into the Myla craving. The round object changes from regular wood to a glowing baseball of crimson death.

Yes. This is getting good.

I raise my hands. "Toss it here."

Peli chucks the carving into the air. I don't even bother trying to catch it. My tail swings out and whacks the sphere, baseball style.

The carving whizzes across the wasteland to slam onto the slimy bark. The trunk opens slightly. My igni speed to enter, but the bark seals up too quickly.

"Again," I command Peli. "And this time, put more of my life force into it."

Peli shifts his weight from foot to foot. "I can drain you easily, but taking just a little of your life force? I've never cast a spell like this before. I don't know what will happen."

"Do I look like I care?" I point to the carving. "Do it, Peli. Now."

LINCOLN

*D*arkness surrounds me. My lungs ache with the need for oxygen. Wood presses against my skin, tight as a vise.

Orange light burns into my eyes. I wince against the assault. One moment, I'm being crushed inside a tree. The next, I sit at a table in a familiar space. It's the meeting room where the one-time Quilliam held court with other regents so long ago. There's no mistaking how the walls are lined with the carved peaks of so many wizard staffs.

My chest aches as I try to pull in air. On reflex, I set my hand on my throat.

There's only one other being in the chamber with me. Quilliam. He appears just as he did in the first vision: a lanky humanoid with a monkey's face and tufts of hair on his cheeks.

"This is an illusion," says Quilliam. "You're still dying."

It takes some effort, but I'm able to squeeze out a single word. "Yes."

Turns out, it's hard to speak without air. I resolve to keep the chatter to a minimum.

Thunk.

Quilliam sets an object onto the tabletop. It's the peak from his wizard's staff—the same item Aldred was using to control the Contagion. Quilliam grins. "I have this back."

"So I see." If my lungs ached before, now they positively burn with the need to breathe.

"You can have all the oxygen you want," says Quilliam. "But convince the demon girl to hand over her life force."

"No." Although my air is running out, I've still enough to state that word with full solemnity. Maybe giving Myla's spirit to the Contagion will kill him, but it would destroy her as well. There is another way.

"I'd planned to sit here and watch you suffocate." Quilliam rises. "On second thought, I'll do the honors myself."

I lift my chin, all the better to give him access to my throat. "Go on."

What Quilliam doesn't know is that Myla will send me fire. I have every faith in my girl. Myla won't give up until she figures it out. The pain in my rib cage turns excruciating. Spots of white dance in my vision.

I don't have much longer.

Quilliam strides across the room, pausing beside my chair. Little by little, Quilliam sets his hands against my throat. That's when it happens.

A ball of red light punches through Quilliam's chest. And in the center of that sphere, I see Myla's face.

Beautiful.

Myla must have gotten Peli to charge up that carving with her life force. Two emotions battle it out inside me. First, there's the warm joy that I might live through this moment. That's quickly followed by a second feeling. Namely, an icy fear.

How much life force did Myla give?

Is she all right?

After the fireball punches through, there follows more flames. Igni. They speed into the room, filling the air with heat and light. A strange pulse of energy moves through me. Looking down, I see what could be a halo of red magic surrounding my body. It's gone too quickly to be certain, though.

Quilliam howls with pain, interrupting my thoughts. His cry mixes the voice of a living being with the distinct kind of squeal that happens when you place fresh logs on a bonfire.

The illusion of the meeting room vanishes. Once again, I'm back inside the tree trunk. Wood crushes in around me. Igni press against my skin. Like before, the flames don't burn.

This isn't helping my oxygen situation any. The spots in my vision spin faster. The pain in my lungs fades. Not good.

Somehow, I manage to croak out a single word. "Wings."

Igni speed around my back, taking the form of wings made from flame. I have my own ceremonial wings, but in the after-realms, they don't empower me to fly.

Let's see what happens in the Primeval.

I call on my new wings. The muscle movement is natural, as if I've been flying my whole life. I picture my wings spreading wide. That's just what they do. Even better, they burn through the wooden confines all around me.

Somehow, my after-realm powers are merging with the unusual qualities of igni in the Primeval. Together, we're tearing through the prison that is the Contagion's trunk.

My inner Guide knew it all along.

I command my wings to beat. They do as requested, burning through wood along the way. A weightless quality fills my body as I move upward. It takes what little energy I have left, but I force myself to keep flying.

Higher.

Higher.

Crash!

With a great heave of effort, I break through the treetop. Clean air rushes into my lungs. I drink it in greedily. My vision clears. My chest ceases to ache.

Even better, the connection with Aldred snaps. I no longer feel the dark craving for power that eats away at him. that freedom combines with my wings to make my body feel even lighter.

Still, not everything has improved.

Below me, the Contagion looms, his face twisted with rage. Long branch-like arms swing beside him. Smoke curls from the new hole I created in the top of his trunk.

The Contagion is hurt, but still ready for a fight.

I'll give him one.

"Fists, little ones." Bits of igni break free from my wings to surround my hands with bright flame.

Perfect.

I soar down to the Contagion, my fists ready and wings blazing. Using the extra momentum from my flight, I punch into the Contagion's side. A huge chunk of wood breaks free to whip across the ground. There it smolders to ashes.

Myla stands nearby, her arms raised as she lets out hearty whoops of joy. *That's my future wife, ladies and gentlemen.* I've sprouted fire wings and am taking down a tree monster. She's doing her happy dance. How lucky can one man get?

Pumping my wings, I arc in for another attack. As I swoop down toward the Contagion once more, I make a silent vow.

This is for Peli's family.

I smash through the Contagion's body, time and again. The branch-arms try to grasp me, but they burst into flames when we touch. As more of the massive trunk breaks apart, something remarkable happens.

The others who were consumed by the Contagion step free. They stagger out, their eyes glazed and bodies stiff. Yet they are alive. And they depart in the reverse order that the Contagion took them in.

Aldred.

Elyse.

Spivey.

Zoar.

Rule.

Of course, Rufus is already free. He's woken up and waits on the ground, his chin resting on his front paws.

As for the non-lion folks, most stand mutely in the wasteland, their eyes wide and mouths silent. For his part, Aldred folds his arms over his chest and glares daggers in my direction. I've seen inside his soul. He doesn't categorize *escaping with my life* as a win. All Aldred senses is the pain of losing.

As I pummel the last of the Contagion apart, one final figure steps out from the very base of the trunk.

It's Quilliam.

The wizard raises his fist, ready to rail on about something.

Before he can get out a word, his body freezes. Where once his skin color was golden, it now turns a charred shade of orange.

Then it crumbles.

Quilliam no longer just looks burned out, but his body also takes on the properties of ash. Little by little, bits of Quilliam fly away in the breeze, collapsing down until there's nothing left but a small charred mark on the soil.

Couldn't happen to a better wizard.

73

MYLA

Some people will tell you the best sight in the universe is the human's Grand Canyon. Others are fans of the Incaenda, which is Antrum's magma river. More chat up the Spires—that's supposed to Heaven's finest city.

Me? I'm a fan of watching my guy swoop around with fire wings while he punches the Contagion into dust.

Good times.

My guy lands. The moment his boots touch the wasteland, all the igni vanish. Lincoln is no longer the man with fiery wings.

He's just mine.

Racing over, I check Lincoln's shoulders and legs. "Are you all right?" I run my fingers across the body armor on his shoulder. Totally shredded.

Lincoln frowns. "It doesn't hurt any more."

"Well, your body armor looks like Swiss cheese, but the skin beneath is fully healed." I lean in closer a closer look. "There aren't even any scars."

Lincoln pulls his brows together; it's what I call his *thinking face*. "Inside the Contagion, I saw red power around me and felt a surge of strength. I wasn't certain, though."

"Red." I nod slowly. "My carving turned red when Peli sparked it up."

"The healing power must have been yours." Lincoln gives me one of those smiles where it's like I hung the sun and moon.

Not gonna lie. I love this look on him.

Next it's Lincoln's turn to check me carefully. "Are you well? How much power did Peli take from you?"

"Not much. I barely felt it." I bob my brows. "Seems I pack a huge amount of energy into a relatively small amount of real estate."

Nearby, the other Contagion survivors sit around. Soft moans sound from their direction, followed by meaningful glances. They want answers. For his part, Rufus seems happy to have a nap.

Well, they're all alive, thanks to me and Lincoln. They can wait while my guy and I catch up. Especially Aldred.

I refocus on Lincoln. "And you made wings with my igni. Who knew?"

"Who indeed?" A sneaky gleam lights up Lincoln's mismatched eyes. He's holding out on me. *Meh.* At this point, I'm just happy that Lincoln is here and unhurt. My guy can keep his secrets.

Aldred stomps over because that's just what creeps like him do. "You ruined this for me." He pounds his chest with his fist. "Me."

"Yeah, we got that part." I don't say anything else, though. It's clear Aldred wants to get into a fight about who ruined what. Not playing. There are two reasons for this. First, it's a no-win battle. Second, it will irritate the earl far more if I stay silent and check my fingernails.

Huh. Still clean.

Aldred stalks into my personal space. "Kill me. You want to."

Lincoln moves so his body separates mine and Aldred's. "Leave Myla alone."

I check the fingernails on my opposite hand. "I know you want me to attack you. Won't happen. We—" and here I gesture between me and Lincoln for emphasis "—will take you down the Rixa way, my friend. That will be much sweeter."

Aldred narrows his piggy eyes. "What do you mean?"

Ha. Like I'd just announce we're taking Aldred to court for all his misdeeds. The earl has enough connections. He'll figure it out on his own. Besides, we have bigger things to worry about right now.

Ignoring Aldred, I look to Lincoln. "We need to check on Nat and Baptiste."

Peli scampers over to pause beside us. "Great idea! I have loved ones to visit as well."

With that announcement, Peli gets to casting another one of his orange colored spells. Before, the sight of Peli's magic wasn't exactly a signal for *happy fun times*. But now? A sense of warmth and well-being streams through me.

Peli is about to be reunited with his family. It's a beautiful moment.

Until Aldred ruins it.

"Halt!" cries the earl. Peli stops casting.

What a dick move on Aldred's part. Peli hasn't really seen his family in forever.

The earl marches up to me and Lincoln. "You've forgotten about the rest of us, haven't you?" To emphasize this point, Aldred stomps his foot. I haven't seen that move performed so perfectly since the first grade. Or maybe Lady Adair. It's hard to keep track.

I set my fist on my hip. "By the *rest of us*, you mean the ones you didn't kill, right? Because last time I checked, Drunk Thrax Grandpa got stabbed and magically erased."

On a side note, it's becoming very clear where Lady Adair got her big attitude from. These two hams are sliced from the same hock.

Aldred turns to the other survivors, who are now clustered in a group. "She's only joking."

I raise my hand. "Not joking."

Lincoln nods. "Agreed."

Aldred lowers his voice so only Lincoln and I can hear. "What will you to say? That I killed someone who doesn't officially exist, and use your invisible monkey pal and a magic lion as witnesses?"

"Dude, you've done so much awful stuff, Lincoln and I have a punch list of things we could bring to the Arbiter." I pop my hands over my mouth in mock-surprise. Remember how I vowed not to say anything about taking Aldred to court? Change of plans. It's just too tempting to watch him squirm.

"Oops, did I say that out loud?" I ask.

Aldred pales. "Arbiter? Have you gotten a codex to gather evidence?"

Lincoln straightens his stance. It's Prince Time. "We are not having this discussion right now. The priority is to check on Peli's family, get the others home, and then head back to Antrum ourselves to ensure our loved ones are safe, in that order. Am I clear?"

At this point, my semi-demonic heart goes pitter-pat. I may lose my *cool chick card* to admit this, but I do so love it when Lincoln gets bossy. Yum, yum.

Aldred rounds on the other Marked Ones. "Great news! I have negotiated your safe passage home." They all look pleased. Rufus yawns.

I fight the urge to groan, but not too hard. A little baby growl escapes my lips. I lock gazes with Lincoln. "Promise me I'll be there when one of us kills him."

"You have my solemn vow."

Peli tiptoes nearer. "Is everything all right? May I go ahead and open the gateways?" He bounces on all fours, clearly anxious to see his family again.

"Go to town, Peli." I can't help but smile as I add six more words. "I can't wait to meet them."

74

LINCOLN

A minute later, a round gateway stands in the clearing. Peli's family steps through. Nora is first.

"You wouldn't believe the day I've had," she says.

Peli beams. "Let me guess. The Contagion burst into the house and froze you?"

"That's it." Nora narrows her eyes. "You look terrible. How long have we been frozen?"

"A few hundred years." Stepping forward, Peli wraps her in a big hug. It's sweet.

"Tell me you killed that wizard," whispers Nora.

"Absolutely dead," says Peli with a chuckle. "With some help."

The twins leap through next: Mlinzi and Walinzi. As always, I have a hard time determining which one is speaking.

"Daddy! Daddy!"

"We got poked by the Contagion."

"But we woke up."

Peli kneels before them. "I missed you both." His big blue eyes line with tears as he scoops them both into a hug. Nora joins the embrace as well. Not going to lie. I'm getting a bit misty myself.

Here. This moment. It's what we fight for.

The twins have been doing that kid-thing where they scrunch up their faces during the hug. Now both open their eyes and scan the scene. Their chatter strikes up once more.

"Who's the lion?"

"Why are the weird people here?"

"How come that old guy's so fat?"

And then, in unison: "Can we go home now?"

Peli chuckles again. "We can certainly go home. After I take care of everyone who helped me, we'll do just that."

"And I am not overweight," grumbles Aldred.

Peli steps away from his family and raises his hands. A spell is doubtless about to begin.

"Before you start," I say. "May Myla and I have a word?"

Peli jogs over to us. "Sure."

Myla and I discussed this beforehand. It's always good to have your scenarios set up. "We wish to return home," I state. "But not before we're certain that you're all right. What will you do now?"

A slow smile rounds Peli's mouth. "After this, I might become the Simian Wizard King. Seems like the job's open. And the newly freed apprentices will certainly need some guidance."

Myla shoots him a thumbs-up. "Good plan."

Rufus lopes up to our group. "Please know that I won't be returning to Antrum. I'll remain and help my people heal." Rufus glances at Peli. "Perhaps I'll even help the future Simian King."

"Were you eavesdropping?" asks Peli.

Rufus gives one of his lion-yawns, which show off an enormous number of teeth. "I have excellent hearing."

"And you're tricky," says Peli. "We'll get along well."

With that, Peli opens the gateway and sends the others home. Elyse requests that she be dropped off somewhere called Viking Village Towne. It's an historical recreation community with a repetitive name that's located outside Akron, Ohio. Not sure how she found out about the place, but they seem to welcome her without question.

For his part, Spivey asks to be dropped off at a DIL community on the outskirts of Hell. It's mostly Whinus demons like him, so that's a good start. Plus DIL stands for Demonic Insect Lovers. Spivey is set for life.

Me, Myla, Rule, and Aldred... now we're the only ones left. Peli opens a fresh gateway. Inside the window-like center, a scene appears: the Acca cavern in Antrum. *Back to where we started.*

"Not sure why we had to go last," grumbles Aldred.

At this point, Myla's tail takes charge.

And by *takes charge*, I mean it punches Aldred in the gut.

"Nice work, boy." Myla pats the arrowhead end.

"Ooooooooooow," moans Aldred. "I was viciously attacked."

Myla rolls her eyes. "Don't get near the tail, don't get punched by the tail. As a super important demon hunter, I'd think you'd know this."

I pat the arrowhead end, too. Myla's tail really is a treasure.

Peli opens his arms wide. It's his way of saying, g*ive the monkey a hug before you go.* So that's what I do. Meanwhile, Myla and Peli's tails share a modified high five.

A sense of satisfaction warms my chest. Peli has his family back, not to mention Rufus along for extra support. My little orange friend should be more than fine.

I take Myla's hand. "Ready?"

"Absolutely."

Together, we step though the gateway.

Antrum, here we come.

75

MYLA

Lincoln and I step back into the Acca cavern. After the gateway vanishes behind us, I take a moment to I scan the cavern.

Huh.

When Lincoln and I left this place, it was totally empty, except for Octavia and the statues of Nat and Baptiste.

Not so any more.

The audience has returned. Everyone stands in neat rows. Any signs of panic are gone. Lady Bentford is back as well. Now that old bat waits beneath Aldred's yellow canopy, alongside the minstrels that had been following Aldred around the Primeval.

Hold on, there.

My skin prickles over with surprise. In all the excitement, I'd completely forgotten about all the thrax Aldred was dragging around the Primeval. How did they return early?

Octavia steps up to our group, which still includes Aldred and Rule. "So nice to see that you've all returned safely." She looks to Aldred. "We received your messages. Everything is in place."

"Messages?" asks Lincoln.

"Yes," replies Octavia. "Aldred said he'd come back with new powers to show everyone."

Translation: Aldred figured he'd have the Contagion's magic by now. He was planning a triumphant return. How very Aldred of Aldred.

"My message said nothing about new powers," lies Aldred. "You must have read it incorrectly. I merely wanted to complete the Trials of Acca."

"Ah," comments Octavia. She gives Aldred a pointed stare that says, *watch your ass.*

"How long have we been gone?" asks Lincoln.

"A few hours," replies Octavia.

Nat barrels up to us. Baptiste follows close behind him. "What an odd battle earlier today! Baptiste and I got frozen but we're fine now." Nat hugs us both in turn. "What happened in the Primeval? Lincoln and Myla, off on another adventure. Tell us everything!"

I haven't known Nat for long, but there's no missing his love for adventure stories. This will be fun.

"We have no time for such foolishness," pronounces Aldred.

Or not.

Lincoln and I share a dry look. Heaven forbid someone else get attention during Aldred's triumphant comeback party.

For his part, Aldred moves to stand before the yellow canopy. "Everyone!" He calls to the audience. "Welcome!"

The crowd cheers. However, the sound carries less enthusiasm than before. Nothing like being locked in a cavern with a tree monster to make you think twice about something.

"The Contagion is indeed dead," announces Aldred. "I killed him. And I saved the ghoul Captain of Thought Police!" Aldred waves to Rule, who's been a rather silent ghoul this whole time. "Come forward, Rule, and say a few words about my rescue."

Rules moves to stand beside Aldred. "Greetings, everyone. I'm simply grateful to be alive."

"Hear that?" asks Aldred. "He's grateful." Aldred claps a meaty hand on Rule's shoulder. "You're welcome."

Rule squares his shoulders. "I'd like to make an announcement before the trials restart."

"Sure, sure. Anything you want." Aldred elbows Rule. "Only don't talk too much about everything I did to help you. It would simply be too embarrassing."

Translation: I did nothing to save you. Even so, I want you to make up a bunch of garbage now to make me look good.

"Thank you," says Rule. "I hereby choose this moment to formally announce my support for the new soul processing bills before Purgatory's Senate. I shall organize a gathering of the greatest ghouls in order to craft the finest—and most specific—Thought Mandate ever created. That way, we shall provide optimal support."

I clap my hands raw at this point. Even add in a few cheers. This is awesome news. Who would have suspected Rule to be awesome?

Aldred frowns. "What about me? Don't you wish to tell everyone about how I saved you?"

Rule folds his arms over his chest. "No, I don't."

Well, that told him in three words or less.

"What a fine joke." Aldred laughs. "My ghoul rescuee has quite the sense of humor. Yet we've other matters before us today. Now that I have killed the Contagion as promised, I do hereby declare the Trials of Acca officially open!"

The cheering strikes up again. This time, there's a little more excitement behind it. I guess watching me get humiliated is a popular idea with some of the nobility. Not a surprise.

That said, it *is* a pain in my ass.

Bottom line? What a crap week. At this moment, I have zero desire to deal with the Trials of Acca.

I round on Aldred. "Now? We're really going to do this?"

Octavia steps up once more. "Of course, the trials shall begin immediately. This is important, Myla."

Lincoln's mother works her *queenly vibe*, which is where Lincoln inherited some of his bossy edge. On my guy, it's a bonus. From Octavia? Not so much, considering how she glares down her nose at me. That hurts.

Bone-deep weariness seeps through every molecule in my body. The thrax, quasis, Avians, Reptilians, and Icythians... everyone wants me to change. Even the Contagion wanted to suck out my life force.

A weight of sorrow settles inside me. *Cissy was right after all.* Everyone has limits. In this moment, I'd sell my soul for a brownie and a nap.

Aldred eyes me from head to toe and smirks. He totally knows I don't have any more fucks to give on this one.

"Come forward, Lady Bentford!" calls the earl.

Lady Bentford moves to stand beside Aldred. With a flick of her wrist, she sets loose a super-long scroll. *Impressive.* This thing puts Santa's Naughty Or Nice List to shame.

Lady Bentford clears her throat. "I have a few questions for Miss Lewis about the Rixa Way. As the representative of the thrax royal court, it is my duty to ensure any future member knows our values and traditions."

I hold up my pointer finger. "One sec." I sashay closer to Octavia. "I thought this was going to be three questions, tops."

"Lady Bentford asked for ideas from other houses," states Octavia. "Things may have gotten a little out of hand."

"A little?" I hitch my thumb toward the Santa list. "Nothing about that looks little."

"Please. It is the Rixa Way."

And in this moment, I realize there is a side to Octavia I've never seen before. She has the ability to beg. Right now, she's got her hands clasped beneath her chin, lower lip wobbling, the full deal.

Gah. Where is my brownie? When can I take my nap?

LINCOLN

I've seen Mother work her big guns when it comes to manipulation. After all, she can make almost any rank and file thrax weep within two minutes. Only rarely have I seen what's happening now.

Mother's going nuclear.

For Octavia, this means everything but all out bawling. It's extraordinarily effective. As for Myla, every part of her seems washed out and exhausted. Circles under her eyes. Colorless skin. Slumped shoulders.

My girl needs real food and sleep. Which is why Mother's pulling out all the stops.

A memory appears. I'm back in the woods with the Guide, only it doesn't turn out to be him at all. It was Lady Bentford. Back then, I'd tortured myself about what the true threat against me and Myla.

At last, I see that risk clearly.

Even better, I know what to do about it.

Striding over to Myla, I pull my girl into my arms. For a long moment, I just feel her melting into my embrace. Long seconds tick by before she speaks.

"I'll do it," she whispers, her voice hoarse. "The stupid trials. Lady Bentford's questions, the Igni Validation test, everything. Just get it over with."

"No, you're not. We will fight this."

She sniffles. "I've got a big cry coming on. I'm talking snot strings galore. I have so had it here."

"Understood. Which is why I'll make a speech and end this abomination."

More sniffles. "I don't need you stepping in to fix my problems."

"But they aren't your problems any more. They are *ours*." Setting my knuckle under her chin, I guide Myla's gaze to meet mine. "Everyone gets tired. That's why we lean on each other."

"When you say sweet things like that, it just makes me want to bawl. I'm being a total weakie here."

"What did I say?" I run my fingertip along her jawline. "We all have our moments. You may not fully realize this, but you give me strength every day. My life was a colorless drudge before you came along. As you know, I almost sold myself into a life with Adair. That's how low I'd sunk."

A smile quirks one corner of Myla's mouth. "That's pretty low."

"You trusted me with the Contagion. I ask that of you again, because the same thing is happening now. Evil seeks to drain my girl of her life force. I won't allow it."

"Do you really think that's what they're up to? Octavia looks truly miserable."

I kiss the top of her head. "This won't take long. All right?"

She sighs. "Agreed."

Lacing my fingers with Myla's, I turn to face the audience.

Here goes.

LINCOLN

The cavern turns silent. All eyes lock on me and Myla. My people love a good battle and this will be a major fight, even if swords aren't involved.

"Greetings, everyone," I begin.

"Now, Lincoln," says Aldred. "There's no need to grandstand."

I round on Aldred. "I will speak my mind now. During that time, here's what you'll do: Step away." I pack all the malice in the after-realms into those last two words. Rage careens off me and runs straight into Aldred.

The earl shuffles backward.

As I suspected he would. After all, I've seen Aldred's soul. At the end of all things, he's a coward.

I return my focus to the crowd. "My fiancée and I are here today for the Trials of Acca. This event has two official goals." As I go through each point, I raise a finger. "One. Show that Myla knows the Rixa way. Two. Force Myla's igni to display whether they approve of her involvement in combat."

The crowd's attention stays locked on me. The air turns heavy with anticipation.

"For the second item, the request is ridiculous. Myla has served on dozens of demon patrols. She's taken down thirty-six Class A monsters. No one needs to approve her involvement in combat. She's already doing it."

Taking a moment, I scan the crowd. Some nobles nod. Others shrug. This is as expected. The Igni Validation test was more something Aldred pushed on Purgatory. My people appreciate demon fighting. They won't stop Myla when it comes to battle.

"Which brings back to the first point. The tests for the Rixa Way. Listen to me carefully. Those are a lie."

Gasps echo through the air, mostly from Lady Bentford and her cronies. That's to be expected. After all, this is the true threat here.

"I've been told this test is to rate Myla's ability to memorize trivia about manners. It is not. This display seeks to tear down Myla's very nature. My girl is aggressive. Dominant. Now Myla must call Lady Bentford Mistress before the whole court? My own fiancée is to be forced into admitting humiliation? That's beyond outrageous. And because of the threat of the Contagion, it's an outrage that I allowed to stand for far too long."

No one in the audience says a word. Many stare at the ground or shuffle their weight from foot to foot.

They're embarrassed.

As they should be.

"Some here wish to change my Myla into a thrax lady with a tail. Listen to me carefully. I won't have it. I adore my Angelbound love just as she is. You will never change her."

I draw Myla closer to my side. Her body feels warm and firm against mine. "Many of you don't know this, but I almost lost Myla once to poison. At the time, I vowed that nothing would be more important than our love. And so I declare to you now the same thing I announced back then. Accept us or move on. There is no saying, *you are fine to rule*, and then whittling us into something else afterwards. Drop that battle tactic."

I scan all the faces. No one says a word, especially Aldred.

"No one wishes us to leave? Good. I have chosen my bride. If you desire to join our future court, then spend your time figuring out how to make Myla feel welcome and comfortable, rather than focusing on your own petty ends." I round on Lady Bentford. "And in that spirit, saffronia does indeed taste like urine."

With a gasp, Lady Bentford drops her list. It's a rather satisfying sight.

I turn to Myla. "My future queen, is there anything you'd like to add?"

Myla inhales a shaky breath. "Only that I love you as you are, too." She grins and it's a smile that sparkles with all that's lovely in my world. My heart warms.

"I hereby declare these trials to be officially over. Everyone, go home." I look to Myla. "That means us, too."

Turning, I loop my arm around Myla's shoulder. She sets her hand at my waist. Together, we walk back to my chambers.

I've felt in love before. Now, I know what it is to be a husband and partner. This isn't only about her and me anymore. It's about cherishing the new entity that is *us*.

And that's a beautiful development, indeed.

EPILOGUE

THREE WEEKS LATER

1

LINCOLN

Three weeks ago, Rule promised to endorse the new soul processing bills before the Senate. As part of that, we agreed to have a day-long conclave in Antrum in order to figure out the particulars. It seemed like a nice idea at the time.

Now the day in question has arrived. Rule has sent over four boxes of detailed minutiae in preparation, all of which we'll discuss. A classic example:

> *If the soul to be processed lost more then 21.1 grams at death, should form 827-A be completed or form 1367-B?*

Needless to say, today promises to be the definition of tedious. Myla's parents are attending, so there will be folks present who can actually speak to Rule's concerns. Still, a full eight hours of this?

I'd rather snort lemon juice.

After our adventures in the Primeval, all I want is more alone time with Myla.

Speaking of my betrothed, Myla now stands framed on the threshold of the Starlight Conservatory, one of the many reception chambers in Arx Hall. While most of my home is decorated in medieval simplicity—meaning wooden furniture, tapestries and

Persian rugs—this particular space is designed to impress. Gold, crystal, and enamel cover virtually every surface.

Yet my fiancée outshines it all.

After closing the door, Myla turns toward me. A mischievous light shines in her blue eyes. Interest sparks in my soul. *This will be good.*

"I have an idea," Myla whispers.

The magnetic pull between us draws me closer. "Yes?"

"We're supposed to attend the…" Myla snaps her fingers, trying to recall the right name. "Meh. I call it the *Rule Thing*."

I tap my chin, as if genuinely thinking this through. "If by the *Rule Thing*, you mean the day-long event to secure his endorsement for your parent's Senate bills? Then yes, that's next on our schedule."

Myla huffs out a breath. "Mom and Dad say it's a lock. They don't want us wasting time with Rule."

"We agreed to join him." I'm a firm believer in keeping your word, by the way. Trust is the bedrock of effective rule.

"And now, we can un-agree to attend. I've found us an out."

"I don't know. My parents already sent five messages this morning to ensure we'll be on time. They don't wish to be alone with the ghouls."

"Boo hoo. So they'd have to do their jobs."

I can't help but chuckle. "Myla."

"Hey, who covered for me when I was weakening? You. Now I'm returning the favor. You don't want to hit this. I don't, either. It's not like we're spending a day with Peli or something."

Which is true. If Peli needed our tine, both Myla and I would be more than happy to oblige. Since leaving the Primeval, Peli has sent us messages reporting how he's now King Wizard over all lands. He's already set up food redistribution to help those in need. *Good for him.*

All of which brings me back to today and Rule. I step closer to Myla. "Let's hear your plan." *Because my girl always has one.*

"Here's the deal. Nothing's more important to thrax than killing demons. So if you and I are testing weapons today then—VOILA—no more *Rule Thing*."

"That could be true." I exhale a slow breath. "Unfortunately, we thrax haven't added a new weapon since the crossbow." And even that addition remains controversial. Mostly because anything with moving parts tends to jam up around demons. It's one of their evil superpowers.

"Uh, false." Fresh excitement pours off Myla in waves. It's contagious. "You just added a weapon when I became your fiancée." She gestures across her Scala robes. "These can change shape. Body armor is one option. There are other things I've tested out, too. Which brings me back to my idea."

"And that is?"

"Three words: Weapons. Fashion. Show."

I beam with delight. Leave it to Myla to turn a humdrum day into something wondrous. It also strikes me that Myla and I are now alone in the Starlight Conservatory. This scheme gets better by the moment.

"You're brilliant," I state. "We're definitely released from today's unpleasantness."

"Hey, it's my job to make sure our lives don't suck."

I chuckle. "Now I'll do my bit as well." Pulling open the door, I address the guard on duty. Although the visor's pulled low on the helm of the knight in question, I already know his identity.

"Greetings, Igor."

"Your Highness."

"Please transfer a message to my parents. The future queen and I will skip today's ghoul conclave."

"But Walker also said you must attend. I'm to ensure you leave on time. He's back from his cruise and most anxious to speak with you."

I fix Igor with my most regal stare. "I'm overruling any other requests on this matter."

"But Walker—"

"No interruptions for the next hour," I continue. "If anyone approaches the door, inform them the future king and queen are focused on weapons testing. Under article 2,867-A of the *Statement on Royal War Readiness*, we cannot be disturbed."

"As you command."

"Thank you, Igor." After pulling the door closed, I focus on Myla. "Now."

She blinks at me dramatically. "Yeeeeeeeees?"

"How about that fashion show?"

And I lock the door with a gentle click.

2

MYLA

This is so awesome, I can hardly stand it.

For weeks, I've been practicing conjuring my Scala robes into different forms. At the same time, I've also been hoarding up the whole *weapons fashion show* idea as the perfect *Get Out Of Jail Free* card for the right opportunity.

And today's when opportunity knocks. *Yeah.*

Lincoln slides onto a black velvet bench. He wears his medieval best, which means chain mail and a tunic. Setting his silver crown onto a nearby table, my guy fixes me with a stare that's can only be described as *seriously hot*.

"Show me," he commands.

The words rumble with just the right level of growl. My inner lust demon wakes up, big time.

Closing my eyes, I picture my Scala robes in a new shape. The threads instantly realign around my body, changing from a white sheath dress into pale body armor. Hefty boots now cover my feet, replacing the sandals I usually wear.

Lincoln gives me the barest of nods. "Good."

There's an unspoken challenge in that word, though. Why? I change into this particular vintage of body armor all the time. Lincoln is waiting for a new creation.

Have I ever got something for him.

This brings me to the tricky part of my Scala robe situation. My garment can take different forms, but I can't eliminate the number of threads in the final creation. For instance, when I tried to create some hefty knightly armor, it cut off around my thighs. That was awkward.

"Here's the thing," I say in my own version of a growl. "There are multiple ways to go to war."

Closing my eyes, I ask the robes to take the form of a human style gown with a plunging neckline, no sleeves, and a long train behind me.

That's precisely what happens.

Lincoln sizes me up for a long moment before speaking again. "Turn around."

Good call. No self-respecting fashion exists without a catwalk. I step in a slow circle. "Well?"

Lincoln rises. "Dangerous weaponry, indeed."

He stalks toward me, every line of his body taught with focus. My blood rushes while my tail flicks behind me in a predatory rhythm. Lincoln pauses once we're almost—but not quite—touching. With slow movements, he pulls off his tunic and chain mail, exposing his bare chest.

Mmm-mmm. My guy is ripped. Even better, he's got a series of battle scars across his skin that are just so lickable, it isn't even funny. My inner lust demon roars her approval. Lifting my hand, I slowly run my fingertip over the trio of silvery scars that mark his shoulder. Lincoln shivers at my touch. My core tightens, seeing how I affect him.

Clasping my wrist, Lincoln pulls my hand to his lips, where he places a gentle kiss on my palm. The touch of his mouth sends a jolt of desire through my body.

Things get a little crazy from here. In short order, we're kissing each other's faces off. My legs wrap around Lincoln's waist while he presses my back against the wall. Somehow my gown gets half-removed. The garment now pools around my waist while Lincoln's rough hands do positively eye-crossing things to my nipples.

It's official. I love *warrior fashion show*.

As we kiss, I run my hands across the shifting muscles of

Lincoln's back. The experience is mind numbing. I barely register the low hum in the room. Well, not beyond a single thought.

Fuck that noise.

Lincoln drives me harder against the wall. Our bare chests press together while his hands grip my thighs just a little too harshly.

All of a sudden, a familiar voice echoes through the room.

"Oh, no."

My stomach sinks. I know that super-deep tone.

Walker is here.

In a single swift movement, Lincoln flips to face Walker while placing me behind him. I quickly order my Scala robes to back into their regular full sheath shape. Scooching closer to Lincoln, I peep over my guy's shoulder. Facing Class A demons in battle? Not a problem. Thinking my honorary older brother just saw my boobs? I'd really like to find a place to hide for about a thousand years, minimum.

Walker stands in the center of the room. I'd say all the blood drained from his body, but as a ghoul he's already deadly pale. Still there's no denying the way Walker sets his palms against his eyes. The guy is freaked.

"Ow, my retinas," moans Walker. "That was more than I needed to see."

Unlike us, Walker's dressed casually, meaning jeans, a black T-shirt, and hefty boots. Behind my honorary older brother, a large door-shaped hole blinks out of existence. Unbelievable. Walker opened a freaking ghoul portal into the very chamber where I was having sexy time.

When Lincoln next speaks, his voice is ice. "Then don't barge into places where you've been specifically forbidden."

Walker sighs. "Like I'd let Igor stop me."

Lincoln glances over his shoulder. When my guy addresses me, his voice softens. "Are you all set now?"

"Yup, fine." Unless you count the layers of humiliation encircling my soul.

"My sincere apologies," says Walker.

"It's totally cool," I lie.

Lincoln doesn't move an inch. Normally, I'd appreciate the

ongoing gun show, but this is getting awkward. "Why are you here, Walker?"

"I just returned from my trip and wanted to chat about the new orphan home I'm designing for Nat. I think it will perfectly suit all the freed orphans, but I want your ideas."

When Walker's really freaked, he babbles. Right now is shaping up to be a classic example.

"Oh," continues Walker. "I also wish to show you pictures from the cruise. The buffet was amazing."

"Walker," says Lincoln.

"I took snapshots of all my drinks, too. The cough syrup cocktails were—"

"Walker!" Okay, my voice came out on the loud side that time. *Sorry not sorry.*

"Fine," says Walker quickly. "I'll catch up with you later."

Another hum sounds. Walker opens a fresh ghoul portal, steps through the door-shaped hole, and vanishes.

Boo. What a mood killer.

I frown. "Maybe we should go to the conclave."

"Not a chance," says Lincoln. "Someone made me promises."

"I did?"

Lincoln turns until we're chest to chest once more. Wrapping his arms around me, he pulls me close against him.

"Promises," I say slowly. "I like where this is going."

LINCOLN

Myla runs her fingertips down my bare chest. "Tell me about these promises… in a minute." She lightly scratches my six pack.

"Here I am, wanting to talk." I mock-sigh. "Yet to you, I'm merely one big slice of man cake."

Myla lifts her hands. "Not true. I'm so done with obsessing about your abs."

"Really."

"I've moved on to your super personality."

"And?"

"Maybe your glutes."

"To refresh your memory, you promised to give me details about BAEJS."

"Oh, that." Myla worries her lower lip with her teeth. "I don't know what to say."

"How about I kick things off, then?" I gently rub my nose along the length of hers. "I'll share the things I like about you first."

"Oh, I love this idea."

"To begin with, I worship your curves." To accent this point, I brush my fingertips over Myla's breasts. She lets out a low moan and Heaven help me, I crave that sound. I glide my hands lower. "I adore your responsiveness." Myla's moans turn even deeper. "And then, there are your lips." I gently kiss the corner of her mouth. "You make me crazy, Myla Lewis."

She looks up at me through her lashes. "My turn, I guess." Her irises flash crimson.

"Your eyes are sparking again."

"They only do that for you, Lincoln."

"And *those* may be the sexiest words you've ever spoken. Consider your promise kept."

We share a kiss, slow and deep. Hours pass with nothing but each other. And with each passing moment, I am thankful beyond words for a partner beyond compare.

∽

The End

The adventure continues with BACULUM (Angelbound Lincoln Book #3). Order today!

BACULUM

Lincoln's adventures continue with BACULUM (Angelbound Lincoln Book #3). Order today!

ALSO BY CHRISTINA BAUER

ANGELBOUND

Revisit ANGELBOUND, the kick-ass paranormal romance with more than 1 million copies sold!

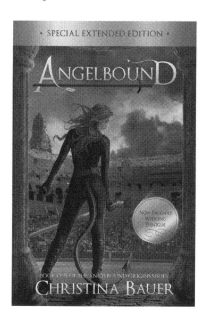

OFFSPRING

The next generation takes on Heaven, Hell, and everything in between with MAXON!

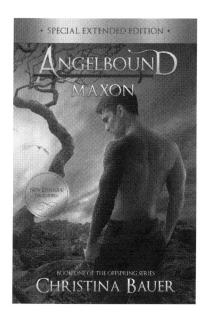

FAIRY TALES OF THE MAGICORUM

A modern fairy tale that *USA Today* calls a 'must-read!' Check out WOLVES AND ROSES!

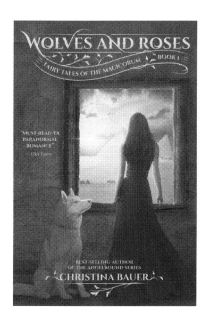

DIMENSION DRIFT

A kick-ass heroine + a swoon-worthy prince + an all-girl heist = the DIMENSION DRIFT series!

BEHOLDER

Medieval mages… Slow-burn love… And heart-pounding action! Check out the BEHOLDER series!

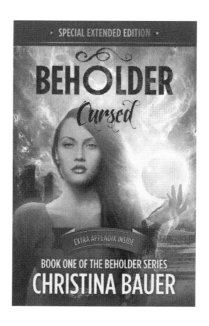

PIXIELAND DIARIES

PIXIELAND DIARIES tells the story of sassy pixie Calla and 'her' elf prince, Dare.

APPENDIX

IF YOU ENJOYED THIS BOOK...

...Please consider leaving a review, even if it's just a line or two. Every bit truly helps, especially for those of us who don't *write by the numbers,* if you know what I mean.

Plus I have it on good authority that every time you review an indie author, somewhere an angel gets a mocha latte. For reals.

And angels need their caffeine, too.

ACKNOWLEDGMENTS

If you're reading my freaking acknowledgements, chances are, I should thank you for something. So, for the record: you are awesome, dear reader.

That said, huge and heartfelt thanks must go out to my husband and son for their rock-solid support. Being an author means a lot of early mornings, late nights, long weekends, and never-ending patience. You two are the best guys in the universe, period.

After that, I must thank the extensive network of reviewers, friends and colleagues who helped me build my writing chops in general. Gracias.

Finally, deep affection goes out to my late, much loved, and dearly missed Aunt Sandy and Uncle Henry. You saw the writer in me, always. Thank you, first and last.

COLLECTED WORKS

Angelbound Lincoln
   The Angelbound experience as told by Prince Lincoln
   1. Duty Bound
   2. Lincoln
   3. Trickster
   4. Baculum *(future)*
   5. Angelfire *(future)*

Angelbound Origins
   About a quasi (part demon and part human) girl who loves kicking butt in Purgatory's Arena
   1. Angelbound
   2. Scala
   3. Acca
   4. Thrax
   5. The Dark Lands
   6. The Brutal Time
   7. Armageddon
   8. Quasi Redux *(coming 2020)*
   ALSO: Origins Box Set *(Books 1-5)*

Angelbound Offspring

The next generation takes on Heaven, Hell, and everything in between
1. Maxon
2. Portia
3. Zinnia
4. Rhodes
5. Kaps *(future)*
6. Huntress *(future)*
ALSO: Offspring Box Set *(Books 1-3)*

Fairy Tales of the Magicorum
Modern fairy tales with sass, action, and romance
1. Wolves and Roses
2. Moonlight and Midtown
3. Shifters and Glyphs
4. Slippers and Thieves
5. Bandits and Ball Gowns *(coming 2020)*
6. Evil Queens and Goblin Kings *(future)*
ALSO: Magicorum Box Set *(Books 1-3)*

Dimension Drift
Dystopian adventures with science, snark, and hot aliens
1. Scythe
2. Umbra
3. Alien Minds
4. ECHO Academy *(coming 2020)*
5. Drift Warrior *(future)*
ALSO: Dimension Drift Box Set (Books 1-3)

Pixieland Diaries
Sassy pixie Calla loves elf prince Dare. Too bad he hasn't noticed her. Yet.
1. Pixieland Diaries *(coming 2020)*
2. Calla *(future)*
3. Dare *(future)*

Beholder
Where a medieval farm girl discovers necromancy and true love

1. Cursed
2. Concealed
3. Cherished
4. Crowned
5. Cradled
ALSO: Beholder Box Set *(Books 1-5)*

ABOUT CHRISTINA BAUER

Christina Bauer thinks that fantasy books are like bacon: they just make life better. All of which is why she writes romance novels that feature demons, dragons, wizards, witches, elves, elementals, and a bunch of random stuff that she brainstorms while riding the Boston T. Oh, and she includes lots of humor and kick-ass chicks, too. Christina lives in Newton, MA with her husband, son, and semi-insane golden retriever, Ruby.

Stalk Christina on Social Media

Blog:
http://monsterhousebooks.com/blog/category/christina

Facebook:
https://www.facebook.com/authorBauer/

Instagram:
https://www.instagram.com/christina_cb_bauer/

Twitter:
@CB_Bauer

VLOG:
https://tinyurl.com/Vlogbauer

Web site:
www.bauersbooks.com

COMPLIMENTARY BOOK

Get a FREE novella when you sign up for Christina's newsletter: https://tinyurl.com/bauersbooks

AFTERWORD

Dear Reader,

If you're still reading at the end of the book, I thought you might enjoy some extra insights on how and why I wrote TRICKSTER.

Before I get into that, I first need to provide some context on how I interpret the hero versus heroine's journey.

Some Stuff on the Heroine's Journey

In my interpretation, a hero's journey can be experienced by a man or a woman. It's about the underlying energy, not your physical form. In this sense, heroes are about saving the status quo from threat. For instance, think *Jack and the Beanstalk* or *James Bond*. The fabric of society doesn't get rewoven because a giant was killed or Doctor Evil didn't blow up another atomic bomb.

This isn't how it works with a heroine's journey. Heroine's energy (which again can be expressed by a man or woman) is about re-imagining society. Think Star Wars. Luke learned to to feel his feelings and as a reward—WHAM—he got to wear a dress and upend the evil government! the classic example through time is the story of Isis, but her tale isn't as popular as Star Wars, so there you go.

Heroine's journeys are extra tricky because you need an inner change to match with the outer one. In other words, it's not like

James Bond is a different guy at the end of each movie. But Luke Skywalker certainly became a new man by the end of the first trilogy. In my opinion, I think this is because as you change the outside world, it's a symbol for altering your inner life. So heroine's journeys need a strong character arc.

The Bitch About Writing TRICKSTER

Now we get to the tricky part. Some of the most fun and engaging character arcs take place when your heroine falls in love. But what about after? Isn't that where most of life takes place anyway? What about that?

Not gonna lie. There aren't many new character arcs for committed couples... after they fall in love.

About Test Pilots (Seriously)

Which brings me to test pilots. (Hang in here; I do have a point!) A regular person says, "holy fuck, I've got three seconds before this plane crashes!" A test pilot says, "cool, I've three seconds to fix this." I think there's a similar thing happening in writing. I think there are authors who say, "no one's writing stories like this? Run!" While another type cries, "No one's doing this? Count me in!" I happen to fall in this latter category. It's how I got into story telling about kickass chicks in the first place.

My Final Point (And I Do Have One)

In TRICKSTER, I wanted to tackle the problem of finding a fresh inner journey for both Myla and Lincoln.

In the end, the arc in TRICKSTER became one where our hero and heroine needed to ignore the world and support each other. And not in the sense of a mother supporting a child, but specifically for a white dude supporting his partner outside of saying *let's fall in love* because, dammit, that's a good story to celebrate.

We all question ourselves sometimes, and having a strong and supportive life partner can help you stay on track. In TRICKSTER, no one's trying to fix the other person. Both Myla and Lincoln love and protect each other *as is*.

And that's a symbol our relationship as well, dear reader. I'm so thankful that folks like you exist. You enjoy reading stories about this kind of love and journey as much as I like writing them. You help me stay on track, too.

See you at the next book!
CB

Printed in Germany
by Amazon Distribution
GmbH, Leipzig